Distinguished Praise for

"Marlene M. Bell is a master storyteller when it comes to the cozy mystery genre."
—**Book Review Directory**

"*Copper Waters* is an entertaining and fast-paced mystery, where small-town intrigue, family drama, and a high-stakes whodunit will deepen readers› affection for the tenacious Annalisse.»
—**Self-Publishing Review**

"*Copper Waters* is emotional and thrilling, surprising and life-changing.»
—**Book Excellence**

"Marlene M. Bell's COPPER WATERS is a well-written murder mystery with descriptive scenes, an intriguing setting, and enough push and pull between the characters and within the plot to keep readers engaged."
—**IndieReader**

COPPER WATERS

A NOVEL BY

Marlene M. Bell

Ewephoric Publishing

Cover by Rhett Podersoo – Machine Room Design, London
Book design by Kevin G. Summers

ISBN: 978-0-9995394-9-1
ISBN: 979-8-9863409-0-6 (eBook)

For my sheep family

From Northern California to Maine, we've met many
dedicated sheep breeders willing to help out fledglings on
the sheep show circuit. Your camaraderie and expertise
throughout the decades have taught me so many life lessons.
The sheep community has its own unique rhythm and I'm
blessed to be a part of it. With gratitude.

CAST OF CHARACTERS
COPPER WATERS

Annalisse Drury—Filled with trust and commitment issues, she uncovers mayhem and foul play at every turn while love takes a rear seat for this gorgeous, green-eyed antiquities appraiser.

Alec Zavos—Family money and fame drive him from his true calling—but for a wavy-haired Greek with a soothing baritone voice and killer smile, he has no trouble attracting feminine attention.

Generosa Zavos—Grand dame and keeper of the keys to Zavos Gallery, she influences her way around Manhattan's art world, not to mention those closest to her.

Katharine (Kate) Walker—Too opinionated and secretive for her own good, she wins the award for how to ripen and age while misleading family and friends.

Chase Miller—From his sandy hair to the signature pink tie he sports at the gallery, he helps the Zavos clan manage their own shortcomings.

Bill Drake—On past missions, running into burning buildings to save humanity was his thing, but today, he examines clues from those who leave their lifeless bodies behind.

Ethan Fawdray—He carries a Kiwi accent as he spends time counting sheep below the equator—a world away from Walker Farm.

Olivia Hyde—Just because she's barely old enough to earn an entry-level career at an ice cream shop, doesn't mean it's all sugary cones and tasty flavors for the public.

Ellen Hyde—Pretty and fresh-faced as a sunrise in New Zealand, there's fear she's a tad too perfect as a mother and station owner—to be the real deal.

Sutton Hyde—It's great to be a carefree Hyde child as long as bugs and plants can't offer a final say in the matter.

Alastair McGregor—He's tanned, in his early sixties, and prefers public transportation over traveling on foot, because championing controversial causes can ruffle the town's feathers.

Cooper Dunn—The fiery-eyed and wild-haired station manager harbors more than a headache when it comes to his daily chores.

Finn Hyde—Politician first, husband and father second, his three-piece suit and perfect haircut send a strong message where he would rather reside.

Commissioner Karena—Top brass for Temuka's police force; his primary goal is superior community service as long as some departmental affairs stay sealed and out of view.

Tane Otene—His pockmarked face is a bumpy as his job as head of Temuka forensics.

Virena's Noah—A naïve child apparatus built to strain and test relationships between adults.

CHAPTER ONE
Disruption and Enlightenment

It's six a.m. on a dismal Saturday. I'm standing in awe of a memo sheet jumping across Alec Zavos's desk blotter in his freezing barn office across from his residence. My breath forms vapor from the cold as I reason out what's underneath. I lift one corner of the paper and spot a pair of antennae belonging to a silent cricket taking refuge.

"Sorry, cricket guy, you need new lodgings." I slide a manila folder beneath the memo sheet to capture the critter, then place the bug in the spacious barn breezeway. "It's safer out here. In the mood I'm in, you're bound to wind up as my next victim, smashed under my coffee cup."

While Alec answers emails inside his Brookehaven estate, I plan to spend time with Harriet, my thoroughbred mare, a gift from Alec. He keeps her in his stable of racehorses because my Greenwich Village brownstone in Manhattan isn't the place for farm animals. In the presence of livestock, my insights come alive, and

I'm able to see his point of view before I take actions that can't be undone.

Alec and I have been on the outs since my thirtieth birthday party last December, and I'm desperate for a new beginning with him. We're in big trouble; he's adulting while I'm being extra—and always—over the top.

"Annalisse, you're my next breath, my next day, my forever. I love you."

Weeks have flown by, and Alec's magical proposal speech during the party skips through my thoughts, reminding me of how close I came to accepting his ring. The sapphire-and-diamond engagement ring he's tried to give me twice, or was it three times? I've lost count. Each proposal came during my open questions about our relationship. At some point, he'll stop asking me to marry him. Waiting for the perfect moment to tell him *yes* will never arrive if I keep bouncing away from commitment.

I sit and pour the last few ounces of orange-and-clove tea into my mug. Cinnamon hits my tongue, then the tart singe of clove as the stable's office chair teeters on its springs, breaking the silence with a high-frequency squeal. The sound sets off guttural noises from Harriet, who's waiting for me in the adjacent stall. I've made my escape to Alec's stable to think about his ex-girlfriend and her nine-year-old boy that she *says* is Alec's son. That was Virena's birthday present to me when she interrupted Alec's proposal in such an ugly way.

I don't believe her story.

She's an intruder messing with our future, and I don't like it one bit.

Harriet whinnies again to be sure she gets my attention.

"Okay, girl. Give me a second to grab the curry and brush."

The last of the tea slams against the back of my throat and I stuff my shoulder length hair beneath my hooded sweatshirt, snugging the drawstring tight against my head, sorry for leaving the heavy coat on a hook in Alec's mudroom. We have the entire weekend together—a quiet two days. Time alone we need to sort out our problems, he said.

"Brr." A shiver rattles my teeth. "Darn it, I brought the wrong gloves too. That's what I get for hurrying out of the house."

Winter in upstate New York is stimulating, but cold when there's a foot of snow on the ground because of a blizzard kicking up from the south, as often happens in January. The toasty fireplace in the drawing room and Helga's pastry platter on the counter try to lure me there, but those comforts have to wait. Harriet needs my attention, and I need her today more than ever.

My breath forms a cloud bank at the front of the desk, and my knuckles stiffen beneath the equestrian gloves. Having my hands on Harriet's hundred-degree body will circulate heat and oil my joints.

The mare does her side-to-side hoof dance when she catches me standing in the breezeway with her halter in one hand and comb in the other. It's a ritual for her that makes me grin. Animals have their habits, just as people do.

Entering her stall, the aromas of horse hide, copper pennies, and clean pine shavings bombard me, notching down the strain from another disagreement with Alec about Virena's boy, Noah. His sudden appearance on Alec's property during my party is a constant reminder of Alec's short fling almost a decade ago.

Harriet's more antsy than usual, bobbing her head at the halter.

"Easy. Stay still, girl. I can't buckle it while you're moving."

Harriet complies as if she understands what I'm asking and follows me through the door to the breezeway tie-out. We've done this routine many times; I'm surprised she's so agitated with me. She might feel the storm's bite like I do, or she senses Noah's imaginary shackles on my ankles, making it hard to move forward.

"That's right; you miss your girl in the other stable, don't you, Harriet?"

Alec weaned the foals from the mares last week, including Harriet's filly. She doesn't have a name yet because Alec doesn't care for my ideas. The Jockey Club has strict rules requiring all registered horse names to go through the association prior to approval. For now, she's merely, "Harriet's foal."

Harriet flinches, showing me her gums when the curry comb's teeth rake her skin, removing the flyaway undercoat, and leaving a path of shiny, chestnut hair behind. I'm lucky to stand almost as tall as Alec to reach such a tall mare for grooming.

"Sorry, girl. We haven't done this in a while." I gentle the pressure and slow the comb on her skin.

With each pass, a movie plays out in my head where Alec and I hurt each other because of outside forces pushing in on us. My relationship with Alec grows more fragile in favor of strangers appearing and disappearing from the scene, using mind games to destroy us. A cute kid enters out of nowhere to weaken and threaten our bond, as Alec moves toward him and farther away from me.

I shake the images away and change grooming tools, starting at her mane between the ears, then traveling down her back to her hindquarters, using the stiff palmyra brush. Who could blame her preference for bristles over sharp curry comb teeth?

"Let's stick with the brush, shall we? I like it better too." Sweeping her powerful muscles, my arm thaws out somewhat. "What should I do, Harriet? We can't blame the boy for this. Alec has to figure it out, but he's ignoring the obvious." I gaze into Harriet's soft, twinkling eye. "The more we talk, the more he pulls away from me."

Harriet exhales as if she empathizes, and I go back to brushing her flank.

My pocket vibrates from a text message.

I draw out my phone and find a few words from Chase, asking me to call him at the gallery when I get time. I do and set it for speakerphone.

Chase picks up on the first ring. "You're up early, Anna."

"A lot on my mind. It's Saturday; why come into the shop so soon?"

"I couldn't sleep. A package came in yesterday's mail for you. Gen stuck it on her credenza. It's addressed to Personal, Annalisse Drury—not the gallery."

Gen Zavos is Alec's mother and our business partner at the Zavos Gallery in Manhattan. She allows me the freedom of days off from my usual duties of valuating antiques for the shop to spend quality time with Alec.

"Hmm. Is it from Kate? Read back the return address for me."

Paper rustles in my ear.

"No one's heard from her since she and Ethan left last summer. Please let it be Kate." I drop the brush and work a hand into my sweatshirt pocket.

Ethan Fawdray, who came from New Zealand, used to manage our farm, the family enterprise belonging to Kate and Ted Walker. The Walker farm in Goshen, New York is where I spent my teen years to adulthood, once "Uncle Ted and Aunt Kate" took me in after the death of the Drurys. They were made-up parents who played a scripted part to cover for Kate's affair with another man while she was still married to Ted.

"Hang on. The print's hard to read." Chase crinkles what sounds like a shipping envelope. "It's an international envelope from New Zealand. Yeah. Someone by the name of… Fawdray."

Ethan. We assumed he left with Kate after Ted's arrest, telling none of us their final destination. It's possible that Kate went to New Zealand with him, and it gives me hope of finding her now that Ethan's made contact. Kate's running instincts must be where I get my urges…

As a child, Kate raised me to believe she was my aunt, but the letter she left behind before she left said *she* was my true birth mother, not her sister Amy Drury, whom I've always known as my mother. The terms *aunt* and *uncle* were turned upside down after Kate and Ethan departed from Goshen. Kate added one more thing in her handwritten note; I shouldn't try to find my birth father because he doesn't know I exist. Amazing. Does she care what I want? Demanding answers to the many questions I have is on hold until my mother decides when we can talk about it. On her own timeline and no one else's.

"Huh. It's a small three-by-three box wrapped in newsprint." Chase interrupts my daydreaming with his report.

"Is there a note inside from Ethan or Kate?" I pat Harriet's cheek and lean into her musky muzzle. "Forget looking for a note, just open it. I'm dying to know what's inside." My lungs swell with relief. We're confirming Ethan's whereabouts, and he'll know where Kate is.

"No note that I can see. It's tied in twine. I'm gonna put the phone down."

I stroke Harriet's long neck with a gloved hand. "Maybe we'll get some good news for a change, Harriet. I could sure use some," I whisper.

"A weird gift." Chase has a lilt to his voice. "There's something else in the box. A note. Want me to read the note first?"

"Just tell me about the box. I'm standing in the middle of a freezing barn with a horse—turning into a Popsicle."

"Oh, got it. There's a skeleton key inside. The note says you're invited to Wool… comb Station. It's signed Ethan. Isn't that who worked at the farm for you guys?"

"Yep. That's him." I'm jazzed about staying on a sheep station, ready to do my version of a happy dance. "Did he leave a telephone number?"

"Skipped a part. He said it's the *station cottage*. No phone number, but there's an address for the cottage."

"Is there an email address?"

"Aren't you and Alec going on your flight to New Zealand soon?" Chase asks. "Alec knew you wanted to see that country in the worst way because of their sheep. He asked me if you'd be willing to fly that far for your birthday. Stop in and visit Ethan then."

I untie Harriet's lead rope and walk beside her to the stall. A hundred questions flood my mind while unclipping the rope from her leather halter. "I'm going to sign off now and put Harriet away. Would you give the box to Gen and ask her to bring it when she comes? She always stops at the gallery before she leaves for Brookehaven. Alec said his mom was dropping by the estate today."

"Doesn't Alec's old girlfriend drop her kid there on weekends?" Chase utters a disgusted sigh.

"Yeah, Alec's on babysitting duty again. To Gen, she treats Noah like her legitimate grandchild, but there's no proof of that without a test. I wish Virena and her son would stay on the coast where they belong."

"You're it!" The words jar my ears from behind. Little knuckles barrel into my frigid thigh.

Harriet bounds into the corner, whinnying; her ears flatten to her head.

In the cold, a fist punch stings my skin, a surprise attack from a healthy boy.

"Noah, step out of the horse stall. She doesn't know you." *Or like you.* Clenching my teeth with one eye on the kid, I calm Harriet. "Shh. Easy, girl."

The blond hellion in jeans and cowboy boots sticks his tongue out and stomps into Alec's office.

"Chase, I've gotta go. Talk soon." Stowing the phone, I limp to the doorway, rubbing my leg, and slide Harriet's door shut with a glance at the latch. "We'll finish brushing later, Harriet." I turn to Noah. "The highway in front of Alec's house is dangerous to cross alone in the dark. Where're your snow boots?"

Noah sinks into the chair in front of the desk, gathering a notepad and pen. With a smile on his face, he ignores me when witnesses aren't around.

"Did Alec come with you?" The vacant breezeway howls in a gust of wind. "Never, ever go into a horse stall when someone has their back turned. Horses are big animals, and they can hurt you."

"Duh. I'm not stupid." He scribbles while making faces at the page.

"Look, it's too cold to play tag in here, and it makes the horses nervous. If you want to, we can play a game inside before breakfast. Any board game you want."

"Board games are lame."

"How about making peanut butter buckeyes with Miss Rissman, Alec's housekeeper? It's candy. Wanna learn how to make them?"

All kids like sweets, but I have no experience with little brothers or babysitting boys.

"Hellie's fat and talks funny. Hard pass, Bi—"

"Stop. Her name's Miss Rissman and she's a German lady. She tries very hard to speak English." I hold my breath in another jaw clench and talk myself out of dragging his disrespectful bones outside by the jacket collar. He uses gutter language to get attention, except around Gen. Noah knows when to sugarcoat words for the most gain. "Where'd you learn to talk like that?"

"It's what Mom calls you." Noah giggles aloud, coloring inside the lines of his horse drawing.

There it is. I'm sure he's referring to the *B* word, not the weight comment, or maybe the weight too. A jealousy remark I wouldn't push past her. I work hard to keep my lean figure. His mother, Virena whatever her last name is, nudges Noah's opinions. Her knowledge of the dangling marriage proposal might be driving her to push Noah on Alec and against me. The possibility of Alec's child with this *person* who's dropped in from the past keeps me from accepting a marriage proposal until we know for certain that Noah is his.

I tolerate a lot from this boy, but now's not the time to stand aside and allow Noah's smart mouth to go unanswered. Trickery is needed.

"I'm going back to the estate to play Xbox with Alec. Wanna check it out?"

"He has Xbox?" His eyes widen at my lie, and he drops his pen.

"Yeah, I saw it in one of the guest rooms. We can hook it up and play; it's up to you. The fort game is the bomb." My brows bump for effect.

"Really? Awesomacious. Let's go."

"Stick close to me and wait until it's safe to cross the highway."

In a shocking move, Noah takes my hand, walking in silence from the horse barn to the road and looking both ways as he's been taught. He crosses the frozen asphalt, with a layer of ice glistening crystalline in the sunrise, without words, gripping my hand.

I act on my plan as we approach the house, but Alec won't like my deceit with the mood he's in. Navigating Alec's past from his college days is wearing me down more than I'm ready to admit. Either Noah is his son, or he isn't. A DNA test is the only way to confirm for certain.

Alec's wearing a dazzling smile and a turtleneck sweater when he greets us at the estate door. His gaze holds mine for the longest time, and I detect a mixture of curiosity and pride. Noah and I, hand in hand, must look like an unconvincing team, me in my tea-stained sweatshirt and double-layer sweatpants, and the kid in his new puff jacket and fancy boots, thanks to Gen.

"I spotted you guys at the barn. You must be freezing, Anna. Where's your barn coat?"

"It's colder than I expected. Excuse me, Alec. I'm going to stand in front of the fire." Sliding past him to the entry, I hear Noah mention the Xbox. My grin is unseen and as wide as Alec's was earlier. Fireworks are sure to begin after I thaw.

The peaceful warmth of Brookehaven Estate doesn't stop my shudder.

CHAPTER TWO
An Unveiling

Alec's recognizable Cucinelli moccasins slide along the hardwood hallway to the awesome sanctuary I call his 'drawing room through the ages', and it's where I'm waiting for the guillotine to drop.

Antiques and hand-crafted furniture from the Renaissance to the Victorian era surround me with less than comfortable fainting couches and claw-footed mahogany tables holding several gleaming Victorian brass case clocks. The room is replete with work from French artisans who had a flair for the ornate. River stone covers one entire wall from corner to corner. Alec's fireplace and hearth are of unforgettable proportions. As an antiquities specialist, being in the company of historical objects is my thing, so it's no wonder I'm laid back in this place. I spend as much time here as I can.

Ted Walker, a mason and the man I knew as my uncle, would be proud to put his name to that stony wall if he weren't awaiting trial for murder from inside his jail cell. When I consider what he did to get back at Kate for having an affair—I try not to think about it often. Ted treated me with disdain when we all lived together on Walker Farm, and now I understand why.

The heat from Alec's rock fireplace is blazing at my back—a cozy hearth to warm the ice in my veins while awaiting Alec's interrogation. I wonder if our intimate weekend upstate is a huge mistake with Noah here. Alec forgot to mention that we wouldn't be alone.

He closes the double doors behind him and stuffs one hand into a pants pocket.

The snap ripples down my spine, and I stand for my accuser. "Where's Noah?" My inquiry's meant to break the ice. I couldn't care less where the boy is.

"Playing with his Xbox." Alec takes me into his arms and laughs. "A curious choice when we don't own a single video game. Wish I'd thought of it." He buries his face in my hair and sighs. "Provence lavender fields. My gorgeous brunette with hair that reminds me of France. Considering what Noah put you through, you handled the situation to perfection. How's your leg?" His thumb sensually glides down my thigh, his dusky, silver eyes finding mine.

"You know about that?" I rest my hand over his and, without thinking, kiss him. "I could've used a referee out there."

"Noah confessed he punched you and called you a bad name. He apologized for it."

"Imagine that." *The sugarcoat king.*

Alec stretches back to observe me as the golden highlights from the fire sparkle in his dark, wavy hair. "You're losing weight. I hope you aren't dieting on my account." He rubs my cold hands for extra warmth. "About earlier, I'm sorry. I have no right to pick the name for Harriet's foal. She's yours, and you should be the one to do it."

I smile at the apology. "I get busy at the gallery and forget to eat sometimes."

"Please don't." He covers my throat in kisses and inches his way to my earlobes until I can no longer contain the goosebumps and break into giddy laughter.

"I hope you'll stay in your playful mood. Let's sit on the couch." I draw him away from the spectacular fire to the cooler area of the sofa, lining up bullet points in my head. "Naming a filly isn't the problem. Your old conquest is."

Alec opens his mouth to reply, but he gets the message when I rise from the couch with my hands on my hips.

"This isn't the time to take a side against me when there are little ears nearby." I don't want to be angry with him, yet I feel the explosion edging toward the surface.

"Don't shut me out, babe. I want to hear what's on your mind." He reclines against the cushion, hands clasped in his lap.

"I understand how badly your mom wants to be a grandparent. I do. She looks at this little boy as her only shot at being a grandmother because she doesn't trust you—trust me—to deliver. I've said this before: We have plenty of time for children."

"Do you want kids?" Alec's question is sincere. "We've never talked about it."

"I'm warming to the idea, though Noah's not the ideal example to get me to the finish line. You're thirty-one, with lots of plans, Alec. Let's work on being a couple first."

He nods, smiling.

"I'm not happy with *me* lately. Virena and Noah have turned Annalisse Drury into an overdramatic loon."

"Not true."

"Yeah, it is. Noah's a wedge between us, and he's straining my friendship with Gen. She doesn't view the boy through objective eyes while she showers him with toys and clothes. Virena sees where this is going."

Alec takes my hand and squeezes. "Virena's a blip from my past."

"She's in the here and now, pushing herself at you. The Zavos name, family wealth, all that, isn't a secret. Not now, and not when you were in college. She knows how powerful you are. Why would Virena keep your child from you for so long when she had so much to gain by telling you in the beginning?" I hold up a palm to still Alec's protest.

Here goes.

"It's because you aren't Noah's father. Putting off the paternity test changes nothing. I've watched Noah interact with you and Gen. He has none of your personality traits, and his scary blue eyes don't belong to you or Virena. You might think this is crazy, but I wouldn't be surprised to learn that he's not even her biological son."

Alec looks up at the ceiling. "How can you be sure he's not mine?"

You're losing his support.

16

We have no background on Virena since Alec stopped dating her, and she later left college. Noah as Virena's ex-husband's biological son is a theoretical possibility. After an unplanned pregnancy, she would need financial support and might have married, or she hooked up with Noah's true father, who skipped out or left them through a divorce.

I take his hand as I drop beside him on the couch. "Things don't line up. If you think about her sudden appearance, why now? Why not after the baby was born, or before? Paternity tests are easy and painless. A swab inside the mouth, and the answer arrives in a few days, or hours if you know someone who can push the findings through." My throat dries and tightens from his reaction.

He's making circles on the velvet armrest with an index finger, still avoiding eye contact. "Do you have any idea what this will do to Mom if Noah isn't mine?"

"She'll be sad and disappointed. Any grandmother would be. I don't want to hurt her. I love your mom, too, don't forget." I sigh. "I'm worried that another Tina Gold Digger, like your ex-wife, has the potential to take advantage of a pair of loving people who are honest to a fault. Think about how much worse Gen will feel if you discover the boy's not yours, years later. Verify *before* Gen forms a deep attachment to Noah."

Alec, an only child, lost his father while sailing their yacht on the Aegean Sea outside Crete two years ago. When Pearce Zavos died that day, Alec's mother became his primary concern, with me a close second. We were all on the yacht together, and Gen has welcomed me into the Zavos clan ever since.

17

The three of us are emotionally linked due to a terrible experience no family should have to endure. I regret our trip to Crete and feel somewhat responsible for how things turned out on their boat.

Alec drags his palm over his hair and withholds a response.

"You have so much on your plate and deserve a break from my constant hounding. I have the perfect solution. I'm going to take a leave of absence from the gallery for a couple of weeks while you work through the Noah thing without my interference," I say. "Chase can cover for me at the shop."

After Chase and I joined Gen in her generous partnership offer, I no longer worry about losing my brownstone. Her art gallery proposition and increased income came at the right time.

"Leave the gallery now? Mom didn't mention it."

"An opportunity came up today, but I have a big ask of you. Can our New Zealand tickets be exchanged for an earlier date?"

"Anna, I have furnishings arriving for the vet clinic next week."

When Alec sold his father's Italy-based car corporation months ago, the sale left him able to pursue his training and first love; becoming an equine surgeon and building the clinic close to his estate home.

"This trip is for me only. I've heard from Ethan, and he's invited me to his family's sheep station. I'm so excited to see if Kate joined him there. You know that I want to talk to her in the worst way. Stay here and get your work done while I chill out."

"You're going without me? Where's his station?"

"It's on New Zealand's South Island in the Canterbury region, I think."

"If you wait until April, we can go together. Why the hurry?" he asks.

"Ethan's invitation came to the gallery. For me."

Alec's lips press into a straight line, and the air temperature drops a few degrees. "The invite isn't extended to me, I take it." He huffs. "Did he say Kate was there?"

"Chase found Ethan's package on Gen's credenza when he got to the shop today. Ethan didn't include much of a note inside, so I don't know if my mother is with him. I'd like to go, Alec. Not to see Ethan, but to reunite with Kate, if she's in New Zealand. You're so busy right now with the clinic and... the boy down the hall." I motion toward the double doors. "The time apart will—"

"From your flashing green eyes, I'm not sure if we're splitting up. Are we?" He touches my arm. "Whatever this is, we can fix it without going abroad."

Sadness spoils his handsome, dark features, all because of an old lover and her son and my search for an escape valve.

What happens to us when I leave him?

I'm uneasy just thinking about the separation, and how adding more space might widen the fissure.

"Come here." I encourage him to rise and wrap my arms around his neck. "You're stuck with me, Alec. You aren't losing me, so forget about that." I land a kiss on his nose to lighten the mood, and his soap-scented, shaven skin reminds me that I reek. "How can you stand me? You smell great, and I carry the arousing scent of Eau-de-Harriet."

My French accent needs work.

He surprises me by laughing, and draws me in by the waist until the closeness is too much to bear. Alec growls and snuggles into the hollow of my neck. "I'll worry about you on such a long flight—by yourself, no less. You'll have several connecting flights, nearly a day in the air." His long gaze sends me into his smoldering kiss. "Don't fly out now. Wait for me. I promise you'll have more fun." He lifts his brows for effect.

"Caving a little, but I'm sure this distance is what we need. Boy, that shower is going to feel good, almost as great as your wanting to slay all dragons and keep me safe. You're all I need; I'm helplessly in love with the jet-setting, complex son of Pearce and Generosa Zavos. There's no other man on earth I'd rather be with." A hard swallow later, my chin rests on his shoulder so that he can't see my eyelids filling.

When Alec and I began dating two years ago, I was easily intimidated by his family's business endeavors and how the media pursues Alec in the tabloids. Good looking, wealthy men on front pages help sell their lies to a gullible public.

He lowers to one knee in front of me and kisses my left hand. "Are you accepting my proposal? If so, you've caught me ringless."

My nerves are fluttering like this is a first date with Alec. I want to accept but can't yet when I'm so rattled.

"Let's wait for the ring."

He searches my eyes for more optimism, and when he doesn't find it, he rises. "All right, but I wish you'd let me come along." He glances toward the mantel clock. "Someone should be around the warehouse today to redirect shipments. I'll change them to another week so you don't have to fly alone. The clinic waiting room can hold a few more weeks when the interior decorating is further along." He hugs me tighter. "How will you manage your acrophobia?"

"Like I always do. White-knuckling the armrests seems to help." I smile sideways at him. "Please don't change your deliveries for me and don't put off the clinic. I'll be fine on the flight."

"What if you get into trouble? It's not impossible, you know," Alec presses while fondling a lock of my hair. He takes a deep breath and mumbles, "Can't get enough of that scent. Wait here."

Alec trudges down the hall, making more noise than usual. Is he going to get the engagement ring?

The heat from the fire beckons now that Alec's gone, and my body has grown cool. There's still no sign of him while I pace the fireside, speculating on what's about to drop.

He returns carrying an envelope, not the ring box or the blue velvet bag that holds it, which is a relief.

A part of me is happy not to talk about marriage because there are still too many uncertainties between us. I hate sealed white envelopes. From experience, the darn things carry nothing but problems.

"I vote we go back to bed and start this day over right." Alec sweeps in behind me, curling his muscular arms about my waist, gathering me against his chest.

"I'm all in. After you show me what you have there." We sit on the hearth, the burning oak's flames swirling and popping at our backs.

Alec flips over a standard card envelope with the flap lifted, then points at the corner. Four colorful postage stamps with Polynesian face carvings glare back at me, their ghoulish tongues wagging in a taunt. They look like the tribal emblems of Hawaiian totems. The postage text is in English and marked New Zealand, signifying that the carvings are Māori culture from the region, not Hawaiian. The address label is computer or typewriter generated for Alec at his Brookehaven home.

"I think you're looking in the right place," Alec states.

"For what? I don't follow."

He's stoic and unreadable as he lays the envelope in my lap. He slides the note out and opens it.

I recognize the aging penmanship, and my next breath catches. "You found her!" Intuition gives me the answer before Alec does. "The card is from Kate."

"Seems so." Alec shifts. "I wanted to tell you earlier."

"How long have you known her whereabouts?" I'm trying hard not to lose my cool.

He knows I've been waiting to hear from Kate, where she ran to, and why she felt running out on me was her best option. We have so much to talk about, even though I understand why she had to cover for her affair. My father is out there, dead or still alive, and I'd like to know which it is.

22

"Her note was in with the mail on my desk when we came home from Italy."

We got back from Italy months ago.

Kate should be writing to me, her daughter, not Alec. Why him over me? Blue ballpoint ink rushes past my vision in a blur—I can't read a single word through my fume clouds gathering around us. Kate's taking the coward's way out… again, sending letters instead of facing me with answers about her fling with my father and where he is now.

"Nothing's sinking in." I pass the note to Alec and prepare myself. "Would you mind reading it aloud?"

"She and Ethan traveled together." He gazes at me.

"Okay, we considered that."

"Kate has business to conclude in New Zealand before she returns to New York. She asked me not to mention this to you until she arrives in the States but didn't give a reason. Kate says she'll meet you in person when she's ready."

"Seriously? Where does she plan to live? With me in Greenwich? The Goshen farm could be sold by now. Does she mention if her son found her another place to live?"

Alec scans the page. "No, she didn't."

I scratch my scalp and shake my head. "Then my sheep station trip to New Zealand is good timing. I have to leave now and see if I can catch her before she skips out. Ethan must know where Kate is. If it's all the same, we'll hang on to the tickets for our April trip, and I'll buy my way for this flight." Tugging at my sweatshirt, I take the note from Alec and sail it into the flames, watching paper crinkle and burn on the log.

He steps forward, his chiseled profile gawking at the fire in disbelief.

"Were you ever going to tell me about Kate's message?" A sob chokes my windpipe. "If it weren't for Ethan's invite, I doubt we'd be talking about Kate."

"Babe, I thought by staying neutral…" He twists his lips and looks at his shoes. "Seeing your reaction now, I know it was a mistake not to tell you."

I ball my hands into fists. "You were afraid I'd run down there to find her." I'm mad enough to send smoke signals, so I take slower, calming breaths.

"If I'd told you… Yeah, I worried you'd run off. Your safety doesn't include my encouraging you to hop on a plane to another country so soon after Italy. Waiting for Kate's return felt right to me. At some point, I hope you'll see things from my side. Kate put me in the middle, but it's *you* I worry about."

Willing myself to relax, I take his hand to get him to focus on me instead of the floor. "I know that. After a shower, I'll give your mom a call from the car on the way home. I might have trouble getting a flight out on the spur of the moment, so if I do, I hope you'll help me."

"Anna, we should discuss this." He catches my wrist. "I'd like to go along. Say the word, and I'm on that plane with you. Allow what's happened with Kate to simmer. You might feel differently in the morning."

Kate gave me her personal locket with our pictures when she left her letter behind explaining who she truly was. My birth mother. Grasping her locket beneath my shirt, I slide the chain over my head and cup Alec's hand, dropping the necklace there.

"Hold on to my locket while I'm gone. It's the most precious thing I own. That way, you'll know I'm coming back to you."

On my tiptoes, our kiss calls up a loneliness—in a flash, two people are about to have a hemisphere drifting between them, due to outside influences that want to manipulate them.

"Gen will be here to see Noah in a few hours, and you have him until Sunday. Let me go, Alec, and please wait for me at Brookehaven. I have to make this trip by myself. If there's the slightest chance that Kate's with Ethan or he knows where she is, I have to go. I've already lost precious time."

In a dead run, I'm biting a quivering lip. On the way to Alec's bedroom suite, I text Chase to hold Ethan's box and note for me at the gallery. True to form, Kate shoves us all out of our comfort zones. I'm certain to find a disaster waiting for me to book a ticket to New Zealand in a mad rush.

CHAPTER THREE
Letting Go of Control

Five days ago, I was in Alec's incredible home. That cozy sanctuary seems a world away from the airport now that I'm in my living space for the next day, sweating in the middle of winter. Cold leather chairs smack of antiseptic cleaners and recycled, stale cabin air, but it's the only way to cover nine thousand air miles from New York to Christchurch with stops in between. No choice, no problem.

We're still on the ground at JFK because passengers from connecting flights in bad weather are holding us up. How will I withstand spending twenty-one hours in the air on a Boeing 737? Alec had the keen insight to warn me about traveling alone, no matter how hard I try to blot out his concerns. That realization has me unsure about my decision when I think about where I am; flying solo because I wanted Alec to stay behind. A sense of doom is advancing through my bones that's hard to dismiss.

You're lucky to find a spacious first-class seat on such short notice, a counter attendant remarked prior to my standing in line for invasive TSA searches. I'm so grateful to Alec for honoring my wish when I know he's agonizing over my leaving and stressing to the max. It was sweet of him to pull strings and make this long flight as comfortable for me as possible. Who wants to sit in economy without legroom for that many hours, sandwiched between others like crayons in a tight box? Not me and my fear of heights with all that ocean to ditch into, should we crash.

Gen encourages personal time for mental health, for which I'm a lead candidate in the state I'm in. Chase Miller is our third gallery partner, specializing in security protocols and responsible for the gallery's website. He's covering my antique appraisal duties with potential clients while I'm gone. More important, he's taking care of Boris, my spoiled ginger kitty, while I'm on what feels like an impossible mission to combine a photography vacation with fact-finding about my heritage from a stubborn mother.

Part of me wishes Chase would appear in the seat beside me. Chase is a good listener and never judges—a rare friend to have. He's my sounding board and confidant who knows me better than I know myself. I'm lucky to have his support in all things.

Charcoal-colored leather covers the ten pairs of seats around me, and matching carpet spans the floor. Most of the passengers in this section are already in their seats, except my seat partner. Maybe that person is ill or changed flights?

Using the empty cushion as a prop, I'm digging through my extra-large handbag for a stick of gum to clear the funky taste in my mouth, when a pair of sneakers align themselves on the floor in my view. Stationary feet, not about to pass by in the aisle.

"This must be the place," a cheerful male voice says.

"Sorry," I mutter, not bothering to look up. *Please don't be creepy.*

My giant tote with many compartments lands on the floor with a thud near my feet. I pop a piece of gum from the pack into my mouth and stow the purse under my chair.

"I like that color on you," he confesses.

I swallow my gum, coughing. "Bill?"

It's Alec's detective friend, stowing his suitcase and jacket. He's wearing a dark pocket Henley instead of his usual Hawaiian shirt, but the smiling hazel eyes and neck scars from his time as a fireman are unmistakable.

"How did you—Why...? Alec." I'm withholding a groan because it's not Bill's fault. "He sent you, didn't he?"

Bill's buckling himself in as I plant my arms over my chest. I have to admit, sending a spy in his stead is a ploy I didn't think of.

"I mean it. Emerald green is your color, Anna."

"What cases are you putting aside to be here?" My jaw sets.

Bill raises his hand to the seatbelt. "If having me along is too much for you, I'll leave right now." Then he turns sideways and adds, "I'm here for two friends."

An announcement that the aircraft doors have closed and we're about to depart for the taxiway sounds through cabin. Did he do this on purpose, boarding late? Bill isn't one for trickery. It's time to be grateful for the selfless act. Not many would drop everything to come to the aid of his friends.

Bill settles back. "I almost didn't make it. The roads stink with all this snow. Summer in another country suits me just fine." He leans back and sighs. "Yep, seventy degrees and sunshine like the Keys."

Bill Drake lives in Florida some months, but his office is located in Connecticut, where he and his business partner, Dan, run a private investigation firm. Bill's tight-lipped about his clientele, and he's a great detective, so I have to imagine he's successful. Finding him on the same plane with me says volumes about how tight he is with Alec. They aren't just friends; they're more like brothers who come to each other's assistance when called upon.

We used Bill's expertise to find Kate when we thought she was kidnapped from Alec's stable last summer. Searching for Kate from Goshen, New York, to Lenox, Massachusetts, was my first encounter with Bill. The second was when he came to assist during our bizarre Italy trip recently.

Bill and Alec became friends during college, not unlike how Chase and I met. I know very little about their early friendship, but I'd like to understand their story. On this excursion, I get to fill in the blanks about Bill, the fireman turned detective.

Would I rather make the trip alone next to a stranger, or spend a day in a metal tube with a good friend who's helped us plenty of times? A no-brainer for my weary mind.

I unfold my arms because it's time to send my awesome seat partner a better message. "Forgive my self-righteousness, Bill; it's so misplaced. I can relax now that you're here. You're a good friend and I'm thankful to have you with me."

And I mean it.

Temuka, New Zealand, in the Canterbury region isn't a large community, with a population of around four thousand. Doing a quick search while waiting on Bill at the rental car counter, I visualize several smaller towns sprinkled near the larger coastal city of Timaru. We should have no problem finding Bill lodging in a hotel or renting a guesthouse near the station, unless they're covered with tourists and booked for the season. Home rentals are in demand everywhere because buying a home is crazy expensive. I can't ask Ethan and his family to put up a surprise guest, and I doubt Alec thought that far ahead for Bill's lodging. Without knowing the size of the station cottage, we'll have to wait until we see how many bedrooms it has.

My emails to Ethan's old address have gone unanswered and so have my text messages, which concerns me a great deal. Traveling this far without more details and verification from him is unlike me. I should've taken care of making a connection prior to my hasty departure. We might be sightseeing New Zealand on our own if Ethan is in the habit of extending invitations without checking with family first. If he went beyond his authority by sending me the house key for a cottage that might be occupied, it says that he hasn't changed his casual, carefree ways. I have to prepare for an abrupt about-face if our cottage is no longer available.

Since the gallery's grand opening party two years ago, when Alec and I became an item, we've been thrust together by desire and destiny, again and again. Anyone else would've dropped me and my negative karma by now, but not Alec. Some moments with him have been over-the-top amazing, while other memories are not so great.

During my time by Alec's side, our short relationship has felt a lot longer and gets more complicated as we go. I dare not to think if we truly belong together, because a few puzzle pieces still don't fit no matter how hard I push them into place.

On the plane, Bill says, "Don't stay away from Alec too long, and check in with him often. I've never seen two people who belong together more than you guys do."

He has faith in us during my doubts, so this gives me hope that Alec and I have a chance. Bill has a track record for stellar advice.

I'll tuck Bill's suggestion away for now and revisit it when we're on the road south.

Generosa wasn't pleased to get my call asking for time off. She believes Alec needs me now more than ever, and two weeks away from him will drive a wedge between us. She understands my need for that meeting with Kate, but when it comes to her son, it makes more sense for her to side with him. As she should.

The airport terminal is spacious and modern—not how my imagination captured the scene. For cultural reasons, I expected tiki torches and palm trees, native art, and tribal tattoos decorating the walls. Instead, inviting, curved couches swerve around each pillar structure, and the straight beam and vaulted ceilings are a nice touch against bluish stone walls. I've read about their natural blue stone used in this part of the world, created by the volcanic activity here. Native ferns and pink flowering New Zealand Hebes dot the huge window sills. They're enough to signal a Polynesian attitude without going overboard. An air of English modern meets island paradise explains the ethnic mash-up from European settlers in three hundred years of colonization.

Bill and I are two hours driving time from Woolcombe Station in Temuka and dragging from exhaustion. I'm swollen from retaining water, my usual side effect from too many hours of inactivity in altitude. Bill suggests we try the attached Airport Kovotella hotel, but I won't rest until we get to the cottage and I can speak to a human I recognize, other than Bill.

He's waiting at the rental car table, rubbing his forehead, looking like he's forgotten something important back home.

Surely that doesn't mean we can't drive here, or worse, we have to settle for a compact car on rough terrain. Renting a vehicle ahead of time wasn't on the radar while I gathered jeans, blouses, shoes, and a 220-volt charging device together. While jamming the basics into a suitcase, a check on the rules of the road for visitors in New Zealand shot right past me. I didn't think about driving to and from the station, let alone having someone with me. Ethan should've been at the airport to pick me up, given the long airport drive. It's easy to blame him, but I came here in a rush; that's not Ethan's fault.

Shifting the gouging tote strap to the other shoulder, I glance at our suitcases. Foo-foo designer tapestry with broken zippers makes up mine. Bill brought a black, hard-side case on wheels for maneuvering tight corners. The kind a savvy traveler would bring. I quickly send a one-line text to Alec to let him know that we made it on the ground and stow my phone.

Bill pockets the rental agreement, twitching his mouth sideways, then makes eye contact with me. "Want the bad news first?"

My empty stomach steadies itself for a blow.

"Do you have any experience with a right-hand drive?" His twitch is back.

"Nope."

"Then we probably have two problems. How about driving on the left side of the road? Have you—"

I'm laughing because neither of us thought about the British influence on the culture here. "Not a chance. We're expected to drive on the opposite side of the road from the opposite side of the car? This is so not good. How did you talk me into this?"

Bill's mouth drops when he thinks I'm being serious, then he groans at my joke.

"That's my sleep deprivation talking." I laugh at him again.

"The way I see it, we either drive it or take the bus to Timaru and board another to Temuka. An expensive Uber or taxi is our other option unless your friend Ethan can be trusted to pick us up. Does he know we're here yet?" Bill uncovers his wristwatch and counts on his fingertips. "No wonder I'm starving. The Kiwis are almost a day ahead of the States, and aircraft meals don't cut it." He swivels. "Take a look." He points to the wall clock.

It's midmorning the next day.

"We got ourselves this far." I observe my missing zipper tab and wonder how long the bulging suitcase will stay closed. "Can we get a trolley to cart these cases to the car?"

"Stay here. I'll find the vehicle. At least we ended up with a Toyota SUV. While you're waiting, I recommend trying to raise Ethan by phone, and you might send Alec a text that we've made it," Bill says. "Don't leave the building and stay where I can find you. Back in a few."

He jogs through the automatic doors and almost runs into a gangly, suntanned older man walking into the terminal.

"Boy, he's bossy." I smile and sigh at the thought of my sore behind hitting the vinyl bench.

The suntanned man walks toward me slowly. I guess his age to be early sixties. He's wearing a beige fly-fishing hat with fishhooks stuck into the hat band. He stops and stares my way from the other side of the horseshoe cushions, with anxious eyes and deep wrinkles shaded by the brim.

The first thing I notice about people is their eyes. Too close to their nose and I'm leery about them. When they have expanded pupils, I think about medications or substance abuse, unless we're standing in the dark.

The stranger with a weatherworn face wearing a T-shirt with an ice cream cone on the front is hard to nail down from this distance, so it's better that I don't judge him.

"Are you Miss Annalisse?" he asks me in an accent similar to how I recall Ethan sounding.

"Yes, I'm Annalisse. And you are?" I smile.

"Was that your boyfriend earlier? You make a beautiful couple. He's one lucky man."

I jump to my feet, looking for a way to move our belongings closer to the automatic doors.

The man joins me next to my biggest bag, the one missing a zipper tab.

"Rough handlers in the airport. I see they ruined your zipper. Tough thing, that. If you want, I can fix your case for you." Mr. Friendly bends over and touches the fabric.

On impulse, I swat his hand away. "Please don't. We'll fix it later."

He snaps to attention. "No harm meant, missus. Since you aren't a townie, thought I'd offer." He touches his brim. "Aren't you goin' to Temuka? I'm here to pick up a lady named Annalisse. My daughter and I live in Temuka. I'm on holiday, fishin' ya know." He taps his brim again with an age-spotted hand.

"You came to pick us up from the airport? Who sent you?"

His bloodshot puppy-dog eyes look lost. "One of my gals at the sweet shop asked me to skedaddle to the airport. My cab service is a side job to make a few extra dollars. I'm Alastair, Alastair McGregor at your service, miss." He bows his head for a moment.

How long has he been waiting outside in the terminal parking lot?

"Didn't anyone tell you I'd be here to get ya?" He's wide-eyed as he looks around the terminal. "I'm sure I'm in the right place if your name is Annalisse."

I don't understand the miscommunication, or lack of in our case. "I'm sorry, Alastair. My friend hasn't sent or responded to any messages since we left New York. Who asked you to come to the airport? I don't know anyone at a candy store in New Zealand. Did Ethan call you?"

"The Fawdray boy? Naw, his sister asked me to come. Caught me by surprise, that. Her family doesn't like me much, but it's all good. Olivia works for me at the sweet shop near Main Street. Do you know it?"

"No. Olivia Fawdray works for you?" Alastair's tale doesn't make sense. I didn't know Ethan had a sister. He didn't mention her to us when he was at our farm.

"Olivia Hyde works at Sidney's Sweets. She's Ellen Hyde's daughter," he confirms.

The name is familiar. "Who's Ellen Hyde?"

Alastair rubs his brow. "You weren't supposed to be picked up? Olivia told me to come to Christchurch airport." He kicks at a spot on the tile. "All this way for nothin'. What a waste of petrol."

"Have a seat, Alastair. Let's dig into this some more. You have more information than I have, it seems."

"Surely." He parks on the cushion next to me. "I think I know what happened. Olivia is Ethan's sister, so he must've told her to get a message to me. He's busy on that station of theirs."

"Do you have a phone number for Ethan? He can clear this up. It's not that I don't trust you, but your being here is a welcome surprise. I have a friend of mine

36

along, so there are two of us going to the station, not one."

"I don't have the Fawdray boy's number, but he comes into my daughter's sweet shop now and again to get a Hokey Pokey."

Whatever in the world that is, but this man might be our road warrior rescuer. His story has holes though, like his daughter owning the shop when he said that *he* does.

"Is there any way for your daughter or Olivia Hyde to confirm our pickup with Ethan? He didn't leave a telephone number, or I'd call him myself." I must have an old phone number for Ethan. How did I get to another country and manage to do it without telling anyone at the station that I was on the way? The email might've reached him after all.

"I don't have the boy's number. Sorry."

"That's okay, Mr. McGregor. I can google Woolcombe Station. It'll be easier." A blush warms my cheeks when I open the search engine on my phone.

"My daughter's name is Sidney. She owns Sidney's Sweets on Whaler's Street off Main. Call her."

"No problem." I switch to a search for the store since he doesn't seem to have phone numbers. "Is Olivia at the shop today, or is she at home?"

"She has the late shift, so she won't be at the shop."

"Okay." That's not a help. I find the sweet shop number, and after two rings, a woman answers with the shop's name.

"Hi. I'm wondering if it's possible to talk to someone about Alastair McGregor. He's here at the airport to pick me up, but we weren't told he'd be driving us to Temuka. I'm looking for Olivia or Ethan Fawdray at Woolcombe Station." I pause and listen to her explain who Alastair is and why he's here. "We're from the United States, and Ethan's expecting me to arrive today. Oh, you have his number? Just a minute while I grab something to write it down."

I jot the number on the back of a beverage napkin from the plane. She asks me if I'd like her to call Ethan for me.

"Would you? That's so awesome. My name is Annalisse, Anna from New York. Please tell him that we're in Christchurch with Alastair. Are you Sidney? Jenny. I see. Thank you, Jenny. You've been a huge help. Enjoy the rest of your day."

Shoving the napkin into the inside pocket of my tote and one step closer to reaching Ethan, I find Alastair standing next to the doors, soaking up the morning sunshine. I make a mental note to follow up with Ethan once we're on the road to Temuka.

"Your friend must be lost in the lot," Alastair says. "Good thing I know where we're going. He can follow us in his rental car."

I'm sure glad one of us knows the way.

I drop another longer text to Alec. I promise to send him pictures and a follow up phone call once we eat something and find the cottage, thanking him for sending Bill to my rescue. Even a Hokey Pokey, turn yourself around, sounds tasty at this point.

CHAPTER FOUR
Road Trip

Bill's sitting in the idling Toyota rental car in terminal parking, waiting for Alastair to start his banged-up compact with a dented fender, torn bumper, and mangled license plate. I sure hope that he's not as cruddy a driver as the story his damaged Uber car shows us. We aren't thrilled that Ethan didn't bother to mention Alastair and his cab ride to the cottage on Woolcombe Station. Is our two-hour trip gratis, or do we pay Alastair for the drive? It's not a bad thing to have Bill's rental as a backup since we don't know where he's staying, and I might need a chauffeur going to and returning from the sheep station. I have no idea how far the cottage is from Ethan's homestead or if the little house is within walking distance of the barns. I could kick myself for allowing my emotions to run amok at Brookehaven. We're moving around dumb with blinders on, thanks to my rush out of New York without a plan.

Bill believes Alastair is telling the truth about retrieving us at the airport now that we know Olivia is Ethan's sister. What strikes us both as strange is why

Ethan is so hard to contact and is sending others to connect with me.

"I'm sorry, Miss Annalisse, but it looks like the ol' gal isn't going to start." Alastair closes the hood with a creak and a clunk. "If it's all the same, I need to call the auto club. I reckon the car blokes can fix her. Do you mind waiting so I can go back with you and your man friend in case we can't get it started?"

"Sure, make your call. I see Bill coming this way."

"Car won't start?" Bill asks me, and I nod.

"If you don't mind, I'd like to wait for the auto club. I feel funny taking off in case they don't get Alastair's car started," I say.

"The club isn't far away. Sorry about this." Alastair taps his hat band and smiles at me.

As his fate would have it, we have a reliable, serviced vehicle.

"Did I mention that I drive on the left side of the road?" the man from Temuka asks.

I look to Bill for his recommendation. Dare we allow a stranger to get behind the wheel of our rental, especially after seeing his beat-up personal car? I'll let Bill make the call on that one.

Bill scans Alastair's identification and driving background, then quizzes the heck out of him. He has driver's license validity for cars only, and his birth-date puts him at sixty-four years old. He's a resident of Temuka, so that much is confirmed. Alastair passes his questions with ease, other than random bouts of nervousness during Bill's investigative stares.

Bill determines that Alastair's been truthful with us and seems helpful and harmless. We can't know if he's accurate with his descriptions of Woolcombe Station until we see it for ourselves. He cites local businesses and eateries that I verify, including their storefront descriptions.

Alastair's driving, Bill's riding shotgun, and I'm sitting in the back on a roomy but smoky bench seat. Kids fifteen years and older can smoke in this country, so I'd better get used to cigarette odor inside and outside buildings. For now, having the window down to the fresh air works well enough to clear the stench.

Once we pass Christchurch's city center of ugly parking areas and gray buildings, with Alastair sounding like a tour guide, there's a smattering of New Zealand's founding history of more interest to me as an antiquities expert. Spires and archways enter the architecture, similar to the curves, masonry, and sharp lines in cathedral-like British construction. Old Christchurch appears to have bounced back to modern skyscraper life after its devastating earthquake in 2011 that all but destroyed large swaths of the older buildings.

As we enter the flats and hills of the Canterbury grasslands, Alastair is chattier, having finally relaxed in our presence. Driving south, we have a gorgeous view of the Pacific Ocean, and the mountain range to the west is just as magnificent as I thought it would be. Jagged peaks have a dusting of snow, leaving the white contrasting to the rest of the lavender-forested nooks and evergreen hillsides. Hundreds of crystal-blue ponds dot the scenery on both sides of the roadway. A reminder of the sapphire necklace that Gen gave me for my birthday. Alec's stunning engagement ring reflects in the blue, and a twinge of disappointment knots my insides.

"The scenery isn't what I expected. I've watched movies filmed in New Zealand with little people climbing mountains, in caves, and lush vegetation all around. It's not like that here," Bill says.

"I know the ones. They filmed on the North Island in Waikato." Alastair points through the windshield and says, "Over the bonnet, we're coming up to a nature refuge. Bluebasin Lake is one of my favorite places in Canterbury. Did you notice the blue walls of stone in the airport?"

"Yes," I say. "They're stunning."

Alastair's head bobs. "It's called bluestone and mined from the hillsides at Bluebasin Lake. Miners are destroying the habitat and changing the ecosphere of the lake. Fish are disappearing and no longer spawning like they used to. We're planning protests next week to stop them from strip mining and causing more damage. On top, we have politicians working against the townies' wishes. They want retirement housing, a shopping mall, and an amusement park near the lake. It'll wipe out the countryside for good with shops and high-rises. You're from New York, miss. Can you see tall buildings, footpaths, and parking lots in a place like this?"

"If politics are involved, powerful lobbyists are pushing for the construction," Bill adds. "That's the way it works in the United States."

"Same here." Alastair grumbles something inaudible. "We have our own politician in Temuka. You already know the family. He runs Woolcombe Station with his wife, Ellen. That young man you keep asking about is his stepson."

Bill's head swivels and I lurch forward as far as my seat belt will allow.

"Ethan's dad is a local politician?" I ask. "I didn't know that."

"Not even. I reckon the best place for Finn Hyde is made into mince. It's money over the people with him. He's an En Zed Parliament member and thinks he's king of the South Island. As dodgy as they come, if you ask me. Dirty through and through." He clears the frog from his throat. "Sorry, I didn't mean to go off," Alastair says, white-knuckling the steering wheel.

Ethan's the stepson of a politician. That's a shocker. He was careful not to mention it while he worked at Walker Farm. I doubt Kate would've been happy to hear about his family this way. At least Ethan was smart enough to keep his dad's politics to himself. I have so much to talk to him about when we reach the station.

"Alastair, is it far to Bluebasin Lake? I'd love to get a few pictures for Alec." I'm already fumbling for my Nikon. "Do you mind a quick side trip, Bill?" My stomach rumbles out loud so everyone in the vehicle can hear. Bill has to be as hungry as I am.

"I don't mind," Bill says. He's starving and wouldn't think to disagree with me.

"The turnout is ahead," Alastair says. "It won't take long. The Pohutukawa is choice now." He looks at Bill to clarify. "Our Pohutukawa is a tree with red bushy brushes. Brilliant for taking pictures."

"I think it looks like what we call a bottlebrush," I add.

Alastair takes the exit, and a wonderland of rich colors and fragrances draw us in.

We must've hit the lupine bloom at peak season as I wander with my camera. Spikes of pink, purple, and magenta explode on their clusters of two-foot green stems. Tiny rows of pea-shaped flowers swirl and curl, larger at the bottom to sharp points at their tops. They remind me of wild stock, one of Kate's favorite florals for arrangements. The lupine grows in bunches all the way into the lake, like colorful porcupines wading through the water. The sea of spikes is so vivid and intense, from the dry banks to the lake in shallow areas; it blows me away with each shutter snap.

A majestic mountain backdrop in bluish-gray cordons off the turquoise water, framing it behind the lupine's profuse color. Bright yellow bumblebees buzz from stalk to stalk in their pollination dance as rich, spicy aromas draw hundreds of butterflies to their nectar. I'm taking so many photos that my finger hurts from depressing the shutter button so much. It's a good pain to have.

I spot the giant Pohutukawa that Alastair mentioned, lying almost perpendicular to the water. Its flowering branches remind me of the red spikes and pollen-laden bottlebrush standing tall over the lake. Thick pines stand in an evergreen layer, the last spot of color before the mountain range juts out of the soil.

Walking to the car, I remove the camera strap and lean against the SUV, in awe of this place. "Wow."

"Told ya you'd like it," Alastair says. "It's a place for photographers."

"This lake is amazing." Bill surveys the mountains and turns to me. "Bet you wish Alec could see this."

"We will the next time. Once he gets the pictures, he'll be counting the days till our April trip."

"You're keeping his tickets for a return trip, then?" Bill asks me.

"Yeah. Something told me not to cancel or change the dates. Alec has to see this spot for himself."

I stow my camera in the back seat and get my phone. "Bill, I'm going to try Woolcombe Station since we haven't heard from Ethan yet. I don't know about cell coverage here, though."

"Should be fine, miss." Alastair takes his hands from his pockets and turns for the Toyota.

Copying from the napkin, I tap in the number Jenny gave me at the sweet shop and hit speakerphone.

"Hyde Station," an older woman chimes as if on habit.

My mouth opens but no words come out.

"It's okay, Anna," Bill whispers.

"Is this Woolcombe Station?"

"Yes, who's calling please?"

"May I speak to Ethan Fawdray? My name is Anna, Anna from the US." I shrug at Bill. "I'm a friend of his from New York. Is he in?"

"Not if he's out with the mob."

The receiver hits something hard, then footsteps fade away. This must be a household landline and she's left the phone behind.

"We have the cottage key, Bill, so if Ethan's busy…"

Hard breathing and clomping boots enter the speaker. A throat clears and a door closes.

More laboring of breath. "Annalisse? Miss Drury, is that you?"

"Ethan. Finally." I expel a gush of air and a little apprehension with it.

My smile must be off the charts because Bill's reflects how I feel.

"Did you get my package? You know, with the key?" Ethan's tone is giddy with excitement. He doesn't usually act bubbly, so he's happy to hear from me.

"Yes, thanks. We have lots to talk about, but I don't want to keep you on the phone too long. How far is the cottage from the station?"

"Not too. Over the next ridge. I can't believe you're here already. Crikey dick, I've missed you heaps. Did Alastair find you?" He's still huffing.

Bill scowls at me when Ethan uses his crazy term.

I'm talking through my grin. "Alastair is here. So you sent him to the airport. We appreciate that. Is the cottage hard to find? We're about an hour away from Temuka."

"Naw. It's a cinch. Sir Raleigh Way. Stay on the main road until it forks and take it to the left. You'll see the street sign. Gray wood and a cool porch. The *bach* sits near a pond."

"What's a batch? This cottage *is* vacant, right?" It would be just like Ethan to put me up as a guest in a boarding house.

"Totally, yeah. Our station manager used it, but he's gone."

Bill raises an eyebrow.

"We had a bit of a scrape when he—"

Ethan can get lengthy with explanations. "We'll want to hear all about it tomorrow after we settle in our things."

"Who's we? Didn't you come by yourself?" Ethan asks in alarm.

Bill raises a finger to his lips.

"Gotta go now, Ethan. We're in a hurry to find the cottage. Check in soon."

"Yeah, cheers."

I drop my phone in the tote, feeling better than I did at the airport.

"I'll stay incognito until it's time to reveal myself." Bill's taking a menacing approach.

"Incognito?"

"I'm not here to spy on Ethan. Lighten up. We're on vacation," Bill confirms.

"Who is Alec?" Alastair asks.

Instinct has Bill and I clamming up and we pass a knowing look between us. The less this stranger knows about us, the better.

We're traveling south on the main highway with our driver in cold silence since asking about Alec. Alastair might be radioactive in his connection to the Bluebasin Lake controversy, and it wouldn't take much for him to research Alec and his wealth. The last thing

Alec needs are dirty politicians drawing him into a New Zealand environmental war.

"Where can we drop you off when we reach Temuka?" I ask Alastair, who has complete control of where our Toyota goes.

He doesn't answer.

A huge flock of adult sheep are crossing the road ahead. There must be hundreds in the band of shorn animals. Alastair slams on the brakes, giving them the right-of-way.

"Don't you raise sheep? What breed are they, Annalisse? They're so pink. Won't they get sunburnt?" Bill asks.

"I'm not sure of the breed. It's hard to tell without their fleece, but they look like crossbred Corriedales, maybe Merino crosses. See their dark points?"

"Better explain points, miss," Alastair turns to Bill and chuckles. "Townie here."

"Dark points are a term used if their noses are black or dark. Sometimes solid or sometimes their features are speckled. Hooves can also have dark portions on them. When we get to the station, you'll get a beginner's lesson on raising sheep. Ethan loves showing people his animals. Kate said he spent so much time playing with critters that he didn't have time to finish his chores."

"Do you expect to find Kate at the station?" Bill asks, but I'm still thinking about sheep.

"I hope so, but if Ethan told her about me, knowing her, she's long gone. At least Ethan is the best source I have to find her. While we're stopped, I'll take a few more pictures." I open the door and wrap the camera strap around my neck.

Clicking off shots of little pink bodies on the move, I watch the tail end of the flock cross the road with two black collies pushing the last few stragglers back to the group. I relish witnessing a large band of sheep moving in concert as a flock. Where one goes, the rest follow because they're born with the need to hang together. There's safety in numbers for animals without a defense mechanism against predators.

A pang of guilt for having Alec stay behind strikes me. He should be here to see this. Hopefully, my photos will do this tranquil scene justice, and he'll come to understand why I had to leave.

"Another reason for coming here, Bill. It's not every day that we get access to a spectacular panorama of sheep, and never in Manhattan." I unwind the camera strap from my neck, settling into the back seat for the rest of our road trip through dry grassland that pales in comparison to awesome Bluebasin Lake.

Forty minutes later, we approach the simple roadway marker for Temuka town limits. The first thing I notice is how much this country cares for its birds and wildlife. We pass a yellow three-foot sign demanding drivers slow down because cars kill their beloved, native Kiwi. A strange, flightless bird only found in New Zealand.

Alastair's floppy tan hat has sunk farther over his ears like a cartoon character, or it's my imagination from staring at his neck for the past two hours. He still hasn't given us his drop-off point yet, and I'm antsy to have him drive to his daughter's shop so he can get out there. Beyond that, Bill can attempt to drive on the wrong side of the road for a few miles.

As if he's read my mind, Alastair says, "Here'll do." He swerves into a turnout on the left side and unbuckles his seat belt.

There's nothing here but a stand of trees and a few rocks. We haven't made it to the town yet. What is he doing?

"Alastair, we'd be more comfortable if you'd drive to your business or home. You can't jump out on the shoulder of the road," Bill says with a glance at the dirt turnout.

"Sidney's place is on Whaler's Street." Alastair points to an unknown spot in the brush. "I can walk. It'll do these old bones some good. Now, just up the road on Main, you'll find motels. Not corkers but choice enough when you're knackered. Good as gold. On your right, food. Fish places and lamb joints that'll fill the belly."

Alastair steps out of the SUV on the traffic side. "Thanks for the ride, Mr. Drake." He waves at Bill and stretches over the headrest to make eye contact with me. "Be happy, miss. Enjoy our beautiful country, and don't worry about my car. It's all good. Cheerio." Closing the door and stepping out on the sunny road in front of us, he strides in a jerky gait as if one leg is shorter than the other. I didn't note it earlier.

I open the door to the front seat and slide across it to join Bill. Sitting on the usual driver's side feels strange without a steering wheel to look over.

"What do you think?" Bill asks. "Should we follow him to his daughter's?"

"He might think we're trying to run him down. Let's find a place to eat, then look in on him."

"Fair enough."

We enter a different era as the main drag opens up to us. Storefronts with squared-off wooden posts hold awnings offering shady walkways for browsing shoppers on wide plank porches stretching the entire block. Each shop frontage reminds me of studio sets built for old Western movies; a bank here, and a woolens shop there. Uneven rooflines and giant store windows reflect displays of bakery goods, their cakes and donuts enticing customers into a bakery café with the old-fashioned ambiance of retail stores from decades ago.

"Drive slower, Bill. I feel like we've gone back in time. There's every paint color of the rainbow. A yellow bank, a green bakery, a blue apothecary. Everyone is walking around in shorts and tanks. We have to take a day from the farm to shop Main Street. The buildings alone are calling to me. Who knows what supercool history we'll find inside?"

"The only thing missing are hitching posts with tied-up horses. I wasn't expecting this. Man, I see your camera getting a workout in this town. Pretty amazing, actually." Bill chuckles. "Umbrella tables, and check out the streetlamps lining the road. I wish I were an artist; what a painting this would make. We'll have to settle for your photos." He looks at me and grins. "I saw a fish and chips place back there. Sound good to you?"

I'd forgotten how startling white his teeth are. "I'm more than ready."

The frying oil isn't rancid-smelling or burnt, so we order to go and sit at the picnic table outside. We wolf down the best battered whitefish I've ever eaten, bar none. Flaky and delicate. Tender fish without the briny flavor of the ocean.

"Boy, if the whitefish tastes this good, I can't wait to try their famous green-lipped mussels," I say with one swipe of my napkin. "Bill, I was thinking, before we stow your luggage in any ol' motel, let's see how much room there is at the cottage. We have one rental car for both of us. If you're in downtown Temuka and I'm at the cottage on the outskirts, who gets the SUV?"

"Are you afraid to stay at the cottage by yourself?" Bill asks, grabbing our trash in an armful and dumping it in a bin near the post. "I'm an early riser. Happy to take you wherever you want to go. I don't mind being your driver."

"Did Alec hire you as my bodyguard?" I speak out loud what crosses my mind as I jump into our Toyota and send the window down for another blast of buttery fish oil.

"He didn't want you traveling alone in case you ran into trouble. Are you ready to see what New Zealanders call a *bach*? I hope it has running water."

"Don't worry, we have a pond for a water source." I'm laughing in jest but inside I'm hoping it doesn't come to that.

He starts the Toyota with a push button. "Let's see how well I can operate from this side and if the navigation works. I've seen plenty of motels with vacancy signs. I won't have trouble getting a room. Next stop, the abode on Sir Raleigh Way."

Tires squeal from a section of road we traveled earlier, and not long after, a woman screams.

"Should we check it out?" I ask Bill, who's already swiveling in his seat.

Bill tears out of the space and maneuvers to the right side of the road.

CHAPTER FIVE
Homicides R Us

"Bill, get left!" I yell while checking for oncoming traffic. That's when I notice a group standing in a semicircle near a driveway—around limbs. From here, it looks like a person's body.

"Oh no." I stare through the windshield.

We slow to a stop and park near the curb of a strip shopping area, leaving our engine running.

"We should help." I jump out to investigate. Women wearing rompers and a guy in greasy mechanic's overalls are standing over someone on the pavement.

"What happened?" I ask Bill, jogging to the scene and scanning the narrow two-lane road where no other vehicle has pulled over other than us. A familiar beige fishing hat lies a few feet from the victim.

"A mad driver went on a strop!" a female screams from the gawking crowd.

"It's Alastair," Bill mutters, his words loud enough for me to catch them. "Did he have a heart attack or did someone hit him?"

Bill reaches the bystanders on Main Street before I do and throws his arm out, blocking me with his body and a stern glare.

"Annalisse, would you please wait in the car?"

"Can't someone help him?"

"It's too late for that."

I change my mind about approaching Alastair. He's in a bad way if Bill wants to shield me from viewing him. Travelers like us from the US who allow a local to drive their rental car will shoot us to the top of the authority's suspect list—even if Ethan sent Alastair to pick us up at the airport. Our first day in Temuka and a nice old man is sprawled out dead on the road less than an hour after he stepped out of our vehicle. We're so naive when it comes to learning the customs of another country *before* making the trip. Why didn't I research this?

I can't help but think of the police encounters we've participated in and the hours of interrogation that happened not too long ago. This time we aren't witnesses to the crime and weren't in close proximity of Alastair when he was hit.

Who is Alastair McGregor, really? A chilliness penetrates my hands. Why did he insist on walking along the roadside? Did he want to throw himself in front of a moving car, or is this just an accident?

I wave Bill over at the same time one of the women throws up what appears to be her luncheon salad near Alastair's prone body. I've seen no movement and try not to think about what's staring me right in the face.

Bill speaks to the male witness and returns to the car. "I hope you didn't see him like that. According to one of the witnesses, Alastair was strolling his usual path. He takes this walk each day, rain or shine, and his reputation precedes him. They all know him well—a businessman and an environmental activist from their community."

"Was he hit by a car, or did he collapse in front of traffic?"

"He was struck from behind, then the car came back around to finish the job." Bill shudders.

"Not an accident?" I'm in utter disbelief. "Activists make enemies. Alastair mentioned a protest next week at Bluebasin Lake. I hope someone didn't do this on purpose to keep him from the protest."

"His cranium was crushed. Brain matter everywhere. The crime appears to be more deliberate, according to the ladies who saw the whole thing."

My fish and chips crawl up my throat where I can taste them again. I close my eyes to Bill's description of the crime scene and try not to relive it in my mind.

"There's no chance he could survive?" I ask.

"No way. His head was mashed under the tires. Once struck, he didn't have a chance to get out of the way. Per the eyewitnesses, the driver sped through like a crazy person in a rage." He verifies the navigation while we're stopped and makes his U-turn in the road.

"Shouldn't we wait around for the police?" If we take off, won't that look like we showed up to make sure—"

"This country has a constitutional monarchy where England runs the show here. I'm not familiar with how a monarchy works, not yet anyway—homework for later. Let the police interview witnesses who saw the incident as it happened. We'll go down to the precinct and tell them how we met Alastair and when we saw him last." Bill glances into his rearview mirror. "I should also bone up on the local government in Temuka. We're tourists in their country and should understand our rights before going to the police."

"The cottage is that way." I point over the seat.

"We're taking the scenic route. I don't want to drive past that crowd with police on the way and remind them we could've staged this. It's not like they know us."

Poor Alastair. If he didn't meet us, he might still be alive. "I wish he wasn't sent to the airport to pick us up." I say what Bill could be thinking.

"We didn't do this to him. A person in a dark Land Rover did," Bill announces without warning.

"They saw the car? I hope the driver gets what's coming for murder. Knowing the make of the car will narrow down the suspects. How many Rover models can there be in a town of a few thousand people?"

"Land Rover has an entire line. Remember, we're in a British Commonwealth, and Land Rover is a UK company. You might not have noticed how many Brit vehicles we passed leaving Christchurch. Tons. They aren't all the boxy type we think about," Bill says. "The police will have their work cut out finding the hit-and-run driver if witnesses didn't get a license."

My heart sinks for Alastair's daughter. "Whoever gets the nasty job of notifying Alastair's daughter, I pity that person. Before you returned with the rental car at the airport, I spoke to a woman named Jenny at the sweet shop. She may hear about it first."

"Immediate family notification isn't going to be a problem."

"Why?"

"The women had strange expressions when I brought up his family in a general way. It seems that Sidney and her son died two years ago, with Alastair at the wheel of their car."

My hand flies to my mouth. "You're kidding."

"According to them, Alastair's alone and has no living relatives."

The ache in my heart increases, as does the sadness.

"The family were in a car accident together, and he was the sole survivor? That's painful just thinking about it. Why did he tell us that his daughter owns, *present tense*, the shop on Whaler's Street? I thought Jenny was an employee."

"Jenny could've stepped in to take over the shop for Sidney, and Alastair might've been so lonely after her death that he took on the taxi service to give himself purpose."

"Whoa. It takes a story like Alastair's to remind us not to squander our time with friends and family."

"So true."

"I'm glad we ate when we did because there's no way I could handle food after all this mess. Who ran Alastair down in broad daylight—without fear of being seen and then drove away?"

Bill's detour takes us to the cottage cutoff from the opposite direction. It'll add a few extra miles, but I don't mind when we have so much breathtaking countryside to absorb. I power the window down as we pass gigan-tic, smooth-barked, native trees filled with noisy birds that include hooked beaks and fat little bellies. Purple wildflowers that look like asters dot the meadows, and plants shaped like Scheffleras grow from the bases of those big trees.

A faded green sign marks the dirt road to Woolcombe Station's cottage on an idyllic triangular property marked by old fence posts. Pristine hedges and more flowering shrubs in pinks and yellows line the wooden porch to the main entrance. Shed dormers break up the A-frame roof, a dead giveaway for their heavy snows during winter. As per Ethan's descrip-tion, weatherworn gray planks in vertical lengths give the home a rustic, country feel. Crisscross windows in washed-out white casings add to the ambiance, but the most glorious part of this little house is the pond and stepping stones that wind to the rear. Water spilling over rocks nearby from a stream to our left pulls me in to its sound. The trickle and movement of water is so calming.

We park next to clumps of small pampas-like grass finely maintained by a groundskeeper, I suspect. Not a blade of ground cover is out of place. Mowed volun-teer grass on the outer yard matches what's near the porch—a landscape that looks utterly natural and not at all commercially grown.

"The cottage is larger, and the outside is cleaner than I expected. Quaint and pretty. Ready to check out the inside, or would you rather get some exercise?" I ask Bill.

"Inside first."

Bill's standing behind me as I dig into my tote compartment that holds Ethan's box with the key. I slip the key into the slot and the door opens to a spacious world of twenty-by-twenty neutral tile and monochromatic sage-green area rugs. Two leather armchairs side by side and an exquisite nubby sofa crowd a large, calf-height, wooden coffee table similar in color to the gray exterior of the home. A vaulted ceiling adds size to the space, an illusion of a much larger dwelling than it is.

"Chic. Someone has a knack for decorating." I glance into the ugly mustard-tiled kitchen. "Ugh. Spoke too soon. We have early seventies over there."

"Not a guy's pad, that's for sure." Bill wanders past me, leaving the vast room for a short hallway. "Looks like two bedrooms and a main bath," he remarks loud enough for me to catch his remark from the end of the hall.

The kitchenette is cubbyhole small, as if it's been left that way from a modern renovation of the living room. One bright window has a view to the pond from booth seating made from the same nubby fabric as the couch. The stove and oven are a single-unit throwback from the Nixon administration, with electric elements and a tea-stained, harvest gold range top.

"Not exactly gourmet cooking appliances." My fingernail scrapes off some of the old grease. "I see a lot of takeout in our future. Are the bedrooms nice?" I stroll to the hall and smell the pungent odor of fresh paint.

"Rooms are clean. Dresser, mirror, and a queen-size bed in each."

"I believe we've solved our travel problems, having only one car between us. Since the cottage is in the boonies, if you'd care to use the other bedroom, I'd like you to stay here. Having someone in the house will distract me from noticing paranormal activity at night." I'm holding a straight face but about to burst from his expression. It's priceless.

"Is that right? Alec didn't mention that you see ghosts." Bill settles himself against the wall, with wide eyes and hands hidden behind him.

"Drake, lighten up already. I'm kidding. We have enough to worry about without people in the hereafter joining our vacation."

"If you're sure you don't mind?" Bill's lips flatline. "I don't want to impose." He hesitates as something stirs behind his eyes.

"I'll let Alec know the arrangements, don't worry. Unless he plans on showing up unannounced? I don't know what the two of you talked about."

"He knows he's being slightly overprotective, but it's well-founded. Trouble seems to like you... a lot." Bill shoves a hand in his pants pocket and twists his mouth into a pucker.

Alec does the same pocket thing when he's frustrated with me.

"Come on." I bump him on the elbow. "I want you to camp here. Alec trusts you, as I do."

Bill's serious nature is absorbing everything I say as truth. I'll have to be careful teasing him. He hasn't crossed any line since we met last year, so I feel protected in his presence, as if Alec were here. "I hereby promise not to make a nuisance of myself. Cross my heart." I cross myself and hold up the Boy Scout salute. "Scout's honor."

He looks at the sofa and touches it as if soothing the fabric. "Considering the incident with Alastair, it's a good idea not to hang around town for lodging until we talk with police and explain how he showed up at the airport."

"I agree. The last time you spoke to Alec, what was his general mood?"

"Crazy worried," Bill says. "In his shoes, I'd be the same way."

I drop my gaze to the floor and consider how I left Alec with Noah. "He put you on the flight because you'd keep me from harm. You can't do that from a motel in town. I'll call Alec and give him the details about Alastair and tell him you're staying at the cottage. I considered keeping the hit-and-run from Alec, but he should be told everything."

"I'll bring in our things. Thank you for taking pity on a detective out of his element." He's outside before I can thank him for his mediation.

Homicides R Us is back in business.

CHAPTER SIX
A Lot Can Be Said About Loyalty

It's three p.m. New Zealand time—our first day on the South Island, with one rental car, one station cottage with two bedrooms, and a dead taxi driver-slash-companion we knew for a short time. And we haven't made it to Woolcombe Sheep Station to see Ethan and Kate yet, my entire reason for visiting Māori Aotearoa, the Long White Cloud in God's country. New Zealand.

My check-in call with Alec went as well as could be expected, considering the discussion about Alastair. I kept the conversation short and light with him, trying not to overwhelm his worry reflexes. He was happy to hear from me, and I also feel better having spoken to him. Alec picked up on my lack of sleep, which made it easier to end our call.

How long before the authorities arrive at the cottage's doorstep to question us? I like Bill's action plan better; we voluntarily go downtown to the Temuka Police Station and explain our part in how Alastair met his fate. Bill as an investigator isn't a perfect alibi, even though we didn't see what appears to be a hit-and-run incident, but it's a defense that can work in our favor.

I have no idea how much Bill told the witnesses about us. He's a coolheaded guy who's savvy about how investigations work, so he'd be cautious about divulging too much to the locals. I'm sure my worries about our involvement in the Alastair McGregor death will be baseless once the police interview us and we tell them our story. My staying in the background while Bill handles authorities is a must for this horrible murder case. If Alastair's death were accidental, the driver wouldn't have sped off, leaving the scene.

Having a detective under the same roof for days will be sticky since I know so little about his personal beliefs, background, and what Bill and Alec's conversation was like before he left. That all changes on this trip. Bill is staying at the cottage, where I hope he'll be more forthcoming without Alec around. I've tried to get Bill to open up a few times, but he's protective about his private life. This journey together is an ideal opportunity to ask questions and learn about his real friendship with the complicated man from Brookehaven Estate.

Our friend might have come with me on Alec's behalf, but I believe he also has concerns for my safety, or he wouldn't have taken himself abroad. Money can't be the only motivator for jumping on a plane for a couple of weeks in New Zealand, can it? I'd like to hear how he and Alec met, and why Bill turned to firefighting after college. Putting out flames in burning buildings takes a certain kind of courage.

After we make a trip to the market to fill up the cupboards, how we go forward with Alastair is our second order of business.

"I didn't notice grocery stores at this end of town. Did you see any? I put your bags in the first bedroom, by the way." Bill sinks into an armchair and wriggles into the middle of the cushion. "Comfortable enough to nap in."

"Don't say nap. I could sleep on a bed of rocks. Shopping is the least favorite thing I want to do right now, but the cupboards are empty. We need to pick up drinks and snacks at least." I rub my forehead. "I'm so tired I could drop."

Bill taps his wristwatch, counting out loud. "It's yesterday evening at nine-thirty p.m. in New York. How'd the call go with Alec?"

"On the home front, he's waiting on his vet clinic shipments to arrive in the morning; my sheep are fine in their barn, and the horses are taking the unusually cold weather okay. A pretty mundane report. He didn't mention Noah and barely acknowledged the gallery, so Chase must have it covered to Gen's satisfaction."

"How did he react to the rest?" Bill asks, folding his hands together.

Sitting on the edge of the couch across from Bill, I slip off my booties, scrunching my toes in the rug fibers. It's good to feel circulation in my feet again. "First of all, he's glad you're here and didn't seem shocked about Alastair."

Bill raises a brow. "That's not like him."

I chuckle. "Could it be that he's mellowing with age?" My laughter brings an uneasy smile. "After two years and everything we've been through, from stolen jewelry and Russian Mafia, poisonings, Gen's kidnapping, Kate's revelations, and Alec losing his dad... it takes a lot to rattle him."

"You forgot Virena and Noah and what happened in Italy," Bill reminds me.

"There's that." My sigh is stronger than intended. "It's better to focus on the positive and bring in more good energy. I'm grateful you're here, Bill, and it's a comfort to Alec. He was right to send you. My intuition is rubbing off on him."

"I'd come to your aid again in a heartbeat. So, he's good with my staying at the cottage?"

"Absolutely. He hoped the place was big enough. I could hear the relief in his voice."

"I can't imagine how hard it was for you to make this trip."

"Too headstrong for my own good. Things we say and do in heated moments." I jerk into a cross-legged position on the sofa. "Yeah, I wish he were here and told him so, but why is Alec refusing to take a paternity test? Do you know?"

"For a man who's already lost a child? I think he has issues to sort out first."

"I forgot about Tina's miscarriage. Her drug addiction and mental problems had to be painful for him. It's okay to want kids, but if Noah is truly Alec's, why is he just finding out now? It's not realistic to hide Noah all these years from a rich man who's supposedly fathered him, is it?"

"I agree. He has to come to terms in his own way. Alec's afraid he spilled DNA with the wrong woman and is about to pay the consequences."

"Don't you see? By sitting back, he's not accepting *any* consequences. As long as he's in stunned silence and doesn't make a move, he keeps almost everyone happy. Gen, the boy, Virena, but…" I choke on my words.

"Not you." Bill says it for me. "Look, I've known Alec several years, seen him with several women—"

"I know that," I snap, regretting my sharpness. "Sorry. I get your point."

"Allow me to finish. Alec is totally off that most-eligible list. If you don't know it yet, you're *it* for him." Bill leans forward, his hands together like he's about to make an irrefutable point. "Here's the hard truth; he could've walked away from you when Kate left, and you turned down his proposal. And he proposed to you again during your birthday and stood by your side when you blew off the second proposal. He wants you no matter what difficulties you both face."

"I didn't *blow off* his proposal. No sane woman would've accepted under Virena's bombshell. How much more can our relationship withstand? Are we trying too hard to make something gel that's always going to be oil floating on water?"

Bill's marriage talk is a sore reminder of what I left for Alec to muddle through on his own. Did I make a terrible mistake leaving him behind?

"When a person loves another that deeply, everyone sees it. It's hard to miss unless you're looking the other way. I'll tell you something else. You gave all when you saved Alec's mother from her captors in the Turkish tower and again at Alec's estate. Without you, Gen might have died."

"He told you about that?"

Bill nods. "He's proud to stand beside you, Annalisse. I'm gonna be bold here; stop trying to control everything to an outcome of your choosing. Stuff happens, and we move forward. So will Alec when he's ready. But if you push too hard, against his own needs, he'll leave you behind. Is that what you want?" Bill's glare burns like hot pokers piercing my skin.

Tears fill my gaze, spilling warm rivulets down my cheeks.

"I love him, Bill. I don't know how to stop pushing."

"Pull yourself together, siren in green. You have the world at your feet and don't realize it."

"Siren." I smile and swipe at the tearstains. "I'm glad we were honest with Alec about Alastair's situation and your sleeping arrangements at the cottage."

"Exactly. Keep conversations to the truth as much as possible."

Shaking my head, I say, "Deception isn't my strong suit, Bill. Alec can always see through the smallest white lie."

"Then don't lie. Would you like him to fly down before he's taken care of his business? He would, you know. All it takes is a phone call from you."

"I'm torn between my belief system and my selfish desires. They're in a tug-o-war for the victor. I want him here, but the distractions would be off the charts when he should be dealing with the boy."

"How do you know that he isn't?" Bill lifts his chin. "Discern for yourself. Tell him to join us or forget about it. Alec can juggle more than one issue at a time," Bill says with a smirk.

"I want him here." Taking a deep breath, I hit autodial for Alec.

"I'll be outside." Bill's up and out of his chair in an instant.

Two rings and Alec answers through the speaker, "Hey, babe. Did you forget to tell me something?"

"Sort of. It's going to take three days to get used to losing a day and remembering everything I want to say. It feels like drifting through fog until I can make up for the sleep lost." I set the phone on the coffee table. "I'm looking through tall sliding glass doors to the yard and my eyes are half-closed. Anyway, before Bill and I stock the place with groceries, I'd like to ask you something."

"Did you come down with a cold? It sounds like you're underwater."

I sniff back congestion from my tearful episode with Bill. "Flowers blooming on the porch. My allergies are acting up."

"Are you guys settled in yet?"

"Neither of us has unpacked. He's as wiped out as I am."

Don't dance around too long.

Alec's quiet for a few beats. "So what's up?"

"Other than what happened to Alastair, Alec, I…"

"Anna, what's wrong? Do you want to come home?"

"No, that's not it. When you've taken care of your clinic deliveries, would you have time to see this gorgeous country with me? I left in such a hurry, and well, I'm regretting it. You can't imagine the beautiful lake Alastair showed us. Acre upon acre of wildflower meadows and crazy birds are everywhere. New Zealand is like a huge nature preserve. An exotic zoo without cages or fences. If Kate's here, she's going to skin me for leaving you in New York."

"Anna, I miss you," he says with emotion. "I hope you aren't asking because you think you should. Your instructions were painfully clear—you go there, and I stay here."

"Right. It's just a suggestion. You don't have to come, only if you'd like to, that's all." I choke on the next words and squeeze my eyes shut. "We don't know when the stores close around here, so I'd better get moving. I'll check in tomorrow after I send you some of the most astonishing photos. I haven't reviewed them yet, but I took around four hundred shots. I should be able to find a few decent ones in the bunch."

"Four hundred? At the lake?"

"Mostly." A hard swallow on my end. "Give Helga a hug for me. I haven't had time to check in with the gallery. In case you haven't yet, please let Gen and Chase know that we're here and fine. I'll call them tomorrow when my head's clearer."

"When the trucks arrive at the clinic, I'll drop you a note." Alec's reaching for more topics to keep me talking.

"Get some rest, Alec. It's late. I promise not to call you again tonight—"

"I got the ball rolling on that other thing," Alec blurts before I can hang up.

I take him from the speaker to normal mode and press the screen to my ear.

"On what?" My mind spins through his current projects at Brookehaven. Foal registrations? The new manager headquarters on the east end of the property? Rejuvenating the closed-off solarium that Peter Gregory ruined?

"Noah and I spent time with the horses after you left, discussing breeding and equine genetics. He seemed to grasp the concept and asked how we chose which mares to put with the stallion. I used this as a segue to explain how breeding livestock is similar to how we understand human DNA. He was jazzed about knowing more about himself, so we decided to take saliva swabs to a lab and test each other. I should have the data soon."

His news numbs my hand to the phone. I grab the throw over the chair for warmth across my chilly lap. He did what I asked of him, so why do I feel a hollow cold drench me? Words elude me no matter how hard I try to form them. Nothing but dead air passes between Alec and me for several uncomfortable seconds. Regardless, he's too far away to leap through the phone and tell him how happy he's made me.

I can't say that.

What's the appropriate reaction?

"Did I lose you? Anna?" His voice is far away and puny.

"Whatever you find out will be a relief for you. Have you told Gen?" I hold a breath against a million emotions battling each other.

"I'll wait until findings are confirmed."

The safest and most efficient plan. Alec won't upset his mother if he can avoid it. In his shoes, I'd go about it the same way.

"Noah will tell Virena, so be expecting her to go ballistic." I'm glad I'm not there. The boy's mother is sure to erupt. If she's a liar, the game is almost over.

Alec knows the complications.

From outside, Bill leans against the porch rail, viewing my animations through the glass. Without the speakerphone, he has to make his assumptions what we might be talking about.

"I really have to go, Alec. Sleep well. Love you lots." I end the call before I say something to ruin the moment or he thinks of more to elaborate on. I need unbroken sleep to rearrange my stray thoughts before we speak again.

The slider opens, allowing heat to enter the family room in front of Bill.

"From your brighter expression, I take it things went well?"

I explain to him about the paternity testing.

"Before this week is out, you'll have your answer on Noah. Let's hope you're prepared for it."

"That's ominous. You don't think I can handle bad news, do you?" I ask.

"Handle it, sure. It's how you'll respond that concerns me."

CHAPTER SEVEN
Some Things Never Change

Today, we're on the way to Woolcombe Station and in livestock country big time. I've researched the current sheep population of almost thirty million, at a rate of about five sheep for every person in New Zealand. It began in 1982 as seventy million. Sheep and lamb numbers continue to drop due to the loss of the land needed to produce meat and wool.

The animal kingdom still dominates this nation. From the moment we hopped in our SUV and hit the main route toward Woolcombe Station, the hillsides' deep crevices spill into miles upon miles of rocky pastures less suitable for humans but more to grazing animals like sheep and crossbred cattle. I don't recognize any single cattle breed except perhaps black Angus. Cows of mixed colors and shapes, some with horns, most without, support a hearty gene pool of four-legged critters.

Out my window, red-roofed homesteads nestle at the base of taller peaks, surrounded by large, natural Totara shade trees, owner-operator granaries, woolsheds, and cooking stations. Bunkhouses for workers and shearers are rough and unpainted, broken down from age—a throwback from the war years when the world began to hum back to life in the 1970s after Vietnam.

Bill and I drive past a smaller station, paddocks, and chutes sporting little white bodies awaiting the shearers. I hope Bill will get to see how shearing is undertaken while we're visiting, or Ethan can show us another station with shearers at work. I'd like to photograph them in action.

"This is going to sound like a stupid question, but what exactly *is* a sheep station?" Bill asks. "We have farmers raising sheep in our country, but I've never heard anyone call them stations. What am I missing?"

I smile. "Kate says there's no such thing as a stupid question, and she's right. A sheep station is their terminology for sheep farms in Australia and New Zealand. We'll see how farmers and ranchers make a living in a rough, mountainous country. Their livelihoods depend totally on their sheep and cattle management."

Bill nods.

"With sheep, there's more labor involved because of the shearing. Most breeds grow a fleece that has to be shorn at least once a year. A few breeds in the US no longer grow fleece because the farmer wants to concentrate on a meat market. They're called hair sheep. Small amounts of wool grow but shed off on their own, leaving hair on the hides. In the US, we don't wear as much wool clothing as we did in the 1700s and 1800s. Our founders raised sheep because woolens were in demand for warmth and military uniforms. The price for wool was high back then because society needed it."

"If there's wool in the cloth, I run the other way. It's too scratchy for me," Bill says.

"Mills have an answer to that. It's called worsted wool. It's stronger, finer, and smoother than regular wool that's rough and scratchy. Men's and women's suits are usually made with worsted wool because it has a softer feel. Your short lesson on wool for today." I chuckle. "New Zealand sheep stations take the all-of-the-above approach. Stations employ sheep shearers and rouseabouts sell the wool and raise lambs for meat. They export much of that around the world." I change the subject. "Are you okay with going into the police station alone? If you think we should go in together, I can put off the station visit until this afternoon."

I have a guilty conscience about sending Bill Drake to the wolves once he drops me off at the station.

"It's best that I test the water with the police. See Ethan and meet his family."

Nodding, I say, "I can't get over the price of meat in the market yesterday. I thought local lamb would be cheap. Eighteen to twenty-four dollars a pound for animals they raise themselves is kind of silly, if you ask me."

"It depends on how many middlemen there are. Exporting products is big business. Who knows how many growers can sell locally? When you figure that most everything has to be flown or shipped in from other countries, prices will have to be high. Housing must be out of sight," Bill adds.

"How do you plan to approach the Temuka police about Alastair?" I ask. "I don't mind coming along as moral support."

"After I explain how we ran into him…" He clears his throat. "Sorry, poor choice of words. They may want a statement from you, so be expecting it. We didn't cause his death, but we have to own up to him driving our rental car from the airport. Nothing happened while he was driving. For that, I'm grateful. If the town was aware that Alastair had an Uber-type taxi service, the police will want to know what happened to his car. I don't know where the towing company took it, but his car's whereabouts is easy to locate. A man his age didn't walk a hundred miles, so we have to explain everything from the time he came into the terminal and what followed."

"The authorities can't say we left the scene of an accident because we didn't see it." I add.

"I've got this. You're supposed to be on a pleasure trip, don't forget. There's no need to drag you in unless they insist. Do police know Alastair's story?" He shrugs off his hypothetical question. "It's a small town, so I hope so. There may be more to him than what witnesses know." He stares through the windshield. "I think the station is ahead. I'll get out of there as soon as I can."

"You can clear everything up." I shiver at the thought of that poor old man lying in the driveway of the shopping center. "We just got here, and it feels like Italy all over again."

Bill laughs. "If that's true, Alec doesn't pay me enough."

A reminder that Alec is compensating Bill for his time. I push down an icky feeling that Alec worries too much and trusts his friend more than me. Or I can look at it another way; Alec is protecting me by sending a friend. I'll go with option *B* since it feels better.

"Look out for the donkeys." I point at the junction to our right. "They broke out of their enclosure." My smile is accompanied by Bill's.

A pair of grays with bulging abdomens and slick coats amble by our Toyota as if they know we'll give them the right-of-way. They have no fear of motorized vehicles. A small turn of their heads and twitching ears is the depth of their acknowledgment.

"Cocky, aren't they?" Bill asks. "How'd they know we'd stop?"

"Practice." I laugh. "My first instincts from this wild place appear to be correct. The animals run the show. I thought my cat, Boris, was bad with his snooty canned food preferences. The donkeys win the award. Boy, this is going to be a fantastic getaway." I draw down the visor against the blinding light. "Once you pass the paddocks, I'd say the main house is that white two-story at the end of this dirt path where the picket fence stops."

Like most of the roofs we passed along the way, the homestead has A-frame construction, a red roof, and two porch railings. Turret-style sections with three tall windows in each flank the length, and a veranda divides the middle on the second floor. A young girl with light hair is leaning against the rails, looking down at our car.

I wave, and she waves back.

Bill coasts to the long set of steps and lets the SUV idle. "Be back as soon as I can."

"Can you find the police station all right?" I ask, feeling like I should warn him somehow. It's foolhardy to sweat it because he knows how to talk to law officers.

"The address is plugged into navigation. Hey, don't forget your camera in the back." He lifts my Nikon by its strap and slings it over the seat.

I unbuckle and step into the aroma of eucalyptus and another smell I can't quite ascertain. "Wait. Drive safely and be careful. We don't know a thing about Alastair. If Ted Walker and our trip to Italy taught us anything, it's to hold cards close to the chest until we find out how much the police know. We're visitors in New Zealand for a short time. I'd like to go home on my timeline, not someone else's."

Waving, he leaves in a cloud of dust.

The front door swings open, and a woman, younger than me, steps out of the darkness and onto the sunlit porch, carrying some sort of mop in her arms.

"Do you need something?" she asks, snippier than necessary.

I sense an irritation by my presence. Did Ethan tell her to expect me? They may not see too many strangers at the station, and she's being cautious.

As I stuff my camera into the tote and walk onto the porch of many uneven boards, I see that she's carrying a puppy.

"Hi. What an adorable dog. What breed is it?" I ask, moving in for a closer look. Lumpy white hair hangs in tangles; its dark eyes are barely visible through matted bangs.

"Puli," she finally admits. "You aren't from around here." She's studying my baby-blue sweater and the sapphire-and-diamond necklace that Gen gave me for my last birthday. Since I left Kate's locket with Alec, I feel naked without something on a chain around my neck. This expensive gift might be the wrong fashion choice for an introduction to a girl without makeup in a bandeau top and shorts.

I nod to her. "Hi. I'm Ethan's friend from New York. He managed Kate Walker's farm for us a few months ago. Is he here?"

My heart's chugging faster than I'd like. Did I come here too soon? This person in her early twenties is better than any guard dog sleeping by the door than I can imagine.

A glimmer sparks in the girl's brown eyes while she pats her dog's head. I suspect she's giving herself something to do while considering her options.

"You're *her*," she says as if my first name is a dirty word in her mouth.

I reach for her free hand. "I'm Annalisse. Annalisse Drury."

Her back straightens with her dog tight against her breast—her warm security animal. With that harsh glare, there's no way she'll make a move to greet me. I'm the evil American who's come to invade her private space. She's sending me some nasty vibes, walling me off with a frigid ice fence.

I take a step back. "I may have come at a bad time. Tell Ethan—"

Thumps sound from a set of stairs inside the house, and a small light-haired child runs onto the porch, past the roadblock in front of me. I recognize her as the girl on the veranda who waved at us after we met the resident donkeys.

The Puli pup takes a header to the porch and scampers inside.

"Sutton, see what you did?" The woman tries to grab the child's shirt but misses her mark. "Go back in the house. We're talking."

"Hi, Sutton." I crouch down to the girl's height. "That was you waving when we drove in, wasn't it? My name's Annalisse. Nice to meet you."

"Hey." The girl folds her arms and holds me with big blue eyes. Her smile shows a missing incisor. "Are you Ethan's friend from America?"

Sutton appears to be around seven or eight years old. She has sharp cheekbones similar to Ethan and those of my guardess but with a pink glow on them that spreads joy to my unsteady heart. Sutton might be the best way to reach Ethan.

"You're sooo pretty," Sutton says in admiration. "I wish I had brown hair." She pulls out a stringy straw-colored lock to prove her point. "Are you a movie star?"

Her question melts away her sister's icy greeting. They don't get many visitors here from other countries and have ideas that we're the United States of Hollywood glamour.

"*Fft.* Sutton, stop bothering."

"This is my sister, Livia. She's a grouch." And just like that, Sutton runs inside.

"If you'd like, I'll call my ride back. Let Ethan know that I came by." I pivot on a heel and trudge down the long steps, wondering where I went wrong.

"Annalisse."

Turning away from Livia to the faint call of my name, I see someone waving their arm to get my attention.

Ethan. It has to be him.

The figure rounds one of the white outbuildings, then breaks into a jog. Upon landing nearby, he's winded—in no better shape than when Ethan worked for Kate. We gave him a hard time about his laziness back then. What I'd give to go back to those carefree days at the farm when Ethan spent too many hours reading mysteries and vintage comics, and Kate sat with me reminiscing about the Drurys, on the porch swing made by Ted Walker's own hands. A swing that might be gone by now. Removed by the farm's new owners, like Kate's stories of the Drury family—my fiction fantasy life, set up by my real mother, Kate. If Ethan knows where Kate is, here or back home, I have to know how to find her.

Ethan's stout frame bends, and he's holding his knees, gasping for air. His sweaty hair is longer than I remember, curling over his ears. He's heavier and has several days' worth of a sparse beard—his new fashion statement, or he's too busy or lazy to concern himself with shaving.

A few more gasping breaths, then he looks up, wipes his mouth with a dirty T-shirt sleeve, and grins sideways.

Gestures I miss from our old ranch manager.

"Take it easy, Ethan," I say, laughing at the comedy he's producing. "I'm not going anywhere." I glimpse his sister's back view in time to watch her vanish into the house. As she arrived, she leaves in the same quiet disgust. There's a story in this worth asking Ethan about. Maybe later after I find out more about Kate.

"Annalisse, it's brilliant to see you." He gives me a solid hug. Jumping backward, as if he touched something hot, he adds, "Are you alone?" He scans toward the house, looking over my shoulder and back to me in gleaming approval.

"Bill Drake is with me, but he had a stop to make. He'll be back."

"Alec and… You don't fancy him anymore?" he asks unsure.

"Alec's fine; we're fine. He couldn't make the trip after I received your note, so he stayed home to take care of personal business. He said to tell you hello." I lie to end his line of questioning in a positive way. "Do you have time to show me around? It's so beautiful here, but I don't see any sheep. Are they on another part of the acreage?"

"Liv's Corries are still here in the building over there." He points out the smaller barn.

"Who's Liv?"

"Sorry, Olivia. You were talking to her."

"I met her, sort of. Sutton called her Livia. Are they your sisters? I don't remember you mentioning brothers or sisters."

"Yeah, half-sisters. After my real Da died, Mum married Finn. Who could blame Mum for remarrying? The station's too much for a widow to manage, and

Finn's a good hand when he's not in Wellington. Finn is part of the legislature, the House of Representatives in Parliament."

What Alastair said is true. Ethan's stepdad is in this country's government.

Ethan twists in another direction. "I'll take you to the Corriedales since they aren't far. Oh yeah, how'd you like the *bach*? We had it painted a week ago and changed the furniture. The last bloke smoked inside, or his lady friend did. The pong was bad." He turns around long enough to make a face.

"I don't understand the term *batch*. Do you mean the cottage?"

"Oh, sorry. It's spelled b-a-c-h. It's what we call a little house, like a vacation home."

"It's a cute place, and we appreciate the offer to stay there. Thank you."

Alastair and Ethan confirmed Ellen's second marriage to Finn Hyde and his involvement in New Zealand government. Until now, Bill's research was just a suspicion on our part. Which brings me to another fact that I've always been curious about. When Ethan arrived out of nowhere at Walker Farm two Christmases ago, I didn't understand it. Kate softened to the newcomer on our farm—an unusual move on her part. My hunch told me Kate expected him somehow. She battles heart issues and couldn't do the heavy work on the farm. Doctor's orders. Ethan didn't explain why he appeared in New York, and I'd still like to know his true reason for coming to Kate's rescue. Ellen Hyde knows why.

"Did you talk to Miss Walker?" Ethan asks out of left field, which affirms the card she mailed to Alec.

"You've spoken to her? No one's heard from her or you, for that matter. Is Kate here?" *Please say she is.*

"Not now. She came home with me, stayed a while, and made me promise not to tell you or anyone in New York. I told her she was mad not to tell you, but I didn't want her to rack off, so I did what she asked." Ethan kicks at dirt on the ground. "Sorry, Anna."

"Rack off? That's a new one for you. I should buy a Kiwi language book while we're here."

"It means go away. Make her angry where she'd leave. She and Mum are good friends."

Ethan shows me the front of the structure where I first saw him. A diesel motor powers the shearers quarters, and a stone fireplace is its warmth in the winter. Neither is in use at the moment. This enclosure has to be a cold place to sleep. The shingle roof looks like it leaks from the patches of green moss in places, and the windows are single-pane. There's little insulation here. It has an awning and a short porch at the end of the building that seems to melt into the hillside. New Zealand has a lot of structures that are built this way.

Trees are scarce in clumps where the fence line takes off across the land until the last post disappears behind higher elevation. The empty quarters building hasn't seen a new paint coat in decades. White paint shards curl on every withering post and board like old, gray whiskers growing in every direction. My hopes sink that we're too late in the season to watch shearing and Bill won't see them in action. It was a gamble, traveling on short notice the way I did.

"It's quiet on the station. I take it the shearers have gone to other ranches?" I ask anyway.

"Yeah. Most of 'em moved to the high country. Won't be long and the muttonbirds will be back around for the hoggets. We have thirty-four hundred this time." His hands are animated as he describes how many yearlings they have and why they're shorn later than the flock.

When I think we're alone, a door creak startles me, and I hop in place, plastering my hand over my heart.

"Oh, I didn't know anyone was inside. Excuse us," I say. I'm standing in front of at a great-looking guy with fiery eyes and wild hair, gripping a white bottle in his fingertips. "Ethan was showing me around." I push my warm sweater up over an elbow.

"Coop, what are you doing here? It's too early for a smoko," Ethan asks him through a sneer, not pleased.

"I want to save a trip to the chemist. Feeling crook and have a bad headache." He shakes the bottle for effect and quirks one side of his mouth in a smile. "The shearing gang leaves stuff behind. Don't have a hissy fit, mate. Miss," he says to me while passing Ethan on the porch and lights up a cigarette.

We watch him stuff his checkered shirt into his waistband and take a few awkward puffs.

"What's smoko?" I ask Coop.

"A tea break—a rest period," he says, reaching out to shake my hand. "Cooper Dunn."

His hands are too soft for a laborer. He might be a supervisor here.

Ethan's glare radiates off Cooper.

"I thought the shearers were gone," I say to Cooper. "Are you shearing?"

"No, miss. I'm Woolcombe's manager." His lecherous wink follows. "You're a pretty one. American?"

"I'm showing Miss Drury around," Ethan complains.

Cooper takes a long drag on his cigarette and extinguishes it under his worn boot. "I'll leave you to it. If I can answer any questions, find me at the woolies pen. Cheers." He glances over his shoulder at me, then Ethan, and ambles away.

"Bugger off." Ethan is annoyed by the manager for some reason. "Coop's been here a few weeks since we let the last one go. I told Mum not to hire another dodgy bloke. He's lazy. I can handle the station, but she doesn't believe me." He waits for a reaction, but I hold comments for later as I take it all in.

Ellen hires the managers, and Ethan won't be happy with anyone moving in on his territory; that's the feeling I get. Ethan and Cooper have bad blood between them—a runholder and a new manager who might not see the operation the same way. Both are rebels who knock heads at every turn, I'll bet. I know firsthand how Ethan likes to push people's buttons when he wants his way. He and Kate had conflicts about day-to-day farming activities on occasion.

"Cooper seems nice enough. What happened to the last manager, if you don't mind my asking?" I'm swallowing dust in the dry breeze and have to clear my throat. It can't be more than seventy-five degrees, but the heat is different than at home. The air has no moisture to it, no humidity whatsoever.

"A Māori and a sickie. The snarky bloke wouldn't do his job, so I fired him." Ethan puffs his chest out like a strutting bird. "The station is my responsibility and Coop is a stirrer. I'm watching him 'cause he's trouble."

In the past few minutes, Ethan has taken on the shade of a raspberry and returned to the native lingo he lost when he came to Walker Farm. I need that Kiwi dictionary because some of the language is zipping over my head. The heat appears to be affecting him too, or it's anger about to boil over. This might be a good time to put off the rest of the tour until Bill can come along as the umpire. I'd like to take Cooper's offer and have him show us the station, not Ethan, who seems stressed out with a lot on his mind.

"Instead of looking at your sister's sheep, could I meet your mother if she's here? I'd love to talk with her about Kate, and could I bother you for a glass of water?"

"Yeah, sure. I can show you the Corries later." He checks his watch; the same one he wore from time to time on the farm. An Olympic with a red suede band. "Mum takes her tea about now. It's a good time."

"What's the smell in the air? Like coconuts or sun-tan lotion." I'm picking up a stronger aroma around the shearing quarters.

"Might be the footbath, copper sulfate. We ran the mob through this week."

"No, it's something else." I know what bluestone smells like because we've used it on the sheep's feet on Walker Farm. The solution is a great drying agent during the rains and to treat limping sheep.

"Then it's Rimu." Ethan points to a stand of tall trees beside the building. "See those big Rimu that look like men with shaggy, long beards? We use the bark and sap as medicine and the wood for carving. It's a fantastic wound prep and blood stop for cattle with broken horns and for people too. Here." He walks to a younger specimen in the yard and rakes the branches that remind me of a weeping willow. "Take a whiff."

I reach out and touch soft needles, like new seedling pine trees with longer spikes on the branches.

"Conifer. What an odd aroma. There's something else, though. This isn't it. I'll eventually figure it out. You didn't say where Kate is now. Did she mention going back to New York?"

"Mum took her to the airport. All she told us was Kate had business to take care of on the North Island. She flew into Auckland."

"How long ago did she leave? Is she still there?"

Ethan twitches his mouth and gazes off. "She left in December."

My mother could be long gone by now.

Planting my fist on a hip, I blow out a breath. "I came all this way, and she's already left the station. I'd considered that option. Kate didn't say when she's returning to the US?"

He shrugs. "She keeps to herself. You know how she is; she leaves when she's ready."

Ellen knows a lot more. I don't understand her relationship with my mother and how the two would've met to become friends on different continents. If Kate's keeping more secrets, Ethan would be the last person she'd tell. She liked Ethan, but also seemed guarded around him.

My boots graze over a pod on the ground, and I teeter sideways, arms flying to balance myself from a fall.

"Be careful walking underneath the older ones; they have cones. I've tripped on more than my share. Let's go to the house and get you a cuppa. Oh, before I forget." Ethan draws out a card tucked in a wallet from his threadbare jeans. "Keep my new cell number. It's lucky that your email came in, or I wouldn't have known when you were coming to En Zed. Call if you need anything." He hands his card to me, and I slide it into my bag.

En Zed is the Kiwi name for New Zealand. I take Ethan's arm as we stroll by a group of dog houses shaped like teepees—minus the dogs.

"Are your guard dogs somewhere else?"

"Na. It's for the collies. They're out with the mob where Cooper should be." He mutters something unintelligible.

Cooper left for some unknown barn, but I've felt eyes on us since we left the shearers quarters. There's no telling who's watching our approach from the main house or elsewhere.

CHAPTER EIGHT
Finding Relations in Unlikely Places

We stamp our feet on a braided doormat with a fluffy sheep in the middle and step inside the antique white of painted furniture and old pictures—from the huge family room to the wafting aromas from the country kitchen. A grand staircase with a sweeping banister twirls to the last wooden stair off to my left, and another smaller room with fine tablecloth dining and high-backed, rustic chairs awaits the family's next meal. The home has a lived-in feeling and a quiet harmony, not unlike their cottage on Sir Raleigh Way. The interior designer is the same person with an appetite for palettes of antique white, grays, and muted pastels.

"Sit anywhere," Ethan says, pointing to one of the sofas.

I stop at the nearest love seat beside the door and sit on the end of the single cushion. The coffee table holds stacks of farming magazines and a thin Temuka news journal with the back page facing out. I catch that the journal is a weekly, not surprising for a small-town paper.

I swivel toward the groaning staircase and pretend to be cool, but my apprehension makes me nervous for some reason. Deciding to stand at the last second, I tug at my sweater hem and wipe clammy hands along my jeans.

The woman on the stairs isn't like I thought she'd be. Looking at Ethan, who's well into his twenties, I expected to find a woman in her late fifties or early sixties. She's much younger. I'd guess mid-forties. Something Ethan had said made me think his mom would be closer to Kate's age. At home, Kate's friends were all elderly, which makes her friendship with Ethan's mom more curious.

With one hand on the railing, Ellen's talking before she steps onto the bottom rung. "Hello, Miss Drury. We've looked forward—"

She sees me and stops, closing her mouth tight, unable or unwilling to finish her sentence.

Her reaction is an odd one. It's as if I'm sitting on the wrong piece of furniture or I'm not who she expects. Ellen puts me ill at ease when I'm already nervous about meeting Ethan's mother for the first time.

Ellen Hyde is a stunning woman who doesn't require makeup. She has wavy auburn hair and an envious peaches-and-cream complexion, as if she belongs on a cliff overlooking the Irish channel, not here studying me from a staircase. Ellen doesn't frequent the outdoors, either. She's au naturel, not a square inch of her is bronzed by the sun. A fresh, natural beauty with an elegance about her movements. Her sleeveless powder-blue shift looks similar to the color of my sweater, but the similarities end there.

"It's so nice to meet Ethan's mom finally." I greet her at the bottom and take her coolish hand in mine. "We miss him in New York, but of course, Kate and Ethan have filled you in about his days at the farm."

A sweet smile crosses Ellen's face without a show of teeth. "Son, if you're pouring, I'd like a cup as well. Use the loose tea." She turns to me again. "I hope you like English Breakfast."

"Yes, it's one of Helga's favorites."

Ellen wrinkles her nose. "And who's Helga? I don't know that name."

"The estate's housekeeper. She was the family's villa maid when Alec grew up in Greece. Kate did mention that I've been seeing Alec Zavos for a while?" I have no idea how much my mother has said because Ellen's expression has gone blank. She might not even be aware that I'm related to Kate. "Mrs. Hyde, I haven't heard Kate mention your name before. If I may ask, how do you know my mother from so far away?"

"Please call me Ellen. Ethan's said so much about you that I feel like we're old friends. I must say, you're prettier than he described. Have a seat." She motions toward the sofa I left earlier.

Perhaps Ethan's description of me is the reason for her chilly entrance from the stairs. She's mastered the art of avoidance and shoves my direct inquiry under the welcome mat for a time of her choosing. Ellen has no Kiwi accent, so she isn't a native here, even though her son is. Who knows what Ethan said to his family when he came home? I brace for whatever is coming my way.

Ellen drops into a recliner and crosses her legs. "Forgive my shock, but you bear a striking resemblance to someone you mentioned."

She's feeling out the situation while testing how much I acknowledge.

"Katharine Walker, perhaps?" I hold my breath as I wait for her to elaborate.

Ellen breaks eye contact. "How much longer on the tea?" she asks Ethan, buying herself more time.

"I don't know what Ethan mentioned about his time working for Kate, but I hoped to hear from her by now. No one except for your family has seen or spoken to her since she literally disappeared last July. Frankly, with her health issues, I'm worried about her. If you can tell me anything about my mother, I'd be in your debt."

"Your mm…mum?" Ethan's jaw falls open and his eyes widen. "But your mum is dead, isn't she?"

"Ethan, that's enough! Go out and pick a few lemons for our tea. Do you like lemon, Annalisse?"

Smiling instead of speaking about my preferences for tea, I find it mind-boggling how sharp she is with Ethan when he asks a reasonable question. I'm surprised that Kate never told Ethan about me during their long flights after they left New York. She had plenty of time to strike up that conversation with him. By sending Ethan away, whatever we say will be in confidence and away from her eldest son.

Why all the secrecy? Kate's seventy years old with most of her life behind her. The people who raised me as their daughter won't be telling Kate's secrets anytime soon because they're dead. Who's left to hide me from?

I'm less sure of myself than before I got here. Ellen is acting odd, and I've shell-shocked Ethan who hasn't caught on yet that his mother wants to speak to me in private. Watching him have a small meltdown as he paces the kitchen island back and forth, I'd like to explain everything, and will at some point.

Taking the newspaper journal from the table, I divert my attention from their glances to the local activities and ads in columns. A bold headline on the front page declares a man was hit on Main Street by a driver who left the scene.

Without meaning to, I gasp as I read Alastair's name in the first paragraph where the article explains that the stricken man died at the scene from head injuries.

"Ethan, pick them today, please." Ellen's patience is gone, and she's on the move. "I'll finish pouring. Take your time." She holds the screen door open for her son, who's sighing and grumbling about going outside just when the talk is getting interesting.

I'm gleaning how little the authorities have on Alastair's crime from the latest reports. Bill won't be any help to the police other than letting them know where Alastair started his trip that day, which isn't noted in the article.

Smoothing down her dress, Ellen moves from the recliner and sits next to me on the sofa.

"Such a terrible accident," she says.

Her fresh herbal fragrance reminds me of lemongrass. Not a wonder why she asks for a touch of citrus in her tea.

I stare into her sad eyes, wanting to correct her that Alastair's murder has to be intentional, but I don't. A nagging in my mind urges me to observe and not project my thoughts onto Ellen.

"Did you know the man?" I ask.

"Yes. Alastair's a longtime resident of Temuka. I dare say everyone knew him. It's too bad he wouldn't listen to—"

"To whom? Do you know who wanted him dead?"

"I misspoke. What I meant to say was his accident disturbs me. He was a nice old man. Friendly to everyone." Ellen looks away from the newsprint and studies my hand before taking it. "You are the image of Kate in her younger years. I can't get over it. You look like she did when Thomas first introduced her to me."

Ellen cleverly moves from Alastair's demise to switching the conversation closer to home with Kate.

"How long ago were you introduced?" My ears prick at the mention of a Thomas. "And who's this Thomas? Do I know him?"

Like Ethan said, Ellen and Kate are longtime friends and have a history. That's why Kate came here to her sanctuary and brought Ethan back home. But I think it's more than that.

"Your expressions aren't hers, though," Ellen says matter-of-factly, ignoring my questions.

As I tilt my head to contemplate what she means, she slides her hand from my crown to the end of my hair, fondling its thickness, which is just plain creepy.

"Because they're my expressions, no one else's. What are you trying to say?" Heat rises in my cheeks. I can feel it.

She draws a long breath and says, "I see your father in you."

I'm numb and unable to speak right away.

Ellen Hyde has a connection to my biological father.

"I think… I'm gonna need that, uh, tea… please?"

Ellen goes into the kitchen and returns with a cup and saucer. "Sugar, cream?" she asks as if it's just another routine tea break.

I want to scream that what she's telling me is a big deal. The biggest deal of my thirty years on this planet. My nerves are on their last end, but I have to steady my emotions here. It isn't a good idea to lose my cool in front of her.

"I'd better take it straight up." The teacup handle is small for shaking hands, and I spill some. Setting the saucer down, I take a long sip, not tasting anything but scalding heat, breathing in too much air and swallowing sideways. Coughing hard, I set the cup on the saucer while I clear my throat several times and get my bearings.

"Would you like a glass of water?" Ellen asks with concern written in her eyes.

I reach for the tea again to try a sip, then another. Closing my eyes against spinning scenes in my head, I have so many questions to ask before Ethan or Bill returns.

"I didn't mean to cause that response. I thought you knew."

"Knew? Knew what? Kate made me believe that she's my *aunt,* not my mother. How would I know any of this when she kept my true identity to herself all these years? Why tell you and not me?"

Ellen nods in earnest. "You must be hurt beyond belief. But she told you, yes?"

"If her past didn't roar back to bite her, I wouldn't know to this day. She left me a few lines in a letter that mentioned my father's name, virtually a stranger—and who she really is. A simple letter from her is what I have, nothing more. She couldn't face me, which hurts like I can't tell you. It seems we were meant to meet so I could hear more truth, Mrs. Hyde. Kate must've known I'd come to New Zealand to find her."

"So it seems." Ellen sips her tea and rests her head before saying, "Your father, Thomas Taylor, is my brother. My family name is Taylor. When Kate left her husband, she intended to divorce him. I don't believe she ever planned to return to Ted, but you came along, and plans changed."

I'm so fidgety I don't know what to do with my hands. I feel like running a marathon to burn off the nervous energy. This woman is going to give me facts to build upon.

"She met you and your brother in New Zealand?" I'm hesitant because that doesn't sound right.

"No, not quite. We lived in Ohio at the time. Kate visited a restaurant and sat at the bar where Thomas was sitting. They struck up a conversation and found that they had a lot in common. The shortened version: one thing led to another, and you were the result."

"Is your brother, Thomas, still alive in New Zealand? I can't hear that he's passed on, so if he has, don't answer." My throat clogs, and tears of happiness and uncertainty spill over my cheeks. "Excuse me." Digging into my tote for a tissue, I dab my eyes, wadding and tossing the Kleenex to the recesses of the bottom.

"I've said enough for one visit. We'll talk again. I'm sure you have so many questions. Are you enjoying the cottage?" she asks, and a relaxing smile follows.

"Your cottage is beautiful. My friend and I appreciate your kindness. Sorry for my emotional outbursts a few minutes ago. I'm still very raw." I sniff and rub beneath my eyes. "Please come to visit us in New York sometime so that we can reciprocate. Alec would like that very much." I pull out my wallet and flip to my favorite photo, one I took of Alec sitting on Kris, his stallion, and show it to her.

"Handsome. He looks familiar. What's his last name?"

"Zavos. Alec Zavos."

She nods and raises her brows. "He's a catch. European, isn't he?"

"Greek and Italian. His mother, Generosa, and I are partners in an art gallery. I'm an antiquities valuator. A history buff of sorts." Now it's my turn to smile.

Heavy shoes stomp down the stairs.

"On my way to the shop—the late shift again," Olivia grumbles, spots me, and her face breaks from grim to giving me a dirty look. "I hate the late shift. He's doing it on purpose, and I hate him. Sidney was nice. I hope Da buys the shop so I'll be in charge. It should've been mine to run."

"What shop do you work at?" I ask.

"You wouldn't know it. Sidney's Sweets."

Alastair's shop. I blink a few times, allowing what she says to register.

"The one the McGregors own?" I ask without thinking.

A hand flies to her hip in defiance. "How did you know that? Were you there?" Olivia asks, and I feel Ellen's eyes penetrate me.

It might be a good idea to say little else on the subject. "I'm sure I read it in the newspaper." I point to the journal on the table.

Think of something benign to add in case the sweet shop isn't in print.

"Ethan brags about an ice cream flavor he calls Hokey Pokey. I'd like to try it. Do you recommend it?" I ask Olivia, who offers a one-sided shrug.

"I think that's your friend." Ellen points through the glass behind the sofa we're sitting on. "Bring him inside and introduce us."

"I will another time. We have an appointment this afternoon." Whether or not we did, it was time to go and sort out what Ellen had said.

"Outta here." Olivia whizzes by us and slams the screen door.

"On that note. I'll be leaving too. Bill and I will be back in the morning for a tour of the station, if that's all right with you, Mrs. Hyde?"

"Please, Annalisse. You should call me Ellen. If Kate and my brother had married, you'd be my niece. I feel like we are family."

My heart skips when her words sink in, and I realize the gravity of them. As my mind runs to places unknown, I turn from Ellen and rush to the screen for a quick exit. "Let Ethan know we'll see him tomorrow." I step onto the porch, swishing through my tote for the camera inside.

"We have so much to discuss." Ellen waves. "Tomorrow then."

I get Bill's attention by swinging my bag high above my head, and he comes around to open my door. He's not going to believe the morning I've had. Not only do I have the means to learn more about my father from the best source ever, but I've also gained a paternal relative. My undercover family tree is getting larger and stranger by the day.

CHAPTER NINE
Temuka Police—Canterbury District

Words are in short supply in the car on the way to the Temuka Police Department, where the officer questioning Bill about Alastair asked to see me as well. Instead of asking a flurry of questions about whom I met and what I saw while scouting with Ethan, Bill does none of that and maintains an eerie silence. His quietness could mean that his meeting with the police didn't go well, and he's concerned about my upcoming interrogation.

"Is there anything I should know before talking to the police? I had an interesting visit with Ethan's mother." I watch Bill at the wheel, appearing deep in thought. "Are you okay?"

His long hair sticks together in wavy, golden locks, laying at odd angles on his neck. He's been perspiring since he left me at the station for my tour, even though temps haven't broken the seventies outdoors. As a matter of fact, I can't recall the last time Bill had a case of sweats. I'm not sure what to think.

"Preoccupied, sorry. I'm running over a few things in my head. The commander I spoke to is a slippery dude, and something about him seems off. I want to hear everything from the station, but let's talk about your upcoming meet and greet with the police first." Bill glances my way and gives me a lame smile.

"Seriously? We've been driving for eight minutes, and you're just now telling me this? We're almost to the police station." My palm slides down my jeans from a flash of nerves. "Should I be worried?" Bill is pale and greenish, and he wasn't this way earlier. "What did they do to you?"

Bill flips the turn signal lever and drives into the parking spot outside the police station.

I'm struck by their building and how old-timey it looks. "A picture out of a fairy tale. Police in Wonderland. Wow." I unlatch my belt and notice the park bench on the porch. "Just, wow."

"The Victorian era meets the Edwardian period," Bill says.

Shutters crowd the windows at the glass entrance, and a quaint lamppost acts as a fake streetlight; perhaps it's gas or electric like those on the main drag, but I doubt it. A blue awning extends over the goldenrod brick entry, and surprising gingerbread decor hangs between the posts. Nothing about the police station sends a strong message of law enforcement here. Could this be their way of calming the public—an unthreatening welcome to all who approach the police? Honestly, I'd like to make small talk with the constables on their bench located by the door. It's as if they're expecting the town to relax for a cuppa at teatime or share a mince pie or a biscuit while they wait. If it weren't for the signboard, New Zealand Police-Established 1886, beneath the gable end, I'd never guess the interior had police officers doing their jobs.

Bill slides off his seat belt and says to me, "I've thought about my experience with Commissioner Karena. He'll probably be the one taking your statement."

"Do I have rights like we do in the US?"

"Rights here are typical of all commonwealths worldwide, but we can't forget that we are visitors from the freest Constitutional Republic on the planet. If Alec's familiarized you with Greece's and Italy's governments, no matter who we are as Americans, other countries are more restrictive and may not include *Miranda* rights." Bill sighs. "You and I haven't broken any hard and fast laws that I know of. We've done nothing that would throw us in jail. Be honest, be yourself, and don't deviate from that with Karena. He'll see through someone who's not candid in an interview."

"What's Karena like?"

"He's straightforward, which is good, but he lays mind traps so that you'll add more details, making it easy for him to go down other rabbit holes. They don't know a lot about the driver who ran over Alastair, but witnesses gave them a partial plate number."

"That's good news."

"Karena will try to get you to elaborate on what you know about Alastair. He'll ask you the same questions he's asked me in the hope that our stories won't match up or you'll remember something I didn't."

"We should've come down together." Splitting us up was my idea.

"There's a short time where I wasn't with you and Alastair—when I went to pick up the rental car. I told Karena that. Alastair's car needing a tow to a shop happened while we were all together, and that's where my recollection begins. Keep your answers short to yes or no if you can. If he asks for details on any question, don't add theories or assumptions, even if you have them. Your interview isn't the place to guess or theorize about Alastair's private life, so think before you answer."

It's the same advice he gave to Alec in Italy.

"What things did he ask you about?"

Bill tilts his head back and looks at the headliner. "Karena checked the rental car agreement and walked out to the Toyota to be sure everything matched, which it does. He verified the contract from the glove box with the airport rental agency. Per witnesses, the vehicle that hit Alastair isn't white; ours is. You and I are on the agreement, so we're legal."

"Alastair isn't," I add.

Bill nods. "Karena knows that. I was honest about our hesitancy to drive on the opposite side of the road. Since Alastair offered to drive, and I verified his driver's license, Karena seemed to soften on the point, but cautioned about letting another driver get behind the wheel in any car we rent from now on."

"Okay, so we messed up. Does Karena know we didn't see the incident?"

"He does. When I walked to get the rental car and left you inside the airport terminal, did you strike up a conversation first or did Alastair?" Bill scratches his head.

"He did. Alastair noticed my broken luggage zipper and asked if I was Annalisse."

I explain how we got on the subject of his daughter's sweet shop and about calling there to get Ethan's number at Woolcombe Station.

"Stay brief when you tell Karena about your encounter with Alastair. He'll ask for more if he wants clarification. Stick with the truth and don't volunteer more than necessary."

My hand swipes a pant leg again. "The rabbit holes. Okay. I'm ready. Will you go in with me during the interview?"

"I'll try, but he'll prefer a one-on-one with you." Bill glances at my thigh and twists his mouth.

"What's wrong?" I pull at the seam of my jeans. "Do I have a rip in the fabric?"

He sighs. "It's something you do—you have a tell."

"I don't understand; what do I have?"

"When you're upset or worried, you slide a palm over your leg. If you keep doing that, it looks as if you're hiding something," Bill says.

"I get sweaty hands when I'm nervous. I don't realize I'm doing it."

"Try sitting with your hands clasped or folded in your lap. Don't pull your hands apart."

I drag in a deep breath, hold it, then exhale and look at Bill.

"Let's go," he says.

I step up to the tall reception desk in front of a textured wall with Bill by my side and ask the woman in a colorful pantsuit to see Commissioner Karena. From her nameplate, she's on a first-name basis with the public and goes by Maia. A green leaf tattoo swirls down her forearm, and her dark hair is swept back in a harsh ponytail. The office is remarkably void of noise and police personnel other than Maia. A few group photos of the gang in uniform hang in the hallway behind reception, and two cubbies appear to be vacant. Perhaps the Temuka police force is a satellite group, and they're all out on patrol?

Maia taps with bitten nails on a keyboard, then looks beyond me.

It's Bill who piques her interest.

He notices her slight and jumps in with a smile. "I was in earlier speaking to Commissioner Karena about the Alastair McGregor case. My name's Bill Drake; we spoke this morning." He flips one of his business cards on the laminated wood.

Maia glances at it and plays with her hoop earring. "Of course, Mr. Drake. I'll see if he's available. Would you have a seat?" She motions to him and tunes me out again, leaving her station.

A fit, muscular officer in a short-sleeved blue shirt and navy pants accompanies Maia to the counter. He isn't wearing the dark cap with a checkerboard around the band that most policemen on patrol wear. I made a few internet searches on the way to the office headquarters to know what to expect. Their Temuka website was vague about policing policies, but I did get a good look at their uniforms and learned about the hierarchy in this district.

"That's him," Bill whispers.

"Hello, Mr. Drake." The commissioner acknowledges Bill, then me. "Are you Miss Drury?"

I nod, stopping myself from wiping off more perspiration.

"Thank you for talking with us."

"Is it all right to have Bill sit in?" I'm hoping he'll agree.

"Since he's already given his statement, just you." Karena's piercing black eyes sharpen. "This shouldn't take long," he says to Bill. "If you'll wait here, please?"

I look at Bill's tribal shirt and wonder if he bought it while checking out the town.

Focus. Ask about his clothes later.

The commissioner leads me down the linoleum hall and into an office not visible from reception. The room holds a long table, many chairs, and a whiteboard on an easel at one end. What appears to be a break room has a coffee or tea machine and the accoutrements in one corner. This reminds me of a TV-show-style bull room for meetings involving all officers and staff. The commissioner and I are the only people in a room made of cinderblock walls with a mirror halfway up on the hallway side. One-way glass, I assume.

Karena escorts me to a molded plastic chair and pulls out one for himself across the table from me.

I noticed the absence of a firearms belt on his person and how he didn't offer to shake my hand. It might be customary because I'm a woman, and it's their culture. I'm fine with that. He wears an epaulet with insignia on his shoulders and embroidered white hash marks against a black field. With a tanned, full, and round face, his cheeks have a light dusting of pockmarks. However, he's clean-shaven with a fresh haircut and seems pleasant enough.

I clasp my hands in front of me per Bill's recommendation.

"I'm Commissioner Karena. Thank you for coming in today. As you know, we're looking into the death of Alastair McGregor. I understand that you had an encounter with him upon your arrival to Christchurch."

"Yes."

"What do you think of our fine country?" he asks to put me at ease.

I'm trying not to look nervous, but I might be giving off that vibe. "In our short time here, the countryside is... majestic. That's the best word to describe it. I can't wait to see more of the landscape during our stay."

He slides a yellow legal notepad in front of him and takes out a spiral-bound notebook with a black cover from his pocket.

"Describe your introduction to the victim. How did you meet?" he asks, flipping open the smaller notebook with handwriting flowing on the page.

I explain Alastair's approach and our conversation up to Bill arriving with the rental car. Karena makes a few notes when I mention the daughter's sweet shop. I skip over my reason for being on South Island since he hasn't gone in that direction. My description is concise, which appears to frustrate Karena, from his pursing lips and deep forehead lines.

"Did the victim say his daughter *owns* or *owned* the shop?"

"Present tense. He gave me the impression that she still owns it."

"Did you speak to his daughter when you called there?"

This is a trick question.

"I spoke to a woman named Jenny. Alastair said his daughter's name is Sidney."

"When your friend came with the rental car, who allowed Mr. McGregor to get behind the wheel?"

I worry my hands and catch myself, moving them into my lap. That's when I see the camera, its red light on, by the door.

"Commissioner Karena, we didn't think we were doing anything wrong by allowing a local to drive us when his car wouldn't start. Motoring down the opposite side of the road is intimidating when we're not used to it."

"Yes, I understand." In a severe glare, he asks, "Did you or Mr. Drake verify his license at least?"

"We did. Bill checked him out to the greatest extent and asked several questions in my presence. Believe me, if Alastair had made any reckless driving mistakes, Bill would've changed places with Alastair right away. He's an excellent driver—was, I mean."

"Did the victim discuss family matters at any time prior to reaching Temuka?"

"Only about himself. He drove us to Bluebasin Lake because I asked him to show us. I like taking photos. He mentioned a protest coming up to stop the modernization of the area and gave me the impression he's a part of the environmentalist group trying to stop mining and building there. Other than that, he was quiet most of the trip."

The notes were flying across his yellow pad more than at any time I've seen in his presence. "What happened when you got to Temuka?" Karena asks.

Leaning back to reflect, I say, "I told him to drive himself home, but he did something that bothered us. Alastair found a turnout on the side of the road and informed us he was walking the rest of the way. I objected, but he said it was fine. He thanked us, directed us where to get lunch, and Bill slid in as driver."

"What happened then?"

"We drove to lunch, staying on the same road until we found a great place for fish—the most awesome I've ever eaten." I smile at his chuckle. "We sat at a table in front of the establishment, ate, and talked for a few minutes. After Bill dropped our trash in the bin, we got into the Toyota and set out to find the cottage where I planned to stay. As we backed out of the parking space, we heard tires squealing followed by a woman's scream." A tremor overcomes me. "Alastair had stepped out of our SUV not far from the fish restaurant. Bill took us back to the highway where a few people were standing at the driveway near the shopping center. I felt sure that something had been hit by a vehicle. I couldn't see what until we stopped and saw a person, not an animal."

The commissioner scribbles in his smaller notebook.

"You expected to find an animal?" He puckers his lips like he doesn't believe me.

"I grew up on a farm. Deer or stray dogs crossing the road are commonplace."

"Did you see a vehicle pass by at the time? As you were backing up, did you witness any cars behind you?"

"No. I checked the road both ways. Whoever it was had left the scene while we were backing out."

"Did the victim tell you where he lived?"

"No. We thought he was walking home but didn't know how long a walk that was. I felt awful when he got out of the car. Are we suspects?" I blurt out.

"Witnesses gave us a partial plate number. We haven't run it yet because the system's been down. Your rental car isn't the right color or make, Miss Drury."

"May I ask you a question?" I wonder how much the police know about Alastair's family.

Karena agrees to it.

"*Does* his daughter own Sidney's Sweets?"

I'd like the straight story.

"Tragically, she died a couple of years ago."

"What a shame. Do you know where Alastair lives… uh, lived?" I ask.

"We do. The matter is still under investigation, but I'll say this much. He resided in his late daughter's foreclosed home. The bank resold it. McGregor paid the utilities but not the house payment and refused to vacate."

I rest my elbow on the table and drop my chin in my hand, staring at Commissioner Karena. Alastair's story gets sadder by the minute, but the officer in front of me shows no emotion. It might be training, or his way to remove personal involvement in the case.

My mouth is dry, and fish-and-chips sound good right now. I look up at the dome wall clock and salivate over thoughts of lunch.

"It's late," I murmur. "Is there anything else?"

"If we have any more questions, may we call upon you and Mr. Drake?"

I reach into my purse for the billfold and give him one of the gallery's cards. "My cell phone is listed here. Feel free to contact us anytime. We'd like to help you in any way we can."

My chair legs scrape along the linoleum as I scoot away from the table.

Commissioner Karena holds the door open for me, and as I pass, his cologne or uniform has a cottony smell similar to clean laundry fresh from the dryer.

"Nice scent," I say. "Please find the person or people who did this to Alastair."

"We intend to. Good day."

I find Bill scanning a magazine, which he lays aside when I come around the reception desk.

"Thank you," I say to Maia.

"Enjoy your day," she responds but watches Bill.

As we enter the sunlight, I breathe. "Glad that's over."

"I don't see you in handcuffs, so it went... okay?" Bill is more at ease too.

"Savage. You had doubts?" I jump into the passenger side of the Toyota. "They know nothing more about the culprit, but I did learn a few new things about Alastair."

"Like what?"

"I'll go over it after lunch. I'm starving. Do you mind going back to the fish place? I mentioned it to the commissioner, and it's all I've been able to think about since. When we get to the cottage, I'll tell you about my morning at Woolcombe Station."

"Lunch it is." Bill pushes the SUVs start button.

"I'm going to live dangerously. Fish and onion rings, if you can stand me afterward." I grin and turn on a local music station. "You've uncovered more than you realize about Kate. Remember when you ran across Ellen's name while researching Kate's whereabouts last year?"

We located Kate at a spa in Massachusetts after we suspected she'd been kidnapped from Alec's stables. A clever ruse set up by her daughter to make us look foolish when Kate was safe all along.

"I sort of remember some of it. You might have to jog my brain about that investigation. We turned over a lot of stones trying to locate your aunt, uh, mother. Hey, this is a vacation." Bill scrunches his brow. "Try not to relive ground already covered."

"I also have a hypothesis on Alastair's murder suspects. Ellen might have painted a pitiful picture of *poor* Alastair with me, but she let something slip. With his involvement in a huge commercial development at Bluebasin Lake, I see a potential for—"

Bill groans and shakes his head. "Detective Drury, hold on to that for later."

CHAPTER TEN
Wounded Firefighter Turns Investigator

We're moving around the cottage at low speed, like zombies with bulging bellies in search of relief. Stuffing our way through mounds of battered fish in malt vinegar with glasses of beer on tap leaves us wishing we'd left the onion rings off our lunch menu. Neither Bill nor I ate anything since last night, when the tender fish and onion rings fried to perfection went down fast, with crumbs flying between plates. I'm paying for my gluttony with the worst case of indigestion. This is Bill's field of expertise.

"How's your stomach?" I ask him. "Did you happen to bring any antacids with you?"

He dips into his pocket and tosses a roll to me. "Never leave home without 'em."

I pop two peppermint tablets into my mouth, crunch them both, then grimace at the chalky pieces. "If there's any good news, I'm done eating battered fish. It's time to alter our restaurant fare." I scan through the sliding glass door. "Care to investigate the pond behind the house? A stroll in nature might help our digestion."

"Good idea." He grunts, leaving his lounger behind. "I'm eagerly awaiting your murderer insights. Can't help myself—once a detective, always a detective. I'll follow you."

I lead the way around well-kept hedges via natural stepping stones to the pond. Tiny wakes float on the water's surface from a dry wind that's steadily picked up since we got back from our late lunch.

"Restful. A great place to vegetate. Did Karena tell you that Alastair was a squatter in his daughter's old home?" I look to Bill for a reaction.

"No. How'd you find out?"

"I asked about Alastair's daughter, Sidney." My smile is wide, but Bill's frown says volumes. "Good investigators wouldn't volunteer facts, especially a guy like the commander. He didn't say much, but I'm surprised he told me anything with an ongoing investigation."

Bill listens while I bring him up to date on the rest of my police interview, including what I learned at Woolcombe Station about Olivia's coincidental job at the sweet shop.

"Removing Alastair from a house sold after a foreclosure is a good motive for murder. Money is the best motive. He owed bills to lenders, and the new owners couldn't rent or sell the property with Alastair staying there. Police have plenty of angles to work. Unless Alastair isn't paying Sidney's shop employees, I don't see a relevance to Olivia Hyde working at the establishment; it employs the public and Temuka is a small town," Bill says.

"Jenny at the shop seemed happy enough on the phone. If the staff aren't getting paid, they'll walk out.

There's something else." I rub my forehead and steady my voice.

"Anna, what is it?"

"Olivia's mother, Ellen, recognized me right away."

"How? Did Ethan keep a picture of you?"

"I look like a younger version of Kate, and she's my mother's friend; actually, she's much more than that." I plant my backside on a decorative slab of gray-wacke and swipe my jeans before I can catch the nervous habit. "I know what you're going to ask." A gust blows yellow pollen from a nearby Pohutukawa tree, and I sneeze. I tell him how she relates to my father.

"Is that right? Huh." Bill belches out loud. "Onions. Sorry." He pats his stomach. "Did you find Kate there?"

"What a pair we are. I got the impression from Ethan that Kate went to the North Island somewhere, which confirms the postage on her note."

"Kate might have wanted to scare Alec into keeping you from following her."

"Ethan's invite to the cottage was just a coincidence?" Heat radiates from my cheeks from the realization of a miscalculation. "He waited for her to leave before asking me to come here. Now that she's gone, some of it makes sense."

"Thomas Taylor is Ellen Hyde's brother. I'll put that fact back on the table. The connection to Ethan's sudden arrival in New York is clearer now that we know why Ethan was sent to help Kate. Ellen knew that Kate had health issues. She was alone and required a farm hand on the ranch. Even though we didn't turn up any correspondence between Ellen and Kate during"—he uses air quotes—"*the Aunt Kate Rescue* from a kidnapping, there must be a secret mode of communication between the women." Bill hums as he ponders. "Do you know any more about your father?"

I shake my head. "We didn't get to that, but Ellen wants to talk, and you should be there during that conversation. She might give subtle clues that I miss."

"From now on, we stick together whenever possible. Have you told Alec about the farm visit yet?"

"He doesn't know anything beyond last night. Alec took what happened to Alastair with an unnatural calm. I don't think anything else we tell him will freak him out because you're here."

"He worries. I'm here because he's well aware that trouble seeks you out."

There isn't a truer statement.

Unwelcome events have continued to tag along since my immediate family died during my teen years. After meeting Alec two years ago, the tragedies have been piling up enough to give me a complex if I think about it too hard, so I try not to and dwell on the positive.

"Let's see what the rest of the pond looks like." I struggle to get off the rock, and Bill helps me to my feet. "Can't sit here too long. My muscles aren't functioning after that huge meal."

The waterway narrows behind the cottage. Leaves with starburst white lilies and native water grasses at the pond's edge come into view as we approach the neck of a trickling stream. No aquatic critters catch my eye. Not a single water bug ripples the surface anywhere.

"No way." I scroll my phone to check out the web on what's normal pond habitat. "Frogs are nocturnal, hanging out in the shade during the day. They aren't like ours and have round eyes instead of slits." I show him pictures from my phone. "Most of them hatch fully formed from the egg stage and not polliwogs like we have in the US. Too bad they're hiding."

"This is the end of the line for the stream," Bill adds. "Your phone reminds me of social media accounts you don't seem to check. Zavos Gallery has one; I've seen it."

"Chase takes care of my postings and responds so I don't have to. Other than sending him photos from my phone, he's my media guy for the shop, and posts to Gen's gallery accounts so she doesn't have to. He's tried to show her how to post, but she doesn't have time. Chase keeps us all in line and updated. He's awesome." I smile. "I've asked him not to post anything about this trip until we get back."

We walk the edge of the entire pool, side by side, making small talk, winding our way back to the cottage. Native hummingbirds and many other small fowl with yellow markings perch on fences and cling to the red brush on tree branches.

"Care to try a bottle of the lemon drink we picked up?" I ask.

"As long as it's not beer, I'm game. After you." Bill gestures toward the door and slides it open for us.

With sodas in hand to settle our stomachs, it's my turn to interview Bill for a change. Why he doesn't have a steady partner is a curiosity. He's such a cool guy but spends too much time working, is my guess. Most people aren't loners by nature.

"Tell me." I cross my legs and settle on the sofa. "How did you really meet Alec?"

"In a college class."

"I didn't know you had the same classes as Alec."

"Forensic science only. Alec needed forensics to finish his thesis. We hit it off and became instant friends. You already heard about the week we spent with his parents on Crete."

I laugh. "The sunburn to beat all sunburns."

"Yep. I should've had scars from the blisters." His amusement changes into a set jaw.

Bill's neck is covered in burn scars and not from the sun.

"Forensics makes sense for a detective. Were you thinking about becoming a pathologist at one point?"

"Were you *always* planning to become a specialist in antiquities?" he shot back.

I hit a nerve.

A place that causes him pain.

"Researching art history is my thing. Relic and antique appraisals go hand in hand, so yes, I'm where I feel most comfortable."

He stares at his soda for the longest time, then takes a swig. "I'm not a fan of opening old wounds."

"You have a tell too, Bill. Your hair." I grasp a lock of mine to drive the point. "It covers what's imprinted on your neck. There's no shame in a fireman saving lives."

Bill shoves the ottoman in front of his chair, crosses his feet at the ankles, and downs a gulp of his lemon fizzy.

"This stuff isn't bad." Bill adjusts our conversation.

"You've been so generous with your time for Alec and me; is there any way we can reciprocate?"

He guzzles the rest of his drink and sets the empty bottle beside his chair.

"I found out that PTSD is a real disorder; it's not fiction. Once beams collapsed on me and the innocent people I wanted in my life were taken, I imagined phantom flames that weren't real on every call afterward. Not too many people know what I went through. The team went into single-story house fires with me to bolster my confidence, stuck to me like glue to help me overcome the fear and old memories of Payton trapped and little Ellie in her nightgown blackened by smoke, cradled in my arms." Bill's voice cracks. "Nothing stops the images from that night—knowing I'll never see Payton's hazel eyes gazing at her beautiful daughter and how she used to look at me when I stopped by. It's hard." Bill wipes his hands down his cheeks. "If I had to walk down a hallway, burning or not, I froze, unable to take another step."

My heart is heavy for him. "The mind can be a wonderful or terrible thing. I'm so sorry you couldn't save them."

"Or anyone else. Like I've told you before, a fireman who can't move in a burning building—dies. That career is over for me."

"You were close to Payton?" I ask, venturing further into their relationship if he'll let me.

"Her deadbeat husband had left them, so they moved down to Florida to be with her mother. Betty's grease fire in the kitchen is how I met Payton. She and her daughter were easy to love, and I fell hard for both of them. So much for my big plans." He stops and warns, "Don't get any ideas. I see the matchmaker's glint in your eyes."

I hold up both hands. "I won't go there."

Bill's phone vibrates, and he looks at the screen. "Alec." He sets the phone down. "He must've felt we were talking about him." Bill hits speakerphone and answers, "Alec, you're a mind reader. We were taking a walk around the perimeter of the cottage."

"Thought I'd check in before I hit the pillow. How was the sheep station?"

"Hi, Alec. We're digesting a huge lunch after our walk. Bill gave his statement to the police while I spent a few hours at Woolcombe Station. We're both going back to the station tomorrow to get an actual tour that didn't happen today, but I found out a lot from Ethan's mother, pertaining to me." We talk about how she fits in with Kate, who Ellen's husband is, and toss in a few general comments about where Kate might be.

"I'm not there, so I can't see how Ellen's reacting to you, but try not to interrogate her and put her off," Alec says. "You have an inquisitive mind."

"Yep," Bill interjects into the conversation.

"I gave my statement to the police commissioner after Bill gave his. As of this moment, we are officially done with the authorities." I delve deeper into Alastair's activism about Bluebasin Lake and what

Karena mentioned during my interview, bringing Alec up to the moment on the day's activities.

"You've had a full day. I'll do some legwork on Finn Hyde and see what I can dig up. It might help to know his background. Be very careful around Ellen. Some politicians' wives are well-trained agents for their husbands." The tension in his voice is evident. He wants to be here; I can feel it. Alec's been waiting for more photos. Before I get sidetracked, I scribble a note to send him pics of the cottage and the lake.

"We're still trying to catch up from the plane ride. It's kicked us to the curb," Bill says. "The jet lag is better today, but it's tough getting used to the middle of summer season here like we've skipped over winter and spring."

"Every day, we feel more normal, Alec." I smile at Bill. "By tomorrow, we should be recovered."

Alec mumbles something.

"What's the word on the new clinic? It must look great inside," Bill asks.

"Not exactly."

I meet Bill's glance as he raises a questioning brow.

"What happened? Didn't the shipments arrive?" I ask, squinting at Bill.

"A change in plans," Alec says.

Uh-oh.

Disasters of all kinds parade across my mind. We've been talking about fires. Did one destroy the clinic building? Is Alec hurt? Did something happen to Helga or Gen? I pace behind the couch, following the swirl pattern on the rug with each step, taking slow breaths, trying not to imagine the worst.

"What happened at the clinic?" Bill asks.

"Did they have to reschedule the delivery?" I await Alec's answer with Bill as he shrugs and shakes his head.

Alec is making a calculation. Whatever it is, he's not sure how to tell us, or he's afraid to.

I squeeze the top of the sofa cushion and lean against the frame.

"I sent it all back," Alec says. "Every last carton. Met the drivers and told them to return everything to the warehouse."

"I don't understand. Was it defective?" My train of thought hits a blank wall, and I can't think of what to say to him. This is his dream, so what's stopping the progress?

Bill does a throat-clearing thing. "If the stuff wasn't right, you must have had your reasons."

"I do. I've considered some good advice. Anna, I'll explain it all, I promise. Hey, I'm gonna sign off. Miss you, babe. Can't wait to see the photos you keep talking about." Alec's laughter is less than convincing. "Keep her safe, Drake, and thanks."

"Will do. Good night."

"Wait, what aren't you telling us?" I say to Alec with a flurry of misgivings. "Can't you tell us now?"

"What I did was strictly my decision."

"Okay then. We'll talk more when you're ready. Sleep well."

Bill makes sure the call disconnects and looks to me for answers to Alec's strange actions.

"Is there a vet clinic plan *B* you haven't told me about?"

"I don't know any more than you do. That's a shocking move." Frying oils are churning and I'm tasting fish again, and I'm on the verge of stomach upset. "I'm stunned. He's done a complete about-face, and I hope I'm not to blame. Alec's ambition to become a veterinarian is why he let his dad's car company go. If I were there with him, would he still be returning equipment?"

"I didn't see it coming, especially for someone hell-bent on goal setting. When Alec wants something, he makes sure that he gets it. Not unlike yourself." Bill looks at his watch and gets out of the recliner. "I need to walk off more of my lunch. Maybe I'll figure out what he's doing before he explains himself. Alec has me questioning how well I know him."

"Keep your phone with you. My lunch has been in my throat since he told us he sent his deliveries back."

"Would you rather I stay here?"

"No. I'm going to sit here a while longer and allow everything to sink in. While I'm at it, I'll make some internet inquiries on Representative Hyde myself. If we're going back to the station in the morning... like Jefferson said, knowledge is power."

Bill exits the sliding door, and I go for my laptop.

CHAPTER ELEVEN
Cooper Dunn

Memories of resting against the fence at Walker Farm during bull sessions with Ethan flood my mind as Bill and I stand at the paddock, looking forward to a real tour. Today's guide is Woolcombe Station Manager Cooper Dunn. Ethan said my visit from yesterday continues today, but chores have taken him from us. It's too bad his mother has other plans for him—to deliver supplements to the sheep grazing in another part of the station. Is Ellen manipulating her son to stay away from me? My *inquisitive mind*, as Alec puts it, is running away with possibilities. The deliveries to their sheep could've been put off until the afternoon after we left.

I'd like to quiz Ethan about Kate a little more. He might have information unbeknownst to him. In light of Alec's warning, I have to be careful of pushing Ellen too hard. She knew Alastair, and her husband is involved in the development of a touchy portion of protected land. Are the Hydes capable of ordering a hit on Alastair to stop protestors from getting in the developer's way? I hope not.

I adore clouds for picture-taking, and we have plenty floating in the crystal-blue skies above us. Overcast is best for glare-free countryside shots and a chance to give the Nikon another workout. Alec should've received the first round of photos via email by now. I'll follow up with more from our day with Cooper and call Alec again about sending his deliveries back.

"G 'day, miss. You're stuck with me as your tour guide." Cooper comes up behind us, stamping out his cigarette. "What do ya want to see first? How 'bout the Corries?"

"Cooper, this is my friend, Bill Drake."

Cooper touches the brim of his cap. "Pleasure. How much do ya know about sheep?" he asks Bill.

"Almost nothing. Annalisse is the expert. I'll follow in the background if you don't mind."

Cooper takes us to a new building a distance from the main barn. The Corrie barn has a coat of fresh white paint, but as we approach, nothing auditory sounds from the pens.

"Are you sure the sheep are inside?" I ask.

"Yeah, about forty head. They're bunked down. Taking a smoko." He grins at me.

Our guide opens the access gate to the barn's shelter, and the girls file out into daylight. They're a uniform bunch with a year's worth of fleece covering them. A few are panting, and they all look great. Little ears and dark noses, not unlike the band of shorn sheep that crossed in front of our car when we drove in on the first day. I can't get over how much smaller and meatier these sheep are than what I'm used to seeing.

"They're beautiful, Cooper. And going to feel better once the wool is gone," I say, glancing at Bill, who is mesmerized by the flock.

"I don't know what they're supposed to look like, but they could be clones of each other. How do you get them to look identical?" Bill asks.

"We breed 'em that way. These are Liv's show animals. Uniformity is part of the breeding program."

A single ewe approaches the fence where I'm standing. "Bottle lamb?" I ask Cooper.

"How'd ya guess?" He laughs. "Liv brings out treats for that one. She thinks you have something for her."

I reach over the fence and scratch behind an ear. The grease in her fleece coats my fingertips.

She takes one whiff of me and scampers back to the group.

"That didn't take long to figure out I'm not Olivia." I laugh at the forty pairs of wary eyes watching us and take a few photos of the group. "Thanks for the look at the sheep, Cooper. It's warm in the sun, so we'll let them get back to their morning siesta. If they're going to be shorn soon, I'd really like Bill to watch a little of the shearing."

"We're supposed to hit it with this group over the weekend. If you're still here, we'll be sure to bring you back."

A female calls the manager's name.

"I'd better see what she wants. Follow me back to the big barn," Cooper says.

Olivia Hyde meets us, bringing Cooper a tall mug of tea or coffee. While they're mired in a lengthy discussion, we move away to give them privacy.

Olivia dresses for attention in a low-cut, tight T-shirt and short shorts that show off her long, tanned legs. Her tan might be a natural one, but her thighs have orange streaks that cause me to think otherwise. She keeps touching her face and flinging her hair, giggling, between pivots and pirouettes. The body language says she's open to any advance from Cooper. It's painful to observe, but at the same time, hard for me to look away. What's happening in front of us is a rite of two people in a dating or mating ritual. The attraction seems to be mutual.

She's years younger than Ethan, I'm guessing late teens or early twenties. My patience for her chat with the manager is wearing thin by the time twenty minutes pass. She has no regard for visitors when she has a more urgent agenda. It's clear that we aren't her priority. Waiting for her flirting session to conclude, we might make it out of the homestead by late morning.

I glance at the sun's position in the sky for an estimate of about two hours before noon.

"Should we give ourselves a self-guided tour?" Bill asks. "This show could take a while. Whoa."

Olivia and Cooper meet in an embrace, hugging as if they're longtime friends or perhaps lovers. Their familiarity exposes more than a working relationship. Much more. Does Ellen approve of Olivia's touchy-feely courtship with Woolcombe's new manager? It's liable to affect his work, but that's for them to sort out.

"We'll take the Toyota and scout around the station on our own. I'm sure disappointed that Ethan's mom sent him on errands when she knew we were coming, and now Cooper is tied up."

"Should we tell someone we're leaving?" Bill asks.

"Ellen wants to meet you, so we'll stop in before we go. The station tour is a bust without Ethan as our guide. With what Ellen told me, I'd like to know more about my real father's whereabouts at this very moment. She didn't want to address Thomas, and I don't understand why she's not bubblier and more excited to see her brother's daughter for the first time. Hopefully, her husband isn't coaching her to be cool and evasive."

"I'd like to meet her. We don't have to stay long."

"Ethan's invitation is rotten timing." I sigh, trying not to blame Kate for taking off and leaving me hanging when all this could have been avoided by staying in New York and telling me about Thomas Taylor in the beginning. Making a mental shift in my plans to stay at the station for two weeks, we might see more of the country by going to another spot in New Zealand. I still don't know how I feel about Kate being my mother when all she had to do was tell me to keep it confidential. Drawing things out makes me believe there's more to her and Thomas Taylor. Who is he really? Is he on the run from authorities?

The kitchen entrance is open to the screen, much closer than walking the entire home to the front door.

I knock on the wood frame. "Hello. It-it's Annalisse," I stammer.

A skinny cook or housekeeper in a striped pinafore apron appears at the screen. "Yes. May I help you?"

"We're sorry to be a bother. Is Mrs. Hyde in?"

"She hasn't come down yet. Can I help you?"

I glance at Bill, then the black-haired elderly woman with the bad dye job. "That's okay. We'll drive around the station on our own."

A whistle floats on the air in the distance.

"Breaktime for the manager must be over. It's Cooper, waving to get our attention," Bill says.

"Should she come down, please tell her we're with Cooper." I smile at the cook, and we turn toward the sheep barn.

"Sorry about that," Cooper says to us as we approach.

When he takes his cap off, his hair is a mass of tangles, and he looks like he's been wrestling with more than one straw bale.

A roll in the hay?

"Must be barn-cleaning day. You have more than enough to keep you busy," I say, hoping we won't be waiting for Ethan and a tour tomorrow. "Do you know if Ethan's gone all day?"

"Naw. He got out before I did. He'll be back later." Cooper brushes himself off and fluffs his long hairdo, raining shards of straw and hair to the ground. "No worries. I can show you around the place."

A lot of his hair is dropping on the ground. Maybe it's from an earlier haircut he gave himself.

"Who's that gorgeous fellow in the next pen over? He's amazing. Is he the stud ram for the Corrie flock?" I ask, referring to the sheep standing alone, watching us.

"Yeah. Liv's brute. Be careful of him if you go inside. I don't advise it, though. He can be slippery."

Cooper turns, and I notice a blue rope halter sticking out of his back pocket.

"Is he the same breed as the group we saw?" Bill asks.

"Dax is the farm's purebred Corriedale stud. He's a big one—a champion from another farm. I don't know where the farm is, but he's a great one for strong fleece. The bugger will be easier to shear than a Merino ram; I can tell you that."

"Don't get injured on our account." I nod to Cooper, and he winks at me. "If we could have a closer look at him? We'll stay outside the fence," I say to Bill, who has grown pale.

"Are you sure this is a good idea?"

Bill's out of his comfort zone with large animals.

"Most rams are territorial. Don't be fearful. They're actually easy to handle once you know how and when to interact with them. Never give a ram a target to run at you, and never turn your back on any flock of ewes with a ram or two among them. Good breeding rams guard their females fiercely."

"It's a guy thing; I'll bet." Bill laughs.

While we're talking, Cooper opens a pass gate at our corner of the pen and slips his rope halter over the ram's head. His hands are shaking from too much caffeine, perhaps.

Dax is holding his head up high beside Cooper, walking as easily as Harriet does for me. He's a halter-broken, show-ring, stud buck made for judging.

"Is he strutting, or is it my imagination?" Bill is awestruck by the prancing sheep paralleling the fence line in order to greet us. "I didn't know you could do that with a sheep."

"Greenhorn," I whisper, nudging him with my elbow. "Show animals have to be broke to halter, or the judge won't get a good look at how his structure conforms to the breed standard. Like the Kennel Club does with its dog shows. We halter sheep when they're lambs, and they pick up the routine quickly. It's no different than training a pup to walk at your side on a leash."

Dax comes over and studies me with his shining amber eyes. He has the smallest ears I've ever seen for a Corriedale ram. They're smaller than the ewes we saw in their pen. His broad head is free of horns, typical of this breed, and Dax's wrinkly snout exhibits telltale signs of females in their estrus cycles. He can smell the brood ewes ready to breed from a long distance.

"How do you know so much about sheep?" Cooper's watching me, deciding my experience level. He's all but ignoring Bill's presence.

"I have sheep of my own. A mixed group of several breeds." I reach over the fence and part the ram's lips to check his gums. I spot four big teeth on the bottom. "He's a two-year-old," I remark to Bill.

"How'd you know that?"

"Sheep get two big teeth for every year." Cooper jumps in to answer him.

I scratch Dax under the chin, rubbing across plenty of lanolin. "What a beauty. Whoever chose this guy knows what they're doing."

Cooper uses his hands to part Dax's lustrous four-inch fleece. "Brilliant, eh? He's gonna shear like butter.

Offspring ought to as well. Liv wants *me* to shear her flock, not the shearing gang," he says with a wide grin, throwing his head back.

Dax's wool crimp is heavy for Corriedales I've seen and creamy yellow with grease. The legs on New Zealand sheep are short as are their necks compared to breeds in the US. Purebred flocks stand closer to the ground in most countries. The United States prefers their show sheep breeds to be tall and elegant. Unfortunately, to supersize sheep, crossbreeding with larger white breeds is the surest way to water down their natural characteristics.

Bill reaches over me and rubs the ram's forehead with his fingertips.

I pull my arm away and take a step back.

"Bad move, mate." Cooper tightens his hold on the halter.

A ram will dip his head and strike at any target advancing on them. Dax does what rams do; he rams Bill's palm.

"Hey." Bill jerks away his hand. "Did you see that?"

"He's a handsome guy. Would you mind holding him a minute longer? I'd like to get a close-up." I fumble with the tote on the ground and take out the camera. Bill is in the first shot.

"We're going to step over here, Cooper. We appreciate your time."

I point to the paddock next door, and Bill follows me there. "Back to rule one; never give rams a place to strike. When they can see you, the best place to handle a ram is behind the head or below the chin. Anything coming at their eyes will bring on the fight instinct."

"I didn't know that."

"They're called rams for a reason. Sometime I'll tell you the story about what happened to me with a ram while trimming trees in his paddock." I slip the Nikon back into my leather bag. "When a fence is between you and the ram, petting his forehead isn't a terrible mistake, so don't worry. Dax is aware of the barrier, but I have seen a ram or two drop back and charge out of spite or because he can. Rams are necessary for a group of breeding ewes unless you're a fan of artificial insemination. I prefer the natural method."

I notice questions behind Bill's eyes as if he's picking through the words in my sheep-breeding spiel. It's hard to know for sure where Bill's mind is, thinking about sheep or my last comment on natural breeding.

"Mind out of the gutter, Drake." I shake my head because Alec does the same thing.

Hair lifts on the back of my neck signaling we're not alone. Spinning around to see if I'm right, Ellen Hyde is standing behind us a few paces.

Her eyes lock on Bill as she scans him up and down.

"You have experience with sheep," Ellen says to me. "Kate mentioned that you're a whiz with animals."

"Hi, Ellen. I didn't hear you, or I would've had you discuss sheep with Bill since *you* are the expert here. This is Bill Drake, our... uh, friend." I almost let slip that he's a detective. If something ugly is happening behind the political scenes, she might frown on a detective snooping around the station.

Bill and Ellen talk a little while I stand aside in one of my favorite pastimes, listening to birds chatter in the tall trees. Her careful answers and periodic glances my way remind me of someone evaluating my reasons for being with Bill instead of the wealthy, celebrity boyfriend my mother had plenty of time to speak about.

"Can you tell me where Kate went when she left here last December?" I break in.

Bill steps closer to me and folds his hands.

My redirection has him dropping back into guardian mode.

"Kate said she would call you." Ellen meshes her lips together. "I heard all about her disappearance to that upscale spa in Lenox, and what Ted asked his daughter to set up so he could hash out her affair with my brother. I hope he rots behind bars for that sick stunt. Faking his suicide aged Kate ten years."

"Killing an old man was horrendous too," I add in case she didn't know. "Alec and Bill overheard Ted and Kate arguing at the spa where he'd said hateful things to her. He hasn't forgiven my mother for the affair with your brother and doesn't want to talk to me. I tried to see him in jail."

"Ted is worthless and needs anger management. I never understood how she could go back to him after Thomas." Ellen stares at her feet.

"Was your brother going to marry her or take care of me?" I'm siding with my mother on this one. "She had no means of support other than Ted."

Ellen mewls as if I struck a nerve. "Thomas is a wanderer and not the marrying kind, but if he knew about you…" She raises her hand high. Looking away from us, she barks, "Cooper, wait there." Her voice softens. "Excuse me, Annalisse. He's supposed to be digging nettle out of that pen so we can gather Olivia's sheep for shearing." Ellen stomps away for a talk with the manager, leaving Bill staring at me—with another question about to erupt.

"Okay, what's a nettle?" he asks, gliding my way.

"Stinging nettle is a spikey green plant that most grazing animals won't eat. Sheep won't touch it. The spines are its defense mechanism, and they will sting you. Digging the nettle out by the root is the only way I know to keep it from growing back and spreading into larger patches."

Cooper pushes a wheelbarrow with gardening tools into the paddock next to Dax. A station manager in New Zealand covers the bases; he's not just a sheep wrangler and shearer, he's part gardener too.

"I suggest that we grab the rental car. Cooper's preoccupied." Bill's idea sours his face. "We're better off on our own. Tours are for *greenhorns*, as you say."

He doesn't exude confidence when he marches for the car with his head down.

On the drive over, Bill was less than optimistic about guides since having had so much trouble with Alastair. Plus, we'll be traveling unfamiliar territory.

"I'm happy to switch with you as designated driver," I suggest, hoping for his sense of gallantry to step in.

A boxy vehicle slows and parks at one of the outbuildings. Someone in a white T-shirt gets out.

"Bill, does that look like Ethan?"

"Can't tell from this distance."

I stop and hone in on the place where Ellen and Cooper are standing. "She's walking away. Have you noticed how Ellen can creep around undetected, just like a spirit in free flight? You do know that she was eavesdropping on us."

"Take a look over there." Bill motions toward the figure leaving the main house and about to cross the dirt driveway behind us. "I think the daughter is heading over to Cooper again."

"He'll be lucky to keep his job at this rate. Ellen doesn't want him distracted by anyone, even us. If Cooper can't keep his hands to himself, Olivia will get him fired. It won't break Ethan's heart, though since he and Cooper don't get along. It appears we've dropped in on a down under soap opera in progress. Time to depart." I smile at Bill and sink into the SUV's passenger side. "If that's Ethan over there, we'll tell him our plans have changed for the next few days. Ethan might have overstepped his family by sending a cottage key and asking me to visit this month. Our arrival has been anything but welcomed at the main house." As I pull the seat belt across, I ask, feeling less than enthused, "Would you like me to drive?"

"Let's stick with the same plan as yesterday, shall we?"

Bill turns the Toyota around and pulls up to the dirty four-wheel-drive vehicle that we believe is Ethan's.

"He's already left; we're too late," I say.

"I spot two white shirts." Bill gets out of the car and surveys. "Congregating where Cooper is."

"Leave 'em alone. A note on the driver's seat is good enough. He'll find it." Pulling out one of my gallery business cards, I flip it over and ask him to call me when he has time. "Ethan should have my cell anyway. I'm sure he didn't keep it. If this isn't Ethan's car, someone will get him the message."

"Should we tell Ellen we're leaving?"

"No. For some reason a wall's going up where I'm concerned. Did you feel it back there?"

"They did put us up in a nice cottage, so I don't have complaints," Bill says with a large smile. "Hopefully, Ethan will call you."

I leave the card on what we assume is Ethan's front seat, and return to our vehicle.

"Here I go mentioning food again. How does breakfast or an early lunch sound to you? Did you notice a diner in town?" I ask Bill, as we're about to enter the Temuka City limits with the quaint, colorful buildings on the main drag.

"There's a couple," he says.

With lights flashing and sirens blaring, an ambulance van is approaching us in the opposite direction—flying at a good clip over the speed limit of Highway 1. The emergency vehicle is the most awful combination of colors: large yellow and green squares in a checkerboard pattern. The entire van in daylight reminds me of spinach leaves swimming in vomit.

"Have you noticed that everything has a checkerboard pattern in this town? From the constable's police caps, their cars, to that horrible neon yellow-green ambulance."

"Better to see them at night at a distance, I'd imagine."

I look into the rearview mirror and watch the ambulance's path. It remains on the same highway we're traveling.

"Were there any other homes or farms on this road other than Woolcombe Station?" I ask.

"Forget about ambulance chasing, Annalisse. I know this is your trip, but get real…" His grip slides over the steering wheel. "It's on to breakfast, pay the cashier, and take photographs. This is scenery day, remember? A chance to get out and look around." Bill arches his brows. "You get sidetracked with ease. One of us has to keep a cool head."

"I know, that's what Gen says. All the same, I have a bad feeling about that van."

"Noted." Bill nods.

If something went wrong at the station, Ethan will tell us if he's able.

CHAPTER TWELVE
Instincts Are Usually Correct

Woolcombe's entire sheep flock is out there on a patch of land, but at the rate we're going, we might not get a chance to see them. The hillsides and mountains Bill and I pass along main Highway 1 are parched and yellowish and in need of a large drink to perk up the dry grasslands. Temuka on South Island accumulates the most rainfall during their winter months in July and August. January, below the equator, is smack in the middle of New Zealand's summer. If I kept to Alec's original April schedule, the scenery would have a springtime appearance. If he's still up to taking that future trip, we'll see the landscape from a different perspective.

For a change from our current rural route, we drive into Pleasant Point, another small town of roughly two square miles. Bill slows past their old locomotive, brought over from Scotland in 1884. At least, that's what the billboard says on the museum building. Since the 1980s, the black steam engine has been an attraction for tourists as a fully restored donation to the museum. I relish seeing more of the countryside from an interior destination and not from a roadway.

A tour schedule for January hanging below the billboard, brings hope of a train ride.

The Flyer locomotive isn't running again until April.

Our luck is so disappointing.

It's a shame the rail company chose to close down the train in the middle of summer... and unusual timing. Their historic train, the Fairlie Flyer, will have to wait for another time—during another journey, if that happens. The pain in my selfish heart clutches me in its unyielding grip, and again I regret my departure from New York in January—without Alec—with wild thoughts of finding Kate. I'm feeling remorse for insisting that Alec stay behind, and how ironic it is that I'm here and Alec is no longer furnishing his clinic, part of the justification for making my case to go alone to New Zealand. Did Alec sell Pearce's car company less for him and more for my benefit?

Please don't let that be true.

I'm desperate to know why plans to furnish his vet hospital have changed, but at the same time, I might not like his reasons. No matter how the change in direction is rationalized, the destruction of a dream is devastating for anyone. Alec's trained in veterinary medicine, specializing in horses. What better way for him to capture that reality than a clinic on Brookehaven's three hundred-plus acres next to his stables? He's meant to follow this ideal path.

Having Bill here as a companion is fantastic, but he's hardly a substitute for Alec's familiarity, his caring, and his warm body next to mine. Should we cut ourselves loose from New Zealand and return to New York since nothing is working out as I hoped? Being separate from Alec did work on one level. It won't be long before Alec knows the absolute truth about Virena and her son's parentage.

"The rail is closed down the entire month," Bill says. "Alec would've enjoyed walking through the old station. He's into trains."

"Seriously? In two years, I've never heard him say that." The comment bewilders me. Something else to ask Alec about.

Bill searches for his phone. "I'll get a picture of you by the train. Alec will love that."

He takes it and trades places with me. "May as well get mine too." He grins, and I take the shot just like that. The real Bill. "Where to now?" he asks.

"Let's look for an elusive flock of sheep. With millions on this continent, they can't hide from us forever."

I climb back into the SUV and see a new text came in while we were outside.

"Ethan messaged. He must have gotten the card I left." His note is short. "What's he doing waiting for us at the cottage?" I look at Bill. "Ethan says it's important, and we should drop what we're doing and come back. How far are we?"

Bill hits the navigation button, plugs in our current location, and the cottage-preset address pops up. "We're fourteen kilometers away. Tell Ethan we can be there in ten to twelve minutes, depending upon traffic."

I text Ethan back and talk to Bill at the same time. "He seems upset. Did something happen after we left?

My thoughts keep returning to that ambulance we passed."

My phone rings from a caller with a restricted number who doesn't want to be known. "Now what?" I flip it around and show Bill. "Should I answer?"

"I would. You haven't had a call all week other than Alec. Anyone connected to the gallery knows you're out of the country."

"We're on speaker." I tap the phone. "Annalisse Drury," I say to the caller with a glance at Bill.

"Miss Drury, this is Commissioner Karena. Is it possible to speak to you and Mr. Drake within the hour?"

Bill swivels his head against the idea.

"We're quite a distance away. That won't work for us. May I ask what this is about? Have you had a break in Alastair McGregor's case?"

"Still collecting evidence. When can I speak to you?" Karena asks.

I'm uneasy about the unknown. First Ethan wants to see us and now the police. I agree with Bill; making appointments with Commissioner Karena without knowing why is a bad idea.

"May I get back to you, Commissioner? I'm driving and need to pay attention to the road. Please text your phone number to me. I'll let you know when we can meet as soon as I've had a chance to check in with Bill. Will that be all right?"

"Sending over the contact information now. I'll await your call. Cheers." The commissioner ends the conversation.

Tossing the phone onto my lap, I consider our options. None of them feel good. "Is there a chance that Ethan and the commissioner want to discuss the same thing?"

"We don't know what that *thing* is. Congrats on the smooth way you ended the call with Karena, by the way. Let's hear what Ethan has to say and go from there."

Minutes later, Bill pulls in behind a dirty Range Rover. I don't know why Ethan gave me the impression that he would wait for us outside. There's no sign of him on the porch settee.

"Where is he?" Bill scans the front of the house. "Around back?"

"He must be inside. It's their house." Bill and I have nothing to hide, but still, letting himself in is an annoying invasion of privacy. It might be the Kiwi way. "I wonder how many previous station managers and visitors have their own skeleton pass key for the cottage?"

"A scary thought but a good one to remember." Bill hesitates at the sliding door. "This ought to be interesting." He opens the unlocked slider and follows me inside.

"Ethan, we're back," I say to an empty family room and vacant kitchen.

He appears from the hallway in a daze with both hands in his pockets, staring at the floor like he's lost a family member. Ethan shuffles along the hardwood in his work boots, scraping and sliding his heels. His mussed hair contains a mix of straw and weeds while dirt covers his T-shirt and knees. He wore his hair in a buzz cut when he worked at Kate's farm.

"Where have you been? Rooting around in the barn with Cooper?" I ask the rumpled form standing in front of us.

Ethan is a wreck and teeters in place—on the verge of toppling over.

"Ethan, what's wrong?" I ask.

His eyes are red and puffy, and streaks stain his cheeks.

"Sit down, man." Bill takes him by the arm to the sofa. "Tell us what happened."

I slip into the kitchen and grab a couple of sodas from the refrigerator. "Take this." I hand him a brown bottle and the other to Bill, bracing for impact.

Ethan drinks in silence, then says, "Brilliant. Thanks, Annalisse." He regards me with a faraway look as if he's daydreaming about a memory. "I sure miss seeing you around. Have you been to your farm lately?"

"When you guys' left New York, Walker Farm went on the market for sale. Kate's son has always hated that place, so I'm not surprised he's trying to get the cash out of it. I don't know if it's sold or not. He wants way more than the property's worth." I sit in the armchair next to the sofa, antsy to find out what's eating at Ethan. "Would you like to talk about what has you so upset? Have you heard from Kate?" *Please don't let this be about her.*

"Mum wants to put the Corrie buck down after what he did."

"Kill the sheep we saw today? Dax?" Bill asks.

Ethan nods once.

"What did he do?" I'm afraid to ask because it's never good to cull the flock's healthy stud ram.

"When Cooper was bent over pullin' thistle out of the pen, Dax got in with him and hit him hard across the back of the shoulders. Olivia found bruises there."

"Is Cooper okay?" I ask.

Ethan hangs his head and shakes it. "We thought he was. Liv saw everything and ran over to help, but she was too late and couldn't rouse him. He wasn't breathing when I got there." Ethan's voice wavers, and he recovers. "The medics tried to revive him, but he carked it." He wipes his nose with his sleeve. "Took him away so the examiner could determine the cause of death. If you ask me, he died of a cervical fracture. His neck snapped at the moment of impact, severing the spinal cord."

"Carked it?" Bill asks.

"Kicked the bucket," Ethan says.

How horrible for the station.

"That would require one heck of a blow in just the right spot. Are you a trained medical professional?" Bill pinches his brows as any investigator would. "I'd wait for the coroner's findings before jumping to conclusions, Ethan."

It's best to keep debate to a minimum and humor *Detective* Fawdray when he uses his book knowledge and investigator skills.

"Ethan reads a lot of crime fiction. He's quite the history buff. Personally, I'd like to think there's a chance they brought Cooper back in the ambulance. Paramedics have defibrillators on board."

"Naw. He was gone when the medical team arrived."

"Did Dax break down the fence, or did someone leave the gate unlocked?" Bill asks.

"That's what we're trying to figure out. He won't leave his pen unless he has an open invitation. No boards missing, no fence torn down, nothing. The corner gate was closed as usual. When Liv got to Cooper, she said Dax was charging the wheelbarrow, but we can't figure out how he got in there."

"If *you* didn't see the ram hit your station manager, how can you be sure it wasn't Olivia who accidentally left the gate unlatched when she went to Cooper for one of their chats? You don't know if Olivia went to Cooper's side before or after Dax did." Olivia feels untrustworthy and that bothers me, or it could be her snarky attitude toward me that I don't trust. "Are you absolutely sure Cooper was hit by the ram, or is that what Olivia says? I know she's your half-sister, Ethan, but people make mistakes. Here's another plausible option: she let Dax in after Cooper fell from some other injury. The ram might've been used as cover for an argument between Cooper and Olivia that ended in an awful way." I look at Bill, fearing my own beliefs are coloring the possibilities.

"Unless you saw the ram act up, hearsay isn't proof of what happened to Cooper," Bill says to a silent Ethan.

"Look, Ethan." I gather my thoughts and arrange them. "Dax ran to Cooper through an open gate, or he jumped a sixty-inch fence. That's five feet. Add nine inches to that and he'd have to spring over my head." I use my hand as a marker. "In my estimation, his short legs aren't built for it without taking off the top rail, so I'd rule out the leaping theory. If ewes were on the other side, I've seen stranger things happen, but it's doubtful in this instance. Dax was allowed into the paddock by a human being. Someone opened the gate and shut it behind the ram, or left the gate open. If Cooper was mauled by Dax, the medical examiner will know it from bruising, marks on the flesh, broken bones, et cetera. I'm not buying the sheep acted maliciously on his own unless he was teased." I open my leather tote and search for the Day Runner to make notes.

"You think Liv or somebody else hurt Coop on purpose?" Ethan stiffens. "No way. I didn't like the bloke, but I'd never hurt Coop. Liv loves her ram too much, and she fancied the new manager. Followed him everywhere. Police have been over every foot of the fence for clues, taking prints…"

"Nobody's pointing a finger at you, so chill. Why even go there? I'm not implying that you'd want to harm the guy, but you aren't exactly best friends."

Ethan's guilt mechanism is in high gear. Is he covering for himself or someone else?

"Did you say the police are already involved?" Bill asks Ethan, then glances at me.

Commissioner Karena's call in the car makes more sense.

"Yeah. Two deputies came in behind the ambulance. I told them it was an accident. One cop is still at the house, questioning Mum, Liv, the cook, and anyone else home during the incident. That's why I'm here.

They want to talk to you and Bill. One cop said so." Ethan rubs below his eyes. "I had to warn you."

"We were there before the incident happened. Cooper was weeding the paddock and very much alive. We'll speak to the police. No problem." Bill gives me a knowing look about more interviews for us in the future.

"While we're on the subject of mysteries, what do you know about a man named Alastair McGregor?" I ask.

"He's some old bloke who owned Sidney's Sweets. The sweet shop where Liv works. Why?"

"Did you hear what happened the day we arrived?" Bill asks.

"Yeah. A hit-and-run driver nailed McGregor when he was walking along the road. I've heard people call him a *wally*. A real loser." Ethan flinches from Bill's reaction.

I see it too.

Bill is squinting and squirming in his recliner. I take it as a signal not to delve into our involvement if we plan to stay neutral in the probe.

"Did you know a Rover ran into him, seen by eyewitnesses? Who drives one?" I ask in the most general way possible.

Ethan laughs. "Who doesn't drive a Rover? I do. They're popular."

"Never mind." I scratch my ear and think a moment. "How well did you know Alastair's daughter, Sidney? Since Olivia works in her shop, were they good friends?"

Bill relaxes in his recliner, nonchalantly working on a hangnail, but he's pressing his lips together in a bitter line, sending more signals.

Time for me to end my line of questioning.

"Why ask about that bloke?" Ethan says to me. "Do you know who drove over him?"

Bill has a throat-clearing moment. "His accident happened the same day we got here. Annalisse is just curious. We both are."

Ethan shows us a toothy grin. "Yeah. She's like that. You'll have to ask Liv about the shop owner."

"Didn't you mention once that you had an uncle who was a journalist? He had the same name as the card we found on the victim in Kate's barn. Remember? Thomas, I think." By playing forgetful, I might uncover more about Ellen's brother. I'd like proof that he's my father, other than my mother's mention in her letter and Ellen's careful reference to him. Kate Walker has kept so much from me, turning my world on its head; how do I know this revelation is the truth this time? Ellen and Kate are friends. It's possible they're colluding on another story to hold me back from looking for Taylor.

When we found the corpse in the Walker Farm barn last July, I recall Kate shutting him down when Ethan spoke of his uncle, Thomas Taylor. At the time, I felt the comment was a fabrication due to Ethan's desire to be part of the investigation. In hindsight, Kate shushing him could lend itself to the truth. Given my one talk with Ellen, his remarks back then have merit now.

"Yeah, we haven't heard from my uncle in a long time." Ethan tilts his head as his mom did yesterday. "I haven't seen Uncle Thomas since I was a little bloke. Mum told me he was in Europe on assignment and he liked to hunt for buried treasure."

"In the sea?" Bill asks.

Ethan stands and shrugs. "Not on ships. I think he explores caves, places like that. I'd better go before Mum throws a hissy fit and sends Liv out looking for me."

"Please tell her we'll come by to visit tomorrow, and give her our condolences for Cooper."

A beam of light streaks through the sliding doors. "The coppers are outside. I have to go." Ethan wipes his hands off on his T-shirt and steps closer to the sliding door.

A white police car with blue-and-yellow checkerboard down its side settles in behind our Toyota SUV. The interrogation man comes to us.

I turn to Bill and ask, "Would they show up unannounced without waiting for our call?"

"Seems so. Who's gonna stop 'em?" Bill gets out of his recliner to verify our new guest. "It's Commissioner Karena. He's alone."

"How do you know his name?" Ethan gawks at me. "Has he talked to you already?"

Bill breaks in to my rescue and says, "Ethan, it'll look bad if you leave as he walks up. Wait. If you've been questioned about Cooper, it sends a better message to stay. Ask if you can be of more help, *then* go back to the station. It's only a suggestion, bro; the choice is yours."

151

Bill holds up his hands as Ethan treads the rug in front of the sofa.

"You might want to sit down. Pacing makes you look guilty of something," I say.

New questions hang in the room like storm clouds gathering for rain.

Could Ethan have set up Dax to run at Cooper to scare him into quitting, or are brother and sister joining forces to cover the real murder weapon?

CHAPTER THIRTEEN
Two Days, Two Deaths

Bill goes to the slider and lets Commissioner Karena into the cottage. Removing his black cap, Karena enters, smiling at me and acknowledging Ethan with bewilderment. The entire room is at attention, as if we're waiting for permission to breathe in order to proceed on his terms. Having law enforcement under our roof puts all of us on edge. I recall how I felt when a sheriff came to Alec's estate, asking questions about the corpse found in Kate's barn, and when the Italian police questioned us at the bed-and-breakfast we were staying at in Bari. Cooper's situation is similar.

Officers of the law have ways of making the innocent feel guilty of crimes they didn't commit. Karena showing up here shouldn't be a shock since we were some of the last people to speak to Cooper Dunn before his encounter with Dax.

My nerves are bowstring taut.

The commissioner on his mission to find a killer is shifting his gaze to each of us, and his silence is thunderous.

Without as much as a glance, Bill senses my discomfort and moves in beside me.

"I hope I'm not interrupting. I took a chance that I'd find you here." He has doubt of my earlier story in his probing, dark eyes. He addresses Ethan. "What are you doing with Miss Drury and Mr. Drake?"

"This cottage belongs to his family, Commissioner. He stopped by to be sure that Annalisse had everything she needs," Bill answers before Ethan has a chance to say something stupid or damaging. "Ethan was just leaving. Do you have more questions for him?"

"Unless he's remembered something new, I have no further inquiries. He's free to go."

"I'll see you tomorrow," Ethan says under his breath to me, then marches to the glass door.

"Can I get you something to drink?" I ask, receiving the commissioner's head shake.

"Please." Bill points to the sofa.

"As you're undoubtedly aware"—Karena watches Ethan's vehicle pull forward and drive away—"we are investigating a death at Woolcombe Station. I assume Mr. Fawdray has filled you in on the incident this morning?"

It's best to allow the police to speak their facts. I want to charge ahead and tell the commissioner what we know, to speed this up, but contain my natural urges. Forging ahead, which sounds good in practice, isn't the best approach to staying out of trouble. Trying that before has only made things worse.

Karena clasps his hands and relaxes his jaw muscles. "Were either of you a witness to the death of Cooper Dunn?"

He's certainly direct.

I lean into the armchair, squeezing the armrests, smelling the commissioner's cottony scent, and look to Bill. Should he feel that the police consider us as suspects, he'll shut the interview down, and we'll handle this situation in a different way.

Bill details our station time of arrival and the events prior to our introduction to the Corriedale ram, Dax. As he closes, Karena takes out his notebook and makes random notes.

I sense that we're about to become a central part of Cooper's case, standard procedure with witnesses in any investigation.

Karena isn't carrying the usual officer's poker face. On the contrary. He's allowing us to witness plenty of his facial tics and brow lifts during Bill's explanation so far. I suspect that he's nosing around for new suspects; someone who doesn't buy the simple accident theory the Hyde family is peddling in Cooper's case. His face is too animated, and his eyes are way too eager for another crumb of truth to add to his notebook. An anomaly for the usual slow-burn interrogator, taking his time, pondering the puzzle pieces Bill's laying out for him.

I sit idle in the quiet, sunny room, taking notice of a noisy bird outdoors, while the commissioner records what he feels is important to his newest case of sudden death.

"As you stood at the fence with the ram, did you observe a closed and latched gate?" Karena asks me.

"Cooper went inside and haltered the ram, but I didn't notice the gate one way or the other. It's standard practice to always close a gate behind you when entering a livestock area. No one wants to chase down an animal because a door flies open. Closing doors and latching gates become habit." I lay a finger alongside my cheek when I remember something else. "Cooper's hands were shaking. He was shaking so hard that it caught my eye, Commissioner. I thought it was worth mentioning."

Karena asks, "Did you see anything else that you might consider… let's say, odd?"

"I don't know if this is strange, but when he shook dirt and straw from his clothes, debris rained down, including lots of his hair. Handfuls floated to the ground. It reminds me of someone who's been through a battery of chemo treatments."

Karena acknowledges while writing. "Did he look sick?"

"Other than complaining of a headache the day before, I don't think so. Do you think Cooper was feeling okay, Bill?" I ask.

"He seemed all right. Nothing I'd characterize as signs of an illness."

Karena stews on Bill's answer for a bit while chewing on his ballpoint. "After you were shown the ram, what happened then?"

This time I narrate a shorter version to Karena, beginning with Ellen Hyde's spooky, silent entrance onto the scene.

"Ellen preferred the manager do his menial tasks for some reason, which is strange because Bill and I were there to get a station tour. Cooper was slated to give us the grand walking tour that Ethan had started the first day we arrived, but that all changed when Ellen asked Cooper to weed the paddock."

"Do you have any idea why Miss Hyde stopped your tour?"

Bill shook his head at me, and I remember his earlier warning in the car about offering theories that might lead police down rabbit holes.

"If we stick to the facts, sir, what we *think* has no bearing." Bill shifts his gaze for a millisecond. "As we were leaving the station, we saw Olivia cross the driveway behind us, walking toward where Cooper was working. From there, we dropped off a note for Ethan at his vehicle because he'd left by then."

"Left to go where?" Karena asks Bill.

"We couldn't be sure, but I noticed two guys with white T-shirts at the barn. I have to assume one was Ethan and the other was Cooper," Bill says. "I was specifically looking for Ethan because Annalisse wanted to tell him we were leaving."

"Is Cooper with the medical examiner?" I ask.

"Yes," Karena says.

My cell phone rings inside my bag, and I grab it to check the caller. "Bill, it's Alec. Commissioner, I need to take this, but I'll make it short."

Walking into the bedroom and closing the door, I answer, "Hey, Alec." He jumps right into what he's found out about Finn Hyde, and I stop him midsentence. "Alec, we have a guest, and I need to get back to them. I'll call you as soon as the commissioner leaves." I nod as Alec questions me why the police are here. "There's been an incident at Woolcombe Station. I'll explain it all in a few minutes. Wait for my call. Thanks."

Bill perks up when I return, and Karena watches me stow my phone.

"Excuse the interruption," I say to the commissioner.

"Are you thinking Cooper's death was intentional?" Bill asks Commissioner Karena.

"Until we complete the autopsy and get the examiner's report, I can't answer that. Sheep can injure residents, but being killed by one is rare. We want to be sure." Karena flips his notebook closed. "To the best of your knowledge, are you certain Cooper Dunn was alive when you drove away from Woolcombe Station this morning?"

"Of course," Bill says.

"Absolutely," I say.

He's heaping Bill and I onto his growing suspect list.

Thankfully, Alec isn't with us. Another Zavos scandal is all that Alec needs right now.

As I think about Alec doing research, my curious mind wants to take this conversation in another direction.

"Did either of you witness an argument between Mr. Dunn and anyone else?" Karena continues digging.

I sit back and play out the scene between Cooper and Ellen in my mind. She was frustrated with Cooper, although neither was yelling about it. Ellen was an owner instructing an employee about a duty he overlooked.

"What is it, Miss Drury? Did you recall something?" Karena opens that little black book of his again. "Any small thing might be helpful."

"Have you spoken with Olivia Hyde, the daughter?" I ask Karena. "She brought Cooper... That's right. I forgot that she brought him a tall mug of coffee, tea, or possibly another beverage. Did investigators pick up his mug in the paddock and test the contents?"

The commissioner jots on the page, looks up at me, and continues to make notes.

"Did you find his mug?" Bill asks Karena.

"I don't know, but I'll check with the deputy commissioner on the scene."

"Were you able to run down the license on the vehicle that hit Alastair McGregor?" Bill asks.

"It was of no help. The plate came from a junker. No one has registered it for some time. The last owner of this license is deceased. The car could be an older farm vehicle."

"Wow, that's interesting. It's almost as if the crime was preplanned in advance, but that can't be. Who would know that Alastair would be out walking that day?" I ask.

"Since his auto accident two years ago, Mr. McGregor was known to walk the town. He vowed never to get behind the wheel again after losing his daughter. I was surprised when he offered to drive you from the airport." The commissioner raises his brows.

"Alastair was asked to pick us up, but his car wouldn't start. I thought we mentioned that," I say to Karena, who flips the notebook cover and stows it in his pocket.

"He had a valid driver's license." Bill picks at his thumbnail. "If we had known about his previous accident, I can assure you, I would've driven myself."

"Will there be a funeral for Alastair?" I ask.

"Unknown. His body hasn't been claimed by kin yet. We're looking for extended family members. I hope someone claims him soon. We don't have the space to keep him in cold storage indefinitely."

"What happens to his sweet shop and the people who work there?" I ask.

"That depends on the building owner. I wouldn't be surprised if someone comes in and makes an offer to take over the space. It's a favored shop."

Alastair McGregor's strange ways are starting to gel for me. He occupies his dead daughter's house, can't pay the mortgage, and doesn't have the money to buy a new car, so he settles for an unreliable clunker with mechanical issues and decides he can earn additional money this way. Maybe Alastair chose walking because he had an exercise routine to take a certain route each day. I've known people who can't change their regular activities because of repetitive psychological disorders, or it's just habit.

"Commissioner Karena, have you been to Bluebasin Lake lately?" I ask. "Alastair showed us how awesome a place it is. Why are developers and miners trying to strip that beauty from your country?" I feel Bill's burning gaze on me.

Karena pauses for a long while. "Yes, the lake has created a town controversy."

"If you'll recall, Alastair said developers and others were fighting against environmentalists and that he was joining the group who planned a protest next week. He also mentioned that Ellen Hyde's husband from Parliament is siding with developers." Leaving the door open for more details, I give him the option to expand on the dispute.

The notebook makes another appearance, and Karena flips to a new page. "What else did McGregor tell you about the protest?" He writes lengthy notes.

"Just that Finn Hyde's siding against the town's wishes."

The room goes silent and cold. Bill gets up to stroll into the kitchen, and the commissioner's glower is a sign for me not to venture further into the subject.

"I only bring it up because I recalled it after we spoke to you last. This lake thing might help you in his case since someone might have wanted him out of the way before next week. There's more to Alastair's murder than being a squatter who wouldn't leave."

"That, Miss Drury, is an unknown." Karena snaps his notebook shut and scoots forward.

I look at my watch and calculate the time in New York. "Bill, it's late. Commissioner, I have to make a return call to the States. It's going on eleven o'clock in the evening there."

Karena hooks his pen to his notebook. "Very well. Should either of you remember anything else in the Dunn matter, call me and no one else." The commissioner hands his police business card to each of us. "You've been helpful." He adds with a wry smile, "You may want to stick closer to this cottage for the remainder of your visit, and a word of caution: stay out of Temuka politics. We've had two suspicious deaths in two days in our quiet town. That's a record. I for one will be happy to wish you well for a quick departure from our country. Cheers."

Karena strolls outside, leaving us wordless until he drives away.

"Annalisse, did you have to poke that guy?" Drake asked in a stage whisper. "This isn't any of our business."

"When he clammed up after I brought in Finn's name, I knew that the police know more about these deaths than they're letting on."

"They're ongoing investigations. Cooper's death was an accident," Bill says. "Even if it's premeditated murder, the lake and these deaths have nothing to do with us."

"It's highly suspicious that a friendly show ram would go rogue and beat up someone familiar to him. Rams just don't do that unless provoked. I'll bet you a Hokey Pokey that didn't happen with Cooper." I glance at the wall clock. "It's time to check in with Alec anyway. He might have uncovered more on Finn."

"Fine. I can't stress this enough. Be careful stirring this boiling cauldron."

Bill's real message is if something happens to me on his watch, he'll have Alec all over him.

CHAPTER FOURTEEN
Adventures in Jousting

Karena's wisecrack about our leaving his country soon is a solid reminder to withhold sarcasm toward an officer of the law—in a foreign country. It's doubly true for any traveler who oversteps and asks too many questions. We are short-timers in his nation, and he knows it. What Commissioner Karena said to us on the way out is a jab to our midsections—a Kiwi's way of joking, but not really. He wants us to wrap up our business in New Zealand early if need be.

"What a day," Bill says. "What did Alec want?"

"He's been checking up on Finn. I told him we were talking with Karena and that I'd phone him with more, so I'm not sure what he found. These cases could make international headlines. I sure hope Alec can enlighten us about the politician since Karena isn't sharing the town politics with us. Did you see how he blew me off and the look he gave me? I think he's up to his neck in the Bluebasin Lake dispute. We're indirectly involved in something sticky, or maybe the better word for it is corruption."

Bill swipes his phone screen and scrolls. "Police and politics are good places to shy away from. I'm glad you stopped the inquisition when you did. That was smart." He scrolls some more. "Huh, there's barely a mention on Temuka's local news about Alastair. Nothing yet on Cooper."

"It's early. Once it comes out that Alastair had political enemies—and we can be certain he had a few—the media should be all over this." With an added caveat I continue, "Unless someone has paid off the politically connected agencies to cover any bad press linking a highly respected member of Parliament to any wrongdoing."

"I see where you're going with this. We don't know that Finn is behind any of it, Annalisse. What Alastair told us is circumstantial, nothing more than his word against a politician's."

"A well-connected one, I'd imagine. Okay, I'll try to keep to the facts, but my senses have been tingling and twitching all day."

"Do you know of an instance where a sheep killed anyone by ramming them to death? You have more experience with sheep behavior than Karena does. He wants to pin Cooper's death on a human, not a sheep."

"He can't prosecute a ram as a suspect for murder. What are you thinking?" I ask.

Bill's back in the recliner, drumming his fingertips on the armrests. "We have to get real. I never thought I'd admit this, but since you've hooked up with Alec, I've learned to keep an open mind regarding your intuition and antiquities, especially those with a sketchy past."

I whip hair behind my ears and twirl a pearl earring. "It's as if you and I are in control of nothing. Fate is always the master because we can't change it."

Folklore and art from long ago are interesting combinations. I believe in curses and leaving relics where they lie. Once removed from their sacred resting places, exposing them to the modern world can be a self-fulfilling prophecy of calamitous proportions. It wasn't until my friend's death with her bracelet, and Alec losing his dad that we could truly understand how real curses can be.

"What about the ram killing Cooper?" Bill asks. "Do you buy it?"

"I know of one instance in California where a commercial sheepman in the Mohave was struck by a Suffolk ram and caught between the sheep and his trailer. The ram lunged and broke the sheepman's neck, but the man survived. It was a freak accident that left him paralyzed and in a wheelchair. More than being rammed by a sheep, I'm curious about what was in Cooper's mug. How did you miss the hair falling on his shirt? That's plain weird if you ask me."

"Olivia liked the guy. Most likely, she brought him coffee or his morning tea." Bill stares right through me. "If you're going to call Alec back, you should do it soon."

Taking the phone out of my tote, I autodial him, tapping Speakerphone.

"Hey, babe. Finished with the police? What was that about?" Alec is trying to sound more cheerful than I feel.

I glance at Bill and say, "The manager at Woolcombe Station died today."

There's uncomfortable dead air from Alec's end, then he says, "I'm sure you've already hashed this out with authorities, but I'd like to hear why they're questioning you."

I glance at Bill, and he jumps in to give Alec the details.

All I have to do is make eye contact with Bill and he takes charge. What would this trip be like without him? I have no idea how this latest news will affect Alec, but we're about to find out.

People are dead. We've seen little scenery. It was a mistake to leave you behind. These phrases zoom around in my mind like shooting stars in a constant light show. Alec, please keep an *I told you so* to yourself. I feel bad enough.

"Drake, did you guys see the ram hit him?"

I find another section of the couch and sink into the cushion. "No, the incident with Cooper happened after we left for Point Pleasant to take in the sights. Bill's been on top of everything; don't worry. All interrogations with Temuka police, the works. We're keeping out of the investigator's way, but we have so many questions," I say.

Bill finishes telling the story of Cooper and our short tour with him before Olivia and her mother came onto the scene.

"The hit-and-run and a charging ram are strange stories, but anything is possible when traveling abroad," Alec says. "Italy and Greece have told us that much."

"Have you received a call or letter from Kate since I left? Ethan says she's on the move again. He thinks she may be in Auckland."

"Nothing from her on my end, but I did find a little dirt on Finn Hyde," Alec says. "Would you like to hear it?"

Alec recites online articles and breaking news from media websites and finds that Finn has potential ethics violations. So far, none of those allegations are sticking to him. He was elected to Parliament six years ago, and he's at the end of his second term. Facts are sketchy, but Finn seems to thrive in the cushy lifestyle as a member of their House of Representatives, and he plans to run for another three-year term.

"Alec, did you notice anything about the Bluebasin Lake area?" I ask. "We've heard he's siding against the townspeople, out to destroy a scenic venue with strip mining and recreation areas."

"That's a crazy combination. No, I didn't notice anything about a lake."

"After next week's protest, the news might make international news outlets," Bill adds.

"If Finn's looking for donors to fund his reelection campaign, it's no wonder he's in the middle of pitting builders and miners against the locals. Money usually wins the day." I'm hurting for their community. "Such a shame when the people are on the losing side."

"If you guys dig up anything that makes Hyde one of the lead suspects in Alastair's or Cooper's death, I'd recommend packing up and getting outta there. Anna, try not to dig in places that puts a spotlight on you, okay?" Alec asks.

"If things get too hot, we won't stick around," Bill agrees.

In light of the changes in our scenic vacation and the authorities still questioning us about murder investigations, we can't go home yet. I'm considering asking Alec again to join us if he can get away. He finds ways to liven things up, and I sure miss him, more than I thought I would. By the tone of his voice, Alec wants me to come home. It's wishful thinking to believe he'd fly down to meet us.

"Then wrap things up and leave, Bill. Having Anna tangled with authorities is *exactly* what I feared the most. I can't help you a lot from New York unless I jump on a flight and come down there."

Bill's standing over the coffee table where the phone rests to make his point. "For as long as Annalisse feels she needs to stay, I'll watch out for her. It's under control."

"Alec, we're handling ourselves with the police. Bill's here because you trust him. He won't let me get into trouble." I swipe perspiration from my forehead. I can tell by his words that Alec's in sheer panic mode and it's making him crazy not to be here. "Is there an update from the testing lab?" I leap into another subject of my choosing.

"There's… uh… been a snag—"

"Those pesky chromosomes giving you the slip?" Keeping my snarky attitude under control has its limits, and I've hit them. "C'mon, Alec. What kind of *snag* holds up genetic testing?"

"We'll talk about it when you aren't so stressed out."

Alec shuts me down in a jolt.

Before I blurt out more raw feelings, I lean across the table and say, "Good night, Alec. Thanks for looking into Finn for us." Kissing my fingertips, I touch the icon that turns off the speaker. "We'll check in soon. Sleep well."

"Anna, wait. Don't leave yet." Alec's voice is faint and full of panic.

"It's late, and I have a lot on my mind, so I'll leave you to Bill for some guy talk."

I wave to Bill and exit the sliding doors. Alec's side of the conversation disappears entirely. My racing thoughts require calm and less conversation. Perhaps Bill can find out what the snag in testing is all about.

While outside, I make a mental note to give Chase a call to check on things at the gallery and see how my kitty, Boris, is doing. I miss him too.

Several minutes later, Bill slides open the door, hands over my phone, and stands next to me on the porch.

"That didn't go precisely as I thought it would, but Alec does seem to have mellowed with age. I've watched him throw wineglasses into the fireplace when frustrated." Bill makes a one-arm pitching motion.

"He has his mother's quick Italian temper." I back against the railing with my hands behind me, longing for the honeysuckle fragrance from Walker Farm's porch. The bottlebrush tree isn't smelling as sweet as it did yesterday. "Gen doesn't lose her temper often. Neither does Alec, so that's a positive. I haven't seen him mad enough to destroy his good crystal, though. I hope I never do."

"He hates that he's not here with you. He loves you so much; it's killing him that you left. He feels helpless from the distance, both physically and emotionally. Alec says you're better together than apart."

The familiar phrase forces a smile from the depths of my despair. "Alec said those very words to me when we met. Believe me, Bill, I considered what my actions could do to us the day I left Brookehaven. I had to take that chance. It's the only way to force Alec to objectively look at his situation with Virena and Noah, not just from his heart." I reach out and touch Bill's arm. Were you able to find out what the snag was at the lab?"

He spins to look off into the distance and stares at an imaginary spot somewhere in the skyline.

What does that mean?

Bill mimics my stance, and backs against the rail next to me.

"Bill?"

"Generosa found out, and the test is on hold."

With a long, drawn breath, I exhale all of it in a single gush. "I'm competing with a mother's desire for a grandchild. Since Pearce died, Gen has been everything to Alec, and I want the best for her. But…"

"You're important to Alec; don't forget that. He's struggling to keep the two women he loves happy."

"I know." Turning toward the yard, I hold onto the rail with unsteady hands and finish my thought. "Somebody's going to be the victor. I'm glad I'm not a gambler. I wouldn't want to take that bet."

"My money's on more than one victor." His wide grin is so characteristic of him. Bill looks for the silver lining.

"We'll keep good thoughts then." I navigate the narrow steps that lead from the porch. "C'mon, Drake. I'm getting antsy and need to walk around the pond to straighten my thoughts. Let's find a pizza place with the gooiest pepperoni-and-cheese pies on the South Island. Eating pizza is what the doctor orders."

CHAPTER FIFTEEN
A Cuppa

Returning from the florist in town, Bill and I are parked outside the entry gate to the Woolcombe Station's homestead, discussing how much longer we'll stay in Temuka. The pot of coffee we chose to finish has me jittery and anxious from too much caffeine. What a bad choice to make on the day after Cooper's death.

I'm one giant ball of queasiness because of the deep fried and fatty diet I've been on since our arrival. In case we can't bargain for a broader tour of the station, I hope to get a few more questions answered from a restrained Ellen Hyde.

"It's up to you, Annalisse. I'm here for as long as you need." Bill unsnaps his belt from across one of his signature palm shirts and faces me for a reply.

His expression is a blank page and not that convincing. He doesn't want to stay. Since the encounter with Alastair on day one of our trip, Bill has been ready to end the trip here.

All I have to do is pack my suitcases, and we're on the next flight out.

"Aren't you interested in how Cooper's accident comes out?" I ask him.

"Does it make a difference?"

"I'd hate to leave New Zealand with the idea that a ram killed him in some freakish turn of events. A homicidal nut case who sends Dax in with Cooper to hurt him is a theory that's way worse though. I won't believe that without a lot of proof. The way he went out can't get any crazier." Groaning aloud, I lift the seat belt latch; it clicks and frees me. "Going back to New York while Alec has no answers on the boy's paternity is premature. The whole point of our temporary separation is for him to uncover the truth without my influence."

"Your being away is influencing him already. And if Noah is his, what's your plan?"

"You're concerned for him, but I have to do this my way. Believe me, I've considered the what-ifs. Causing the man I love to suffer alone hurts more than you can imagine. Do you know how many times I've thought about bolting from this place and flying back? You said it's killing him; well, it's killing me too. Let's delve deeper into why I'm doing this." I swipe a hand down my jeans and chuckle at the gesture.

Bill notices it too, and smiles sadly.

"After Alec divorced his wife, she spent her sizable settlement from Alec when she remarried. Tina's second husband is still in jail, I think, but it didn't stop her drug-dealing husband from trying to extort Alec for money from inside prison. Tina stole old photos of Alec when they were about to end their marriage and gave them to a certain scandal sheet where editors add any caption they want. They pay for photos." My nervous hand drifts toward my leg, and I catch myself. "I thought you might've been involved in detective work for Alec back then. I may be wrong."

"You aren't. It was a bad time for Alec after losing their child and watching Tina get hooked on coke."

"Alec said as much. His pain continues while Tina and her felon husband take advantage of Alec's notoriety to enrich themselves with their tabloid schemes." I lean against the headrest and stare at the fuzzy tan liner. Alec's pain. What father-to-be who's lost a baby wouldn't want another chance to experience fatherhood? "Oh, Bill, I've been so focused on manipulating outcomes that I've forgotten what Alec went through with Tina. What you've said is sinking in."

Bill lifts the corner of his mouth in recognition. "I see both sides. From where I sit, you should be on the same side."

"This is the problem for a control freak like me. As long as others stay in line with my belief system... How do I stop pushing so hard?" I ask him.

"Put your instinctive juices to work. Knowing what's driving you in the wrong direction where Alec is concerned is the first step to fixing the problem. Let things happen naturally and make subtle changes if needed. Steamrolling never works out well. Like we talked about earlier, let fate guide you in positive directions."

"Alec and Gen have the same gentle nature and take everyone at face value. I see the potential for another extortion attempt with Virena and Noah."

"Alec isn't a fool. He gets the gravity of making the wrong decision where little Noah is concerned. He told me so."

Nodding, I say, "That gives me encouragement. Thanks for telling me." I take a few calming breaths to drop my heart from my throat—to where it's supposed to be. "Boy, I wish Harriet was waiting in that barn over there." I motion to the white shearing shed across from the Hyde's main house.

"Who's Harriet?" Bill asks.

"My thoroughbred mare. Alec gave her to me after the horrible trip to Crete. Before you and I met." I sweep myself back in time to Harriet's stall, taking a long whiff of her chestnut coat. "Did you know that horse sweat smells like a pile of pennies? I'm sure I mentioned it before. That magnificent horse has a way of making things all right."

"I've never noticed a horse's smell because I won't get that close. Their size is too intimidating."

"It's a common reaction, but keep in mind that horses have a sixth sense and know when they're feared. Alec should teach you to ride so you'll relax around them. You'd enjoy it. The wind blowing in your face as you sit high on their back. The feeling is indescribable." Happy tears fill my lids, and I wipe them away. "The aura animals put out is amazing. I can't say it any other way."

Bill's eyes widen. "Why do they have to be so huge?"

"As Alec told me once, they're noble beasts. His family had plow horses in Italy. They can't drag around a plow without size and scale." I shuffle my purse contents and find the notebook, jotting down a few ideas for the filly. "The words sound good. I haven't come up with the right name for Harriet's filly yet."

"Let me see." He stretches to read my notes.

I close the notebook and drop it into my bag. "It's a work in progress. My ideas keep changing, so I'm not there yet. I should ruminate on it first."

"Ruminate." Bill laughs. "Like a sheep, you mean?"

"When we're in sheep country… Before we get to the house, I'd like your thoughts on something else. New Zealand is a big place. We don't have to stay at that cottage; we can stay anywhere. What do you say about paying our respects to the Hyde family, then packing our bags and going to another part of the island? We've seen all that we're going to here, I'm afraid."

"A fresh approach and a new beginning sound good to me. Are you telling anyone we're leaving?"

"Not right away. Ethan might try to talk us out of it, or maybe not. I can't get a good reading on him. Once we've landed in another spot, I'll message him where we've left the cottage key. The family is damaged and stressed out enough, and I don't want to add more to Ethan's plate. He'll be too busy to play host for the rest of our visit anyway. We've barely seen him as it is. It's time for us to move."

Bill push-button starts the SUV, and we're grinding gravel beneath the tires.

We park at the walkway and gaze at each other without words. Bill's hesitancy is rubbing off; neither of us wants to be here.

Drawing a long breath, I say, "Let's do this one last time. I'll pluck the Dieffenbachia plant from the back."

I get out to open the liftgate and stretch for the plant with giant, variegated yellow and green leaves. If food guru Helga were here, I would've taken her pastries to Ellen instead. For now, a pretty sympathy plant will do.

Their youngest daughter, in an embroidered peasant blouse and shorts, skips out to greet us at the car.

"Hi, Sutton." I'm shaken when the girl bear hugs me around the waist, causing me to lift the plant high into the air. "Careful, we don't want to break the plant. Would you like to bring it inside and give it to your mom for us?"

She nods, grinning. "Oh yes. It's so pretty."

Ellen might have told her who I really am since my first visit. Little Sutton is the only happy person in a family of seriously grumpy Kiwis. Since rejoining his parents in New Zealand, the familiar, carefree Ethan from Walker Farm has all but evaporated into someone who's uninterested in life. He rarely smiles, and he's so sober about the simplest activities. Ethan carries a different burden on his station.

We follow Sutton into the house, watching her drop the potted plant onto the coffee table in a thud, teetering it to one end. Bill catches the top-heavy plant before it spills soil out of its plastic container.

Ellen walks out of the dining room in purple flowered culottes and a lavender shirt. "Good morning, lovelies." She's bubbly, showing no outward sorrow toward the recent death at her barn. Cooper had worked for them only a few weeks so it's likely Ellen and her manager weren't close. "What a gorgeous Dieffenbachia. Thank you both. Sutton, please go upstairs and make your bed. Your room is a disaster, and put your games in the closet."

"Ethan stopped by the cottage and told us what happened to Cooper after we left. We're so sorry to hear about his accident and your loss," Bill says. "Is there anything we can help you with while we're here? Annalisse is as close to a professional sheep woman as you can get, and I've been known to wield a mean shovel. We're at your disposal."

Ellen tosses her head back in joyful laughter that rings false and put on for our benefit. "Thank you. That's so kind of you to offer, but Ethan is stepping up with his da in session. We put word out that Woolcombe is looking for a new overseer for the station. We'll be fine."

My, that's fast. The man's been gone less than a day, and she's turning into the town crier for ranch help. Are they that desperate? I glance at Bill, then smile at Ellen to cover the action.

"Did you say *in session*? What does your husband do?" I'd like to hear how Ellen characterizes her husband's work.

"Finn's a member of Parliament in the House of Representatives." She recites her words with a deadpan expression as if she's rehearsed her answer many times. "He's away in Wellington; that's the country's legislative seat for this democracy. They meet Tuesdays through Thursdays, and Finn usually comes home on weekends, except during heated debates."

"How exciting to be married to such an important man. Congratulations." I'm digging deep to find my enthusiasm but manage to pull it off from Ellen's genuine smile. "How is Olivia taking Cooper's death?" She hasn't come downstairs, and I can't help myself from inquiring about her.

"You noticed my frivolous girl's antics, did you? If only that man had sold us his sweet shop. Then she wouldn't be exposed to men who're beneath her like Cooper Dunn. Rest, have a seat. Can I get you tea? I'm heating the water."

I'm taken aback by Ellen's snooty comments about Alastair and her manager when she was neutral before. "Don't go to any trouble for us. We've had a pot of coffee already."

Someone wipes their feet at the back door and enters the kitchen in sloppy boots.

"G'day, Annalisse—Bill. I didn't see you drive in." Ethan turns to speak to Ellen. "I heard from Da. He called super early. He's going to be stayin' until Sunday, so we'll have to get Liv's sheep shorn next week. I can't do it without him, especially now." Ethan looks like he's been caught in a dust devil, or he slept on his pillow wrong. Hair stands straight out over his ears.

It feels odd that no one has talked about Finn until now. Could the marriage between Ellen and Finn be one of convenience for political aesthetics? It looks better to the public when politicians have a cookie-cutter, perfect family. In comments and actions, the sister of Thomas Taylor is careful not to show her emotions. She's had at least six years to practice being a representative's wife, or longer if Finn began his career in local government.

"Where's the fruit I asked you to pick for Cook?" Ellen asks her son.

"I haven't done it. Coop left the sheep barn wrecked out." Ethan looks at the floor.

"My good Lord. Never mind. I'll do it myself. Cook's waiting on the apples for the festival pies she's entered. Don't forget, you've volunteered to set up our booth on Friday. Do something useful and make our guests tea. Biscuits are in the tin," Ellen says over her shoulder to Ethan then slams the screen door on her way outside.

"You forgot this, Mum." Ethan grabs a wicker-handle basket on the counter. "Be right back." He flies out the door after her.

The teakettle whistles.

"Your turn," Bill says, shaking his head. "What a place."

Running for the kettle, I turn off the element beneath and move it to a cold burner, staring at the pot. Why not? One cup of tea kinda sounds soothing.

"Bill, I'm going to pour myself a cup. Would you like one?"

"None for me."

On the counter closest to the kitchen sink is a collection of white pottery canisters. The tea jar is the largest in the group of four. I lift the lid and sniff the honey and warm toast aroma of breakfast tea in the loose leaves. I hate loose tea with a passion. It's hard to keep the tiny leaves from floating through it no matter what device I've tried to corral them. The whitewashed cupboard doors have glass fronts on them, displaying beautiful rose-pattern plates, bowls, and cherry-colored glassware to match, but no other tea bag canisters are hiding among the place settings.

"C'mon, people. No regular tea bags? Don't they use bags in England?" I ask Bill.

"We aren't in England."

"It's as close as you can get. Wait, here's a box." On my tippy toes, I spot a flat green carton in the corner cabinet.

The words Hibiscus Tea Bags are inscribed on the side. That's a tea I've always wanted to try, so I slide out the box and flip the lid, taking a single bag and dropping it inside a mug by the kettle. Steam rises from the cup, and the bag sizzles as the hot water hits the bottom. The tea steeps for a time and changes color to a pinkish amber as I read the ingredients on the outside of the tea box.

"Are you sure you wouldn't like a cup? Who knows how long they'll be getting apples." Twirling the bag in the water, I smell the unusual aroma and take a sip, swirling fruit notes and other flavors along my taste buds. "Hmm, slightly salty and a little bitter. This one's gonna need sugar cubes." I drop in three to ensure the salt tang is covered, stir, and sip it again as I meet Bill on the sofa. "Hibiscus leaves are more bitter than I'm used to, but it's supposed to be good for you. Smell."

Bill sniffs. "What did you say that was?"

"Hibiscus."

"I'll stick with coffee." Bill sours his lips.

"Flower teas are probably a down under thing. Specialty flavors are available back home but not as much." I drink more with gusto and feel happiness move lower with the warmth. "It's growing on me, but I'm partial to brands with orange and clove."

My throat tingles, and I'm having a hot flash. I rub underneath my jaw, and the sensation turns itchy.

"That's weird. My throat and face feel tight, and they itch." I look at the mug in my hand and set the cup on the coffee table. I recall the same tactile experience from a time when I was little. "I think a case of hives is coming on. Take a look, Bill. Are there bumps on my neck?" I tilt my head aside, exposing more of it.

"Blotches with white patches. Are you allergic to anything?" Bill's looking over the other side of my face.

"Tetracycline is the only thing I'm aware of." Knifelike pains stab my stomach, and I double over. "Ugh." I grasp the table as another wave of gas pummels my midsection. That one's so sharp it takes my breath for a second. "Did you see where the bathroom is downstairs?"

My watery mouth and nauseousness aren't going to wait for a home inspection. I'm flying like I have wings to the kitchen sink, barely making it. Everything I ate and drank this morning splatters the clean, white porcelain in gruesome art.

Bill's beside me, rubbing my back. "Add hibiscus to your list of allergies."

"What a mess I've made." I turn the tap on high, rinse out my mouth, and wash pieces of pepperoni and dough in liquid down the disposer. "I'm churning like an attack of seasickness and I'm lightheaded." Holding onto the tile ledge to steady myself, I add, "We'd better go back to the cottage. I'll be okay in a couple of hours."

Bill reaches for a plastic grocery bag tied to the cupboard door and unties it. He walks over to the counter and, using the plastic over his fingertips, steals a handful of unused tea by the strings. Carefully, he wraps them and slides the bags into a pants pocket.

"Don't touch anything, Anna. Look." He's pointing at an empty syringe inside the tea box.

"What in the world is that doing in there?"

"I'm taking the syringe and your used tea bag. Are you all right for a minute?"

Using longer than usual strides, Bill gets to my mug and plucks at the string, depositing the bag directly into another plastic bag. He slips it into his other slash pocket.

"There's something in my tea?"

"I didn't see a loose needle in the box, but that doesn't mean it isn't there. I don't feel like getting poked. Maybe the syringe was there for a good reason." Bill studies me. "You're more flushed. You might have a simple allergy, but my Spidey senses are activated. I want tests done, and I'm taking you to emergency."

Why didn't I stick to the stuff in the canister?

"Let's leave before I start heaving again." I wobble around and lose my footing on the kitchen rug. On the way down, my forehead glances against the counter's edge, and to the floor I go—one arm out to break my fall. My left wrist takes the brunt of my weight, and I feel it give way in excruciating pain.

"Bill!" I'm writhing on my side, holding my wrist, feeling like I'm going to be sick again.

"Don't try to get up on your own." He stands behind me and helps me to my feet with his arm around my waist. "Can you walk?"

I nod. "Don't go too far away."

The kitchen door swings open.

"Sorry I took so long. Anna, what happened? You're a ghost," Ethan says, running to my side.

"Where's your hospital emergency room?" Bill asks. "Annalisse needs to be looked at by a doctor."

"Why?" Ethan's mouth opens into an *O*.

"Don't have time to explain. Do you have a big flour sack towel?" Bill asks.

Ethan pulls out a drawer, opens a wrapper, and tosses Bill a brand-new towel.

"I'm going to cradle your wrist to stabilize it, Anna. Let me know if it's too tight." Bill folds the three-foot material in half longways, draping it over my hand and wrist in one continuous wrap. "How's that?"

"It's okay, but I'm so dizzy; I don't want to fall again. I can't walk to the car without help." My head is spinning as I fall against Bill.

"Ethan, I hate to take you away from your chores, but you'll have to lead the way to the emergency room. We'll follow you in the rental car."

"I'll drive the rental," Ethan says. "I'll tell Mum where I'm going."

"We take two vehicles. They may want to keep Annalisse for observation. Fair enough?" Bill scoops me into his arms as if I'm a sack of feathers. "No time to wait for you to report in with your mom. Call her from your Rover. Hold the car door open for Annalisse, then jump in your vehicle. Let's go—now."

Praying I don't throw up again, I relax against Bill's chest, trying to ignore the thumps in my throbbing wrist. I think Ethan opens the front door for us, but I'm not sure.

"I'm sorry to be so much trouble," I say to Bill.

"Watch your head." Bill sets me into the seat on the passenger side and belts me in. "If you think you're going to be sick again, tell me, and I'll pull over."

"Thank you. Don't go over too many bumps, okay? Smooth road…" I gaze at Bill and see pain and concern for me in his eyes. Is that how he looked before he went into his burning building for a friend? "Call Alec."

CHAPTER SIXTEEN
The Reunion

A faraway, high-frequency beeping disturbs the most amazing fantasy I'm having in a tranquil forest, where pine needles and pollen from a canopy of monstrous redwoods litter my face and hair like confetti. Time to rise from my restful nap and explore the Giant Sequoias along the path, showing off their outstretched branches to me in a big welcome hug. I've never seen redwoods in person before—I will when I visit the California coast one day. The trees in my path are bigger than I imagine can be real, so I must be dreaming of their splendor.

Pine needles glisten iridescent from an earlier passing shower, crystal droplets I can see myself in. A forest's aroma is almost indescribable; each tree has its own particular smell, depending on the species. I don't recognize where I am in an assortment of dense, wet aromatics that leave a sweetness behind for the senses. Warm sage foliage in the form of moss and Mother Nature's fungus spring from the bases of these trees, mushroom-like in the dampness and humidity. When

I run my fingertips over the texture of their reddish trunks, they have rough bark that scratches in a good way. There's a distinct concoction of cinnamon sticks and Christmas in a bottle emanating from the bark and a fruity flower petal I don't recognize. It's pelting my nose until it makes me sneeze, as streaks of light peek through the extreme treetops' centuries old. Conifer needles are everywhere on the forest's floor…

My throat is itchy and so are my arms. I'm running away from needles raining down on me—no longer a nice fantasy. Instead, the pin pricks are painful and sharp, piercing my wet skin at every angle.

Light creeps in from the corner of my eyes, and the beeps are louder in my ears. I'm in a bed with a side rail and wired to some kind of monitor. Just great; it's a hospital bed. An aroma overwhelms me in an odd combination of citrus scented air freshener mingled with sandalwood. I glance at my arms and legs hidden beneath a light pink blanket. All seems to be where they should be except for the open brace covering my wrapped left wrist and hand—secured across my chest. That's a new addition. My head is heavy but without the usual migraine symptoms, and I don't remember getting here.

Cobwebs are clogging my throat, and I cough. "Can I have some water, please?" My voice sounds no better than that of a toad.

Someone with warm fingers holds my hand.

I know that hand.

"Babe, welcome back."

Turning toward the person speaking, I see Alec in a close-trimmed royale beard. How many days has it been since I drove away from Brookehaven? Ten, twelve, more? How long have I been in this bed?

"You're handsome without a beard, but the new look is so chic," I manage to croak, feeling a little like a bedridden character from an old movie. "When did you get here?"

Alec rubs his whiskers and squeezes my good hand. "Do you like it? If you do, I'll keep it a while. How's your wrist feel? I'll get them to increase your pain meds if you need it."

I gaze around the room for Bill, whose absence unsettles me. We've been together for several days, and it feels strange not having him nearby. He must've gone back to the cottage once Alec arrived or flew back to the States. I can only imagine how much sleep they've lost while I've been lying in the hospital.

"Did Bill fly back?" My tone is a little too sorrowful.

"He's still here." Alec shifts, cupping my hand between both of his. "Would you like me to find him?"

"That's all right. He could use a break from me… I'm so happy to see you." I manage a heartfelt smile. "Coming this far is so selfless when there's so much going on at home." My chest tightens because I'm the selfish one.

He kisses my knuckles. "You know the answer to that. I almost pulled Bill at the last minute to show up myself on the plane, but I didn't want to cause an argument. If I'd known more about the station and Finn Hyde, there's no way I would've stayed behind. The man is corrupt, as bad as they come."

"My head's still foggy, so tell me all about it when I'm clearer." I push deeply into the pillows. "And how in the world did you get down here so fast?" My eyes focus on two gorgeous flower arrangements on a table. One is a stunning group of long-stemmed baby pink roses, and the other is springtime in a vase with multicolored stock, Asiatic lilies, and pastel carnations emersed in red roses and baby's breath. "The flowers, are they from you? Such beautiful arrangements."

"Bill and me. You've been asleep since yesterday. Drake brought you in, and they admitted you to treat your wrist and run tests. Whatever you drank at that place made you extremely ill." He puckers his lips. "You came close to having your stomach pumped, all because Ethan wanted you down here."

Recognizable animosity between Alec and Ethan—forget about that going away.

"The tea. I tossed up everything I ate after breakfast and left an ugly mess in the sink. I'm glad to have missed out on the stomach pump event. Do they know why it made me so sick? I think I'm allergic to hibiscus flower."

"Bill said within minutes of drinking the tea, you got rid of it and everything else you had in your stomach. Bloodwork didn't show anything unusual, and so far, the nurses tell me that you weren't compromised, other than the wrist."

"I'm surprised the nurses told you anything about my condition."

Alec tilts his head aside and dimples one cheek. "I told them you were my fiancé, so technically, I'm a family member. We're as close to that and more, aren't we?" His soft kiss on my hand seals the fact.

"Ah, that would do it." He considers me off the market, just like Bill said to me about him. The warmth pouring through his hands goes straight to my heart. "Thank you for being here, for putting up with me, for everything. I mean that."

I've used the fiancé excuse more than once when Alec was in the hospital, long before his marriage proposals. I can't imagine any nurse refusing a request from a guy like Alec. I admire his new masculine appearance. The beard is a sexy style made for him—more Greek-looking, dark, and devastatingly handsome than before—and he's always looked fantastic.

He observes me for a time. "I'd do anything for you, babe. You're too happy for a lady stuck in a hospital bed."

"Seeing you. Here. I'm so lucky."

Alec leans over and gives me a peck. "I've missed you, Anna from Manhattan."

"You look tired. I'll bet you didn't sleep at all on the plane, did you?"

"Dozed off a few times. I'll sleep better when you leave the hospital."

"Have Bill drop you at the cottage if you aren't there already. Get some rest."

"Forget about me; I'm working to spring you from this place. Your wrist has a solid fracture, but it was too swollen for a cast yesterday; that's why they slapped a brace on you. They'll cast it here or leave it in this brace so that your personal doctor can take care of it. It depends on how long you plan to stay in New Zealand."

Glancing at my captive wrist, I look to Alec for guidance, reading a strong message in his stare. He's waiting for me to tell him we should go at once because that's what he wants. To whisk me back to New York, where he can watch over and protect me from everyone, including myself.

"Two men have died since we arrived. One looks like a straight-up murder, while the other happened at the station where I drank the tea. Don't you want to know why?" It's fruitless to ask because Alec is invested only in my safety. "I can't leave yet, Alec. There's a deeper agenda than simple accidents going on." Sinking into the depths of my pillow with a stabbing in my chest, I ask, "How's your DNA lab work going?"

He releases my hand and straightens his spine. "We'll save that talk for another time."

Rejection.

A knock sounds on the closed door to my room, and Bill enters with a huge grin.

"I heard voices. Either Alec was talking to himself, or you woke up." He radiates, with an even bigger glow of white teeth. "You've been asleep a long time. Stomach still upset?"

"No, and thanks to your trip to the emergency room, I get to test drive this new contraption." I drop my eyes to the brace and sigh. "I don't remember everything after I upchucked. How can you still walk after carrying me to the car?"

"You had to carry her?" Alec is aghast. "I didn't hear about that."

"Alec, I was dizzy and fell with all my weight on one arm. Pain and nausea are a terrible combination, as you might recall."

"Nice to see you've come back, Annalisse. I'll leave you two alone."

"Wait a minute, Bill. Alec, would you mind finding a nurse and asking for a Motrin or ibuprofen? My wrist is beginning to throb a little." Eyelash batting adds a subtle pleading to my request.

"I'll take care of it and bring you some water."

After the door closes, Bill moves to the side of the bed. "Alec's still okay with me staying at the cottage?"

"Yeah, we're good. How did he get here so fast?"

"The last time we spoke to Alec must've been his trigger to coming here. After you fell, I called him, but he was boarded on the plane or in the air. Alec called me when he got to Auckland." His eyes fall to the brace, and he frowns.

"He caught a flight to Auckland on the North Island? Did he forget where I was?" I cringe at his longer roundabout flight schedule.

"It was the only flight he could get without driving to another airport."

"That explains everything. Didn't you pick up some tea bags before we left the Hyde's house, or did I dream that?"

"Karena has your used tea bag as well as what I took from the box. His forensics team is looking at them."

"You bypassed the hospital tox screen?"

"Normally, I wouldn't have, but when your preliminary tests came out clean for substances, I took

192

what I had to the police. If they find anything suspicious, they also have a corpse in the morgue to test."

"Cooper's body." I'm familiar with Bill's methodology. After all, he has the systematic mind of a detective; if plan *A* doesn't work, one goes to plan *B* to get answers.

"The tea wasn't in your system long. And don't forget; you noted things about Cooper that could also be signs of poisoning. Too bad I didn't have the foresight to take the entire box with the tea. I left it beside the kettle for anyone to hide or dispose of." Bill says.

"If they find toxic substances in the tea, won't police have the authority to search the premises?"

"In this case, with your sickness and Cooper's death, my smart money is on the police getting a warrant first. Too much is at stake if authorities can tie what happened to you to Cooper's incident. His death is still considered an accident involving a sheep." He slips one hand into his chinos pocket. "Ellen Hyde can consent to a search without a warrant, but if there's evidence inside, without it, the case might get thrown out in court by a judge. The law of search and seizure here is similar to the States. Let's wait and see what the commissioner's team finds before we imagine what comes next, shall we?" Bill smiles without a show of teeth.

"Does Alec know that police have evidence you supplied them?" I ask.

"I brought him up to date earlier, away from any of the hospital staff overhearing. This isn't the ideal place to discuss a possible homicide."

Alec uses his familiar knuckle-knock and opens the door. He has bottled water in one hand and something else in the other.

"A couple of Tylenol. That's all they'd give me." He twists the cap off the water. "The nurse apologized for not leaving water earlier."

I reach for Alec and take a swig of water that freezes my teeth. "Thanks. Tylenol doesn't usually work on me, but I'll try anything."

"They prefer no more than one visitor in the room at a time. Feel better, Annalisse. Alec, meet me outside for a minute."

"Are you okay alone for a little while?"

"And if I say no?" I let the bottle slip onto the blanket beside me.

"Take your Tylenol. I won't be long." Alec pretends to be upbeat, but I know that clenching jaw when he's chewing on a problem. "Close your eyes, babe. I'll be here when you wake up."

I watch his wrinkled shirt back as he leaves me to my thoughts. It's hard to know what Bill has on his mind, but I have to trust that he knows his friend as well—if not better—than I do.

My hollow stomach growls, and I take another sip of water. A hibiscus flower allergy is a stretch as a theory, not with Bill discovering a syringe in the tea box. Someone is playing with those tea bags. Be patient. The evidence is in good hands.

Gingerly, I roll onto my right side and, with heavy eyelids, close my eyes.

CHAPTER SEVENTEEN
Trust and Mistrust

My arm is numb with a tingling sensation in my fingers as if I've slept on that side too long. I'm in a fresh hospital gown on extra pillows, trying to navigate the sling around my neck and holding my arm in a cast. When did they cast my wrist?

Alec's in the armchair at my right, softly snoring. I'm comforted seeing the rise and fall of his chest. It's a peaceful sleep, perhaps the first real nap he's had since leaving Brookehaven at least forty-eight hours ago.

A gnawing ache plagues me as I watch his slumber.

How can I miss him when he's in the same room with me?

From now on, no more making heavy, one-sided decisions without first considering Alec's side. We both want the most positive outcomes, but that's impossible if I can't see beyond my needs.

He boarded a plane, any plane, bound for New Zealand the night of our talk because Alec refuses to stay at a distance, no matter how much I urge him otherwise. What must he think of my fickle decisions? The turmoil I've put him through since leaving New York was my idea of a well-meaning break for us. The only break anyone truly receives from this hiatus is a wrist fracture.

A pain shoots through my cast forearm. "Ow."

Alec opens his eyes and smiles. "How do you like the new wristband?"

"Ha. I must've been out for a while. I went to sleep with a brace on."

"They put you out to set the bone. The doctor thought it was time to cast it before you did more damage. You were twisting the wrist in your sleep."

"How long do I stay in a cast?"

"About four weeks, then it's back into a brace for another two. It'll fly by, don't worry." Alec's laughter breaks out from the face I'm making. "It won't be as bad as the boot I had to wear on my foot for ten weeks. You've got this."

"The pink roses are from you, and the mixed bouquet is from Bill. Did I get it right?"

He nods. "Red roses didn't seem appropriate. I hoped you'd like pink instead. Softer and more like you."

Alec helps me up because I have a sore back from lying in one spot too long.

Giving him a one-armed hug, I whisper in his ear, "They're perfect. Thank you." I pull back. "What would be even more perfect is a one-way ticket to a wheelchair ride out to the hospital parking lot. I feel strong enough to leave. Mind if I sit in your chair for a while?"

Alec guides me there, and I settle in.

"When was the last time you remember eating?" he asks.

I can't remember. "I've been sleeping too much to notice. If I'm allowed something light, that would be heavenly. Will you check with the nurse?"

As if waving a magic wand, he darts into the hall.

The quiet is restful, and I inhale, relaxing every muscle in my back and arms. Other than the cast, the rest of me has come round to normalcy. If I can speak to a doctor or have Alec speak to one on my behalf, I'm so ready for the drive back to the cottage.

A strong knock on the door startles me.

"It's open, Alec. No need to knock."

A man in the hall clears his throat.

It's not Alec or Bill.

"Excuse me, Miss Drury. Are you up for visitors?" Commissioner Karena enters and leaves the door open behind him. He's carrying a box of what appears to be chocolates. "Nice flowers." He holds up his gift for me to see and sets them near the vases.

"Commissioner, hello."

Karena's in full dress uniform, sizing up the sling. "How are you feeling? Improved?"

"Yes. I'm astonished to see you." A new symptom of the nervous flutters attacks me.

"Mr. Drake came by the station. Did he mention that? He told us what happened at Woolcombe Station and about your fall. Terribly sorry to see you in hospital. I trust you'll be out soon?" he asks with hesitation in his voice.

"Did you find out what was in the tea? I'd like to know what I drank."

Alec walks in with a member of the kitchen staff carrying a cloche-covered plate on a tray. He immediately halts when he notices the uniform.

The care worker in all lavender scrubs smiles at me, setting the tray on the table with the flowers. "We're in between meal service. Here's a little something to tide you over till then." She glances at the policeman over her shoulder and then disappears around the corner.

"Alec, this is Commissioner Karena. Commissioner, Alec Zavos."

Karena extends his hand to Alec; his eyes flicker as they work out Alec's identity puzzle. "Are you with Miss Drury?"

On feet taking flight, Alec's beside me, resting his hand on my shoulder. He's not fast to return a reply, and the commissioner raises a brow. Karena either recognizes Alec or wonders why he's being so evasive to the question about me. Like Bill, after our encounters with the Italian carabinieri, Alec and I elaborate less to authorities during inquiries. It's safer that way.

"Commissioner Karena is investigating the incidents from this week, Alec."

The officer folds his hands in front of him. "I have one question for you. The rest can wait for a better time. We have new developments in the Alastair McGregor case. Did you speak with any of the witnesses personally, Miss Drury?"

"That day?"

"At the site of the incident."

"Anna, I'd advise counsel if you plan to answer more questions," Alec says.

"I don't have anything new to add, Commissioner. Bill spoke to them; I did not. He directed me to stand clear of the body, so I stood at the car while Bill went over to see if he could help the victim."

"Of course. I understand," Karena says in a downtrodden manner.

"Has something happened to the witnesses?" I ask.

Alec exerts extra pressure with his grip, and I roll that shoulder.

I know what I'm doing and pat his hand.

"Relax, Alec."

"It's been brought to my attention that eyewitnesses differ from their original statements. Are you absolutely certain that *you* didn't see the vehicle that struck Mr. McGregor down?"

"As I told you, we were parked for lunch and heard the collision. The two or three women witnesses told Bill they saw a vehicle hit Alastair, turn around, and strike him again. Didn't it happen like that?"

Karena is thinking, staring at the empty hospital bed. "Witnesses sometimes recant what they thought they observed. Striking Alastair once could be that he wandered into the road. Hitting him twice is a malevolent action. Our witnesses disagree on which it was."

"Either way, the driver left the scene, correct?" Alec asks.

"Yes. I was hoping Miss Drury could add another perspective."

"As I understand it, they didn't witness the crime, Commissioner. I don't know what more Anna and Bill can offer on the hit-and-run." Alec squeezes my shoulder then releases it. "Sorry, Anna."

"Did you meet Mr. McGregor?" Karena asks Alec.

"No. I arrived after Anna was admitted to the hospital. I've missed all the fun." Alec's stern face isn't impressing the commissioner's sullen one.

"We're punchy and sleep deprived, Commissioner." I raise my arm in the sling. "Thank you for your gift; it's very kind of you to stop in. Bill might be the better source for details regarding Alastair, should anything new arise."

"Heal quickly, Miss Drury." He looks toward Alec and says, "Mr. Zavos."

Waiting until the officer leaves, Alec reaches out to me.

"Let's get you back into bed before the nurses boot me out of the room. I'm sure your food is cold by now."

"Sure, but I'm not that hungry." I'm back in the mattress rut once again, and Alec fluffs the blanket over my thighs. "Karena is a peach, isn't he?"

"The commissioner is anything but a peach." Alec runs a hand through his hair.

A quick knock at the door and Bill comes in wearing a shade of uncertainty. "Hey, glad you're both here."

Laughing, I say, "Where else would we be?"

"I've been with Temuka forensics most of the day. They have results back on the tea. I thought you'd like to hear them." Bill draws his lips tight.

"Karena didn't say anything about the screening results when he was here. He has to know. You're the investigator, Bill; who does that to a victim?" Alec asks.

"It's possible he doesn't know I'm working with his forensics team and wants to hold cards to his vest until he's certain of the findings. The case is ongoing.

He's trained to withhold the facts unless pressed for information. Karena did the same thing with me during my interview."

"He was close-mouthed with me as well. What did I drink?" I'm tired and want an answer.

"Findings are conclusive enough to go to a magistrate with a warrant request for fingerprints and a thorough search of the homestead and premises at Woolcombe Station."

I slap the bed with my good hand. "Bill, c'mon. What did they find in the tea? Could it have killed me?" My cast grows heavier with the weight of a boulder planting it to my chest.

"Your used tea bag held traces of copper sulfate, and someone had loaded the unused bags with the same substance in powder form."

My jaw slackens from the news, and I look at Alec, who's also agape. He knows what this substance is.

"Are they going to test the water at the station in case it's in the water supply?" I've never been so happy to have thrown up stomach contents in all my life.

"The warrant will cover it all, I'm sure," Bill says. "Although I didn't see a loose hypodermic needle or one on the syringe in the box, it might still be in there. The bags were tainted with powdered copper sulfate on purpose. Injected with a large needle into the thin bags, I believe. There can be no other explanation for a syringe in that box. It held traces of copper even after someone tried to wash it out."

"A deliberately hatched scheme, but why? Hiding the box at the back of the shelf, the person tried to conceal what they were doing. Bluestone is the common name for treating sheep foot rot using copper. Right, Alec?" I ask.

"Yes."

"What about medicinal use, copper-infused tea bags for the sheep?" I ask.

Alec shrugs. "I don't know what use they'd have for that." He drops his head in his hand. "No way. If you found the box in the house and not the barn, the tea isn't meant for sheep. Should we have the hospital run more tests on Anna?"

"I don't think it's necessary. They ran blood tests on her already. The tea was in her system for mere seconds before she got rid of it. I was there, Alec. The copper didn't have time to do any harm to Annalisse. Fortunately for her, she's extremely sensitive to the substance and shouldn't suffer any ill effects, according to forensics." Bill sounds positive enough not to panic, and I trust his judgement.

"The station manager hit by the ram could've been exhibiting symptoms of copper poisoning for some time if he were given the tainted tea on a regular basis," Alec says. "It's a slow process as it attacks the liver. A sheep that ingests too much copper is a goner. That's why sheep and goat supplements must be free of copper. The mineral is added to cattle blocks, so buyers need to be aware."

"Do they plan to test Cooper's body for the substance?" I ask Bill.

"Frankly, anyone who died recently and is still in the morgue will be tested. Especially anyone who got sick and came within reach of the people at Woolcombe

Station." Bill grumbles, twisting his lips. "Which one of the family would do such a thing?"

"I have some ideas," I say. "Ethan mentioned they ran their sheep flock through a footbath just prior to our arrival. Copper sulfate would've been readily available. Hmm." I recall something Ellen said to Ethan on my first day there. "Ellen told Ethan to use the *loose tea* when making my cup. She was specific. That's the Earl Grey or the breakfast tea she offered me."

"You didn't notice anything strange about the loose tea?" Alec asks.

"No. Ellen poured it in the kitchen and it tasted fine. The hibiscus tea sizzled when I poured it over the bag. It seemed strange at the time, but I thought it might be characteristic of the flower." I shrug. "That should've been a signal not to drink it. My favorite orange and clove teas don't release bubbles."

Alec wrinkles his nose and shrinks backward. "Regular tea in a bag shouldn't sizzle or fizz. Oh, babe." He sits on the bed and holds my hand. "You aren't going back to that house again without one of us at your side. Accept no food or drink from them. Whatever is going on is sick."

"I poked around in the cabinet for the tea myself. No one tried to poison me. If I had used the loose tea in the canister, I wouldn't be here." I snap my fingers. "You know what? Alastair mentioned a mining company wants to take the bluestone from Bluebasin Lake. Bluestone covers the walls at the airport. It's a popular building element for offices and homes in New Zealand. The controversy at Bluebasin Lake is something to consider along with copper sulfate. They could be connected if they make the product bluestone from that mountain range."

"Or we can look at it another way. Annalisse might have broken a case wide open for the police. The sheep accident might have been a purposeful murder," Bill says.

"If that's supposed to make us feel better, Drake, it doesn't." Alec squeezes my hand with sweaty fingers. "We're a little tired of black clouds tracking us via their GPS."

My shivers are making me cold. "If it's not to sicken people, what other purpose could the copper be used for? A warning of some sort?"

"The women of the household, Ellen or Olivia, or it's possibly Ethan, who didn't like Cooper Dunn. All had an opportunity and live in the main house with access to the bluestone treatment, and one or more of them could easily have a personal motive," Bill says.

"I haven't seen Anna's doctor since they casted her wrist. They sure treat patients odd in New Zealand. On that note, I'm on my way to hunt down a release to sign. Wanna go with me to the nurse's station?" Alec asks Bill. "Anna has an ice-cold meal to eat before we whisk her out of this place." He makes sure I'm watching and bumps his brows twice, then pats Bill on the back. "Let's run down a doc and get Anna's release papers."

The guys leave me to my thoughts. Does the Hyde family have a dark secret, and I fell into the middle of it during my visit? Poison is the preferred method of murder by women because it's anonymous and blood-less, but Harry Carradine, my old boss at the gallery, was also poisoned—by a man, Peter Gregory, his own brother-in-law. Anyone can carry out a poisoning. Was Cooper's death the perpetrator's goal, or was it something else, like causing him to be ill and quit working as the previous manager did? I'll be curious to hear how Cooper's autopsy turns out. Accident by beast, murder by beast, murder by man, or a combination of the three methods are all possible.

Commissioner Karena is bound to show up with more questions for us.

Gee, can't wait.

CHAPTER EIGHTEEN
Revelations

It's strange having Alec and Bill in the same space at the same time since it's been Drake and me hanging out all week together. I'm taking up the entire cottage sofa, lounging against a bed pillow with a lap robe across my legs, while Bill flips through the sole gardening handbook from a pile of animal husbandry magazines on the coffee table. We gave Alec our last lemon soda when we returned from the hospital, and we lost him in sleep after he downed the bottle. The drink must have an antianxiety effect on the body because soon afterward, he was snoring with his feet up, in Bill's favorite recliner. Alec rarely snores, but I've come to realize that when he does, he's totally exhausted.

I've thought about Alec's new socialite beard and I can relate to what might have sparked his hairier look, discounting the simpler reason—being tired of shaving for his housekeeper and no one else. A fresh face in the mirror does wonders for an ego lift.

It's a bonus for me, too, when he's another notch sexier with the beard than without it. I'm flanked by two great guys willing and more than able to protect me. How did I get so lucky?

Pain meds and the cast on my arm aren't going anywhere for a while, so I might as well get used to the sling for as long as I can stand the sponge baths. I give that about two days.

After a bad breakup in college, I underwent a complete makeover because my friend and confidant, Samantha Freeman, sent me into a forward-looking transformation. My makeover ended with sitting in the beautician's chair for a new bob with bangs. The next day, I had the most wonderful facial peel done at a day spa. It made such a difference in my skin that I felt reborn. Samantha was right; my fresh update gave me the more positive outlook I needed and a boost back into humanity. I miss her friendship every day.

"He's zonked out," Bill whispers. "Are you okay?" He studies me, holding his eyes steady.

"My wrist throbs, but it'll pass." I watch Alec smile in his sleep. "It means so much having him here, Bill. He hasn't slept well since the flight, possibly before that. When I left the estate, I was so angry at him for keeping Kate's note from me. But his being here with us is a comfort. When I asked Alec to leave New York and join us, I doubted that he would, but I'm glad he did." Flailing my legs to get upright, Bill comes to my aid and helps me to my feet. "I don't want to wake him," I whisper and lay the lap blanket over Alec. "C'mon, I need the blood to circulate; it's freezing in here."

Walking into the light behind Alec's chair, the sun drenches my goosebumps, recharging me.

We're standing at the porch railing, gazing at distant unpruned and weedy vegetation at the cottage's perimeter. The cottage surroundings don't thrill me as much as they did since going to the hospital. Where we are is a sore reminder that we're living in a Hyde home on Hyde property.

"Do you think the family will wait for us to fly back before they mow?" I ask.

"They have more pressing priorities than gardening. Karena may already have his warrant from the judge, and the Temuka Police Department is searching the Hyde home for evidence right now. Small-town court systems move faster than those in large cities."

"Are they looking for just the copper sulfate or the box of tea bags?"

"If the person responsible hasn't already hidden or destroyed the evidence, investigators will scoop up anything suspicious. Cooper's mug contents are in the testing phase as well. Now that they have an obvious substance to check for, it won't take police long to determine a possible poisoning or match what they found in the bags. If Olivia gave Cooper a tainted drink, they'll find it."

"If they find a foreign substance, what about someone else making Cooper's coffee or tea that morning? Olivia might be a courier because she was interested in him and looked for opportunities to get his attention." I pick at the wood rail, reliving a little déjà vu. I've used this maneuver on past boyfriends. "She's not exactly a ball of fire around the household that I've seen. Olivia has a job outside the home, and maybe *Mum* considers her the favored child in the family."

"Anything is possible," Bill says.

"Ellen isn't in a position to spare Ethan from the station, yet she sent him to Walker Farm to help out Kate two Decembers ago. That's still hard for me to understand. Ellen hasn't oozed a closeness with her son in any conversation I've overheard between them."

"Be careful jumping to conclusions. Your intuitions are very good, but we haven't exposed ourselves to the interactions between the Hydes for more than a couple of days. We don't know them well," Bill says, watching a dust cloud moving toward the cottage. "Is this a through drive?"

"Not that I'm aware of. Nothing else on this stretch but the cottage. Maybe they're lost."

A dusty, dark vehicle slows and stops on the road in front of the house.

"We're about to have a visitor, and it's not Ethan or the police," Bill says.

I gasp when it's clear who the driver is. "Did Ellen visit me in the hospital while I slept?"

"Not that I saw. Play this cool, Annalisse. Don't mention the police or searches. I don't know how much Ethan told her about your fall. She may not know about the tea, only that you fell. Let her do the talking and follow my lead. We should make this brief."

Sutton opens the passenger side door and runs ahead of Ellen Hyde.

"I'm warning you, Sutton's a vivacious little person who's eight going on twenty-five," I say to him with a smile.

She's wearing a yellow shorts outfit and sandals, scampering up the wooden steps to the porch where Bill and I are waiting.

"Hi. We came to see you, Miss Annalisse. Is your arm hurt?" Sutton hugs me around my hips. "We're sorry you fell at our house. Mum came to give you something."

Does Ellen think I'm going to sue Woolcombe Station for my injuries? The consideration is a new one. She's the wife of an influential politician and lawsuits might be as commonplace here as they are in the States.

Ellen approaches us, taking the stairs on the balls of her feet, one at a time. She's wearing peach lipstick, in a peach-colored shift, carrying a matching purse, and holds a large hardcover book in both hands.

"Sutton, remember what we talked about. Miss Annalisse has a broken wrist. Be careful not to bounce around too much." Ellen holds her hand out to Bill. "So nice to see you again, Bill. Have you met Sutton? This is our youngest daughter."

Bill smiles, close-lipped, and nods in approval but says nothing.

"Annalisse, I came to give you this, but since you're one-handed, I'll leave this heavy thing with you." Ellen passes the big book to Bill, and he rests it on the railing, as unattached to it as he can be. "It's not how I'd planned to give it to you, though. Things have been topsy-turvy this week."

I find this bit of theatrics and her word choice almost comical.

The dead air around us is awkward at best.

"How are you feeling?" Ellen addresses me, glaring at my arm in the sling.

"Clumsy mostly."

Ellen shows off her bright smile as another uneasy, long silence fades.

"When Ethan told us that you fell in the kitchen—I don't know what to say except how sorry I am for your injury. You arrive in one piece and go home in a cast. What you must think of us. Spending no time with you, no station tour, and now this. We are deeply sorry for the unfortunate timing."

Cooper's death is bad timing for him, I would have to agree.

"I'll mend, Ellen." I glance at Bill leaning on his forearm against the rail.

His facial muscles haven't moved since Ellen gave him the book. Not a jaw clench or twitch. He's jumping into investigator mode, the total observer, ever watching his target of interest.

"How much longer will you be staying with us?" Ellen asks me as Sutton drops her tiny hand from mine. "We're entering our busy season."

"Mum, that's not fair. She just got here. Ethan says she has two weeks," Sutton cries out.

"They are very busy at home too. Her boyfriend is waiting for her there." Ellen isn't that convincing.

"No." Sutton covers both ears. "I won't listen. She has to stay." She looks at me with tearful eyes. "Please tell Mum you'll stay longer."

I ignore Ellen's inquiry because this child is starving for affection, and she's upset. She loves to be around people. It's my guess that she came so late in life for

Ellen that she longs for playmates her own age. Older Olivia is self-involved, and Ethan is too busy outdoors to pay attention to a younger sister until he's finished his chores.

Bill stares into the glass doors. "Annalisse, I hate to rush you, but we should go inside and check on Alec."

"Alec's here? Alec Zavos?" Ellen spins a one-eighty and peers into the glass, shading her eyes from the glare. "When did Alec arrive? Kate's told me so much about him. I'd love to meet him." She stretches for the door handle without waiting for a reply.

It's amazing the fuss she's making. She was nonchalant at the farm when I brought up Alec. Why the sudden change in attitude?

"He's asleep; please don't wake him. This is his first good nap in the past three days." My excuse stops her from entering. "Perhaps later in the week. We plan to stay awhile because—" I stop myself from bringing up the police investigation that Ellen might be oblivious to.

How can she be? A man died on her property the day after Alastair was run over.

Ellen's watching me, waiting for me to finish my sentence.

"We'll give you a call, Mrs. Hyde, once Alec's acclimated to the time difference and has caught up on his rest. I'm sure he'd like to meet you also," Bill says, just as Alec slides the glass door open. "Oh, man, I'm sorry we woke you."

Ellen jumps backward three feet with her mouth open in awe at his sudden appearance.

Alec does the hand-through-the-hair gesture, yawns, and eases his killer smile at Ellen.

I think she's melting in a puddle on the porch because he's taken her breath away. Literally.

"He has that same effect on me." I laugh out loud, which brings a self-conscious grin to Ellen's face.

"Hi… Alec Zavos." He reaches toward Ellen and waits for her to accept his hand.

"Alec, this is Ellen Hyde, Ethan's mother."

"Splendid to finally meet you, Mr. Zavos. Kate's description of you is deficient, I must say." Ellen sounds just like Kate. It's as if my mother said the words.

"Is your son here?" Alec scans the landscape for movement or Ethan's shape.

"How was the nap?" I ask Alec. "Too short, I'll bet."

"Who's the pretty one with the beautiful eyes?" Alec crouches in front of Sutton, who's clutching my hand as her security blanket.

"Do you think my eyes are beautiful? No one says that. I'm Sutton. Are you Annalisse's husband?"

"Whoa, there. That's a ton of questions." Alec whispers something in Sutton's ear, and she giggles.

"Really?" Sutton asks him.

I have no idea what he said to her, but whatever it was, he's definitely made a good first impression on the women of Woolcombe Station.

"Well, as much as I hate to, we have to be going. Annalisse, you're welcome at Woolcombe anytime and so are your companions. Feel better, dear. Let's go, Sutton," Ellen says to her daughter. As she passes me, she whispers in my ear, "Good as gold. He's mint, girl."

Sutton squeezes my waist in a goodbye hug and takes her mother's hand as they stroll together to the car.

"Reading material?" Alec asks, staring at the big book on the rail.

"We're about to find out. Ellen brought it to Annalisse," Bill says.

"How do you feel, babe?" Alec asks me. "Meds wearing off yet?"

"I hope so. My head doesn't seem attached. I'll see how it goes without anything stronger than ibuprofen. What's the title on the dust jacket, Bill?"

Alec and Bill huddle over the book.

"It's about archaeology, right up your alley," Alec says.

"Are those ruins on the cover? How cool is that?" I ask, moving toward the book for a better look. "Who's the author?"

Bill checks the cover, opens the book, and skims through the first pages.

Someone has signed or inscribed a phrase in black marker ink.

"It's a first edition," Alec says, sliding me to his side. "You should see this."

Scanning over the title page, I read the inscription out loud. "For my sister, Ellen. My biggest and most beloved fan. I love you, Thomas. He bought her a book, so why give it to me?"

Alec closes the book and points to the author of it. Thomas Taylor.

The author of this book is my father in hiding, if he's even alive.

"How long ago was it written?" I ask.

214

Alec turns to the publishing copyright. "The first printing is 2012. He has a big-five publisher promoting him. Impressive."

Thomas Taylor could be very much alive. It's possible I'll find clues to his whereabouts in the text, but I'll wait for my dull thoughts to settle. The book is the better source for learning more about him, since I'm not too keen on asking more questions of Ellen in light of the swirling events surrounding the people at Woolcombe sheep station.

"I recommend we all wash our hands after handling the book. I don't know what Ellen touched prior to bringing it to Annalisse," Bill says.

Bill's number one suspect for the copper sulfate might be Ellen Hyde.

CHAPTER NINETEEN
Setting the Truth Free

Behind the cottage, I sit with Alec under a huge Rimu tree near the pond where narrow, spikey pipe cleaners hang from branches swinging in the intermittent breeze. The fronds remind me of Norfolk Island Pines in their shape and structure but without the pine smell. Bark is shedding at the massive tree's base in reddish-brown bunches, covering sparse grasses that can withstand deep shade. We had to remove a few thorny seed cones before finding a comfortable spot to chill out behind the cottage after our walk.

The brook empties into the pond not far from us in a weak stream over stones, and the trickle is soothing to my ears now that my head feels normal again. Alec gazes at the area surrounding us, absently picking up smaller cones, tossing them into the pond. The water ripples as the cones hit the surface before they float off. It feels nice to sit and not talk, with Bill inside the cottage giving us quiet time alone.

"I haven't been here that long, but from what I've seen, New Zealand is an overwhelming country." Alec's announcement breaks my reverie.

"It is. I should've touched base with Ethan before leaving, though. Kate's already gone, and we're in the middle of murder investigations *again*. The police can call these deaths anomalies or whatever they want, but I know both men died because someone wanted them dead. April has to be a better month to visit. January doesn't cut it for me."

"You didn't know that," he says, taking my hand. "Don't beat yourself up. We don't have a great track record for magical trips abroad." Empathy is written in his smile. "I'm ready for that to change anytime." Alec's laughter has that old baritone sound to it. "It would sure make things more enjoyable. This will help." He reaches for his neck chain and lifts Kate's locket over his head. "You might be missing this."

I fix my eyes on the gold. "Yes. I've felt naked without it." I turn sideways so Alec can slip it over my hair and place the locket straight. The familiar weight of it relaxes my shoulders. "There's a comforting feeling when I wear Kate's locket. It brings me closer to her."

"Kate has three children, and it's you she added to the locket. She wore it next to her heart for a reason. I took good care of it, but its home is around your neck."

Resting my head on Alec's shoulder, I say, "That little girl, Sutton. Somehow she hurts my heart. She longs for companionship or attention she's not getting. Tomorrow I'll go out and shop for activity books, coloring pens, and cartoon books for her and have Bill drop them off. She can use a diversion and might like the gesture from us." I lift my head to make eye contact with him. "Now that you're here and I'm out of the hospital, we don't have to stay. Would you like to go home? Has your mother said anything about my leaving?"

"You know Mom. She doesn't like to see us far apart. Chase has your back, so your job isn't in jeopardy."

I jerk away at his seriousness. "My trip put the partnership at risk? I thought Gen understood. I love Zavos Gallery and can't imagine not being there."

"Just kidding, babe. Lighten up that bruised sense of humor." His thumb grazes my knee. "I can take care of everything here over the phone or email. Stay to your liking as long as you don't get more involved in either investigation. Although their deaths are tragic, neither concerns us."

I nod. "Karena said as much when he spoke to Bill and me. Ellen acts like she wants us to leave and so do the police. It could be my overactive imagination, but I wonder if they're mixed up in this when their warnings are similar. She asked how long we planned to stay, and in her next breath, she told me that this was their busy season. Karena is anything but subtle with his requests."

"Police don't have to be subtle," Alec says.

"Let's go find Bill. He's been a great designated driver. Sending him was a genius move on your part. If I had to drive around on the wrong side on my own… I hate to think how stressed out I'd be." I trace his beard, then touch my lips to his. "Thank you for doing that, and thank you for being here."

Walking into the cottage, Alec slides the door closed behind us. I notice Bill isn't happy about something.

"Bill, what's wrong?" I ask.

"Nothing and everything. Ellen never mentioned the tea you drank, only your fall. Did Ethan keep that part to himself?"

"He came into the kitchen after I fell. He may not know about the tea I drank." I glance at Alec, who's grimacing at the mere reference to Ethan's name.

The first time Alec came into contact with Ethan was following Kate's disappearance from Alec's estate. I dropped her at his stables, and from there, she vanished. Sometimes personalities just clash with no reason for it. I don't know why Alec dislikes a naive, unassuming guy like Ethan. At first, I thought it might be jealousy, but it can't be that. One day, I'll find out what bothers Alec about Ethan.

"If Ethan's poisoning people, he won't shout it from the rooftop," Alec says with his usual distaste for Ethan. "He's the most probable culprit in that bunch. I've never liked that guy."

"We'll be sure to leave you out of a reunion. He's always been nice to me." *May as well ask him.* "I don't understand why you think Ethan is such a bad guy. Did he do something to you?"

Alec puckers his lips. "He rubs me wrong."

Bill and I look at each other.

"How so?" Bill asks. "He seems harmless."

"It's not that important." Alec drops next to me on the sofa and says, "You don't hear it, but his Kiwi accent is more pronounced around you. I want to punch him out when he does it."

Alec's envious of an accent that Ethan can't help, or he doesn't trust him. It's okay for Alec to feel that way if he senses something is off, but I don't concur in Ethan's case. I had a working relationship with him when he managed Walker Farm; Alec hasn't. My intuition has been there for me many times when certain people strike me as false.

"I don't notice it, but I'm guilty of liking his accent. All dialects are cool to hear when I'm around New Yorkers all day at the gallery. Try not to let Ethan get to you. I don't look at him, Alec. I'm in love with you, not him." I reach over with my good arm and squeeze his knee.

Bill clears his throat. "Getting back to the tea, we don't know if someone's consumed it except Annalisse. The police must have the search warrant in hand by now."

"Ethan's a question mark," I say. "He has a motive because he didn't like Cooper. Did he hide the tea box? Anything's possible."

"Deaths like these rarely happen in Temuka. The commissioner said as much," Bill says. "Ellen Hyde isn't the least bit rattled, so they aren't searching yet. She wouldn't have left the station to make a delivery with her daughter if investigators were swarming the premises unless they told her to leave."

"What do you think is going on at Woolcombe Station?" Alec asks Bill. "Are investigators worried? For small-town cops, they're pretty laid-back about these deaths. From second and thirdhand information, I don't see how the Alastair and Cooper incidents relate to each other. They look like two separate cases with different motives to me."

"I've considered the possibility that both deaths are related somehow. Until the medical examiner gives the police their reports, we can only surmise. It's highly suspect when each death occurred a day or two apart," Bill says.

"Where's Olivia lately?" I ask Bill. "Since Cooper's death, she hasn't been mentioned by any family member. Has she gone back to work at the sweet shop? Is Ellen protecting her because she knows what Olivia might be capable of?"

Bill recites what we know about Olivia Hyde to Alec, bringing him in on all the facts we have on the Hyde family, triggering a back-and-forth about Finn Hyde.

"Finn wanted to buy the shop from Alastair, but he refused, according to what Olivia said on her way to work. We can't forget that important fact," I remind Bill. "Ellen confirmed this too. How far would a man like Finn go to secure this shop for his daughter when the stumbling block is Alastair?"

Alec nods. "Another layer of suspicion. If the Hydes are pillars of the community because of Finn in public office, do you think the Temuka police will prosecute anyone linked to them for crimes?" he asks Bill. "Well-connected people can sweep things aside for the right amount of money. Both deaths can be explained away as unfortunate accidents." Alec looks at me. "Like the bribes we saw take place in Italy. The police openly took gold as payment without fear of repercussion."

"There are connections to Alastair and Cooper," I say to Bill. "Ellen and Olivia connect to both men, but knowing Ethan, he wouldn't care enough about Alastair to run him down in the street. He's not a cold-blooded killer." Bill is in agreement from what I can tell by the light in his eyes. "Alec, Ellen tried to tell me more about Alastair but stopped herself. Olivia said what I think Ellen wanted to say. I believe Alastair refused to let go of Sidney's Sweets, possibly for the income it generates but also because of his late daughter. He was living in the daughter's home for free."

"The bank didn't want the optics of kicking an old guy into the streets, so they didn't try that hard to remove him from the home," Bill adds. "Realtors must be happy to have Alastair out of the house."

"Other than banks and realtors, Ellen and her daughter had plenty to gain by having Alastair out of the picture. Olivia had the opportunity to be a good employee and bring her boss tainted tea. If someone were slowly poisoning him with copper sulfate, he might've been ill and stumbled into the street," I offer.

"If his death was purely accidental, why did the driver flee the scene and not report the incident to authorities?" Alec asks. "Wouldn't any of us have waited for the police and called an ambulance?"

"Honest people do that," Bill says. "If running Alastair down was intentional, the driver didn't want to get caught because of the old, unlicensed vehicle, which feels calculated and premeditated. For all we know, that car could've been repainted by now so it no longer matches witness statements. I hope Karena is checking that option out." Bill reclines noisily in the chair.

"Olivia likes male attention as most young girls would. I didn't meet the manager before Cooper, but Ethan called him—what word did he use? *Sickie.* Yeah, he referred to the last manager as a sickie. He was abruptly fired from his job because of illness. Did they even bother to find out why the guy was always ill? It's doubtful, if Ethan had his say in the matter. His mom hired the managers, and Ethan wanted to run the station himself. He also injected his innocence into Cooper's death when I spoke about his sister, not him. Is he trying to cover for himself?" I shake my head and add, "No way."

"Ellen is a proud woman of means. Is she capable of steeping copper tea bags in Cooper's morning drink to discourage him to leave his job should Olivia fall for Woolcombe's manager? I assume that his salary wasn't much," Alec says.

"Supposing that's true about dear ol' Mama Hyde," Bill says, "it's understandable to want the sweet shop for Olivia and have control over whom she chooses to go out with. A great provider with more clout in the community." Bill rubs his chin. "An interesting theory, Alec, and it goes well with Finn wanting the same thing. Remove the chaff and pick a suitable partner for Olivia."

"Is there anyone else in the Woolcombe household with access to the copper sulfate?" Alec asks me.

"We met a cook or housekeeper the day Cooper died. Sutton lives there, but I don't recall seeing anyone else."

"Can Sutton reach the cupboard where you found the tea box?" Alec asks.

"Not without a chair or step stool. It was in the back on the top shelf," Bill says.

"Let's stick with adults who don't need a booster chair, boys." I can't believe where our spit-balling is taking us. "Other than Bill and myself, we didn't see anyone else enter or leave the Hyde homestead while we were there, but that doesn't mean a person couldn't have come into the house while we turned our backs."

"It won't be long before word gets out that you were poisoned, Anna," Alec says. "Whoever is doctoring the tea bags is going to hear about your fall as a result of tasting the copper-laced drink."

"What would you suggest?" I ask Alec.

"All right. Here's how we play it; from now on, if we talk about touchy subjects, we do it away from the cottage. This is a house provided to us by a politician..." Alec trails off and looks at Bill. "If I haven't told you enough, we're grateful for you being here." Alec stands, and Bill meets him between the furniture. They clasp hands and give each other a cross between a guy hug and a pat on the back.

A shiny glare passes through the sliding glass doors from a moving vehicle outside, and I recognize it. Who can forget the black-and-white checkerboard and lemony colors on the Temuka police cars?

"We have company." I point to the road.

The three of us watch Commissioner Karena get out of the car, and tension thickens the room again. His knock on the glass goes right through me. It hasn't been but a few hours since he came to the hospital. What now?

"Come in, Commissioner." Alec slides the door open for him.

"Excuse the intrusion. I wanted to bring you an update from forensics, Mr. Drake, since you brought the tea bags into our office. We ran tests and found copper sulfate in the used bag as well as the others."

"Thank you, but your team called me earlier."

"I see." He looks down as if putting his thoughts together. "You might also be interested to know that Cooper Dunn's autopsy reveals high levels of copper throughout his body."

"Wow," I say. "Is anyone searching the Hyde home yet?"

Karena pauses, dimpling his cheek. "That's really none of your concern, miss, but yes, I left investigators to do their work."

"What do you mean, not her concern? Annalisse was poisoned by the same substance. She has every right to ask if you're searching that place for clues." Alec's agitated by Karena's flip remark.

"Annalisse has been injured by the same individual who planted the tainted tea in the cupboard. Her situation could've been much worse," Bill adds, staring at Karena.

"I agree. It's fortunate that you had a violent reaction and tossed up the copper tea, Miss Drury. We believe Mr. Dunn was exposed to the substance for many months. His liver is riddled." Karena twists his mouth in disgust. "I'm glad your wrist will heal. Mr. Dunn isn't as lucky."

"Did he die from the copper exposure, or was his injury from the ram the actual cause of death?" Bill asks.

"Both are a factor. At this time, his cause of death is inconclusive. The medical team is considering both the spine trauma and poisoning. The ME says we may never know what killed him for certain. What we've yet to determine is if someone opened the gate and turned the ram in with Mr. Dunn. That will show us intent to cause great harm."

"With a deadly weapon," Alec murmurs.

"Do you have more than one suspect?" I can't help but ask.

Karena checks his wrist for the time. "I'm late for another appointment. Oh, and one other point of fact. I'm telling you this because you were at the scene following Alastair's mishap."

His death is a mishap now.

"The team also tested Alastair McGregor for excessive copper." He rubs his hands together in a washing motion. "We don't know how or why, but he also had the copper in his system. We're checking the buildings in town and the sheep station for water contamination."

Bill shoots glances at Alec and me. "Thanks for the update, Commissioner," Bill says. "Please keep us informed."

Karena waves, leaving us to connect the dots on our own. One family has ties to both men, but if the perpetrators are the Hydes, different reasons resulted in their deaths. Ellen could have made that effort to protect her daughter from getting too involved with Cooper. When Alastair died, he was an environmental agitator who could stop the land development at Bluebasin Lake. Could Alastair have been the protestors' leader? He's also kept the sweet shop out of the Hyde family's hands. Reason number two for Alastair's demise.

Cooper Dunn and Alastair McGregor came in contact with a person or group behind the copper poison. The tea bags are the source, not the drinking water. There are no coincidences as blatant as this when their deaths are a day apart.

"Karena told us just enough to drop both investigations into a vault forever. Did either of you pick that up?" I ask. "Calling Alastair's death a mishap is a red flag for me."

"Yeah, if he wants these cases closed, he has plenty of options," Alec says.

"Olivia works for Alastair. How can Karena not see a connection between the copper tea and Olivia's ability to pass him a toxic brew? Unless someone told him to turn a blind eye or the police department has been paid off." I cross my arms in disgust. "I hope it's not that."

"Police know how connected the Hyde family is to the community, and he's acting as head of the Temuka Police Department. Let's see how hard they look for suspects," Bill says.

"Bill, do you believe these small-town cops have the ability to solve this puzzle?" I ask.

"The real question is, do they want to? Time will tell."

CHAPTER TWENTY
Returning to the Scene

Alec rides shotgun in the Toyota this morning, giving me time to replay our options on the way to the sheep station—whether to stay in the cottage or go home. I want Alec to see the sheep operation we've been talking about and drop off the gifts for Sutton. A force draws me to the Hydes' youngest daughter. The lost, little soul with her oversized heart cries out to me for help. I come with an armful of coloring books, puzzles, and crayons to keep her busy as a remembrance of our visit to her home in hopes that she won't associate any bad dreams with us after we're gone.

Sleep escapes the weary and fearful. I'm more tired from my throbbing wrist and seven fitful hours tossing on the pillow than before I fell into bed late last night. From our discussion at breakfast, the guys are refreshed and ready to explore. Alec and Bill are both sound sleepers. It must be another guy thing because I don't know how men can shut down their minds that easily. I can attest to Alec; he falls asleep immediately, while I stare at the ceiling, sorting through good and bad memories, listening to the rhythm of his breathing.

If we were in New York, and Bill was on one of his domestic investigations, would Alastair and Cooper still be alive? The effects of my karma on others has been anything but positive lately.

"How long do you plan to stay at the station?" Alec asks me. "This desolate road reminds me of the Australian outback. I expected less dust and more forests."

"We'll be there in about five." Bill senses Alec's frustration.

"Just long enough to drop off this stuff for Sutton. I know you aren't crazy about being here, Alec, but I don't want them to think we're ungrateful for our lodgings. They gave up their cottage for us. If you'd rather, Bill can take you back to the little house. You don't have to be here," I add.

Stop the spoiled brat routine. Let him tell you what he wants.

"Alec, please forgive all tactless remarks from the back seat. You know how I get when I'm tired. My brain disconnects from my mouth, and the wrong words pour out. What's happened this week is hitting me all at once." Reaching over the seat, I squeeze the top of his shoulder. "I'm compelled to do this thing for Sutton."

"Don't worry about it, babe. Give the girl her things, and we split. Investigators might come back for another look."

I didn't consider a scenario where Alec followed me to New Zealand, and I'm mad at myself for not being more prepared to have him with me should my situation change along the way. I've gotten used to Bill on this trip because of the hours spent with him in the air. This threesome feels like looking for Kate all over again.

"We won't stay long," I say to Alec.

Alec mumbles a few words under his breath.

Whatever is said brings a chuckle from Bill.

"Must be getting close. I see the Bray sisters coming in for a closer look." Bill points the donkeys out to Alec and then laughs out loud. "They wander the place freely like a pair of giant watchdogs."

"Donkeys are cool beasts," Alec agrees. "But their braying takes some getting used to. The only thing noisier is having a peacock on the property. Tried that once, but couldn't get used to their screeching calls in the middle of the night." The guys share another hearty laugh.

Woolcombe Station looks abandoned. Every car, truck, and ATV must be hidden away in barns or garages. Or did the police tow them off, looking for clues?

I squint through the windows but can't find a living being.

"It's a ghost town. Are they expecting a freak storm?" A police arrest strikes me as a better possibility, but I keep it to myself.

"I think that already blew through. We'll wait here while you drop off the girl's books." Alec glances at Bill, who's still buckled in his seat with the engine running.

"I'll leave my purse behind in that case." I reach for the door handle with my good hand, but before I can grab it, Alec's already outside the car.

"I'll carry. There's a lot here." He gathers the small pile and takes my hand, helping me to my feet. "Wait here, Bill. We'll be right back."

Leading the way toward the bluebird wreath on the homestead door, I climb to the porch but stop short of knocking, spinning a one-eighty instead toward Ethan's empty parking area next to the sheep barn.

"Would you like me to do it?" Alec asks.

"Ethan should be here managing the place." My intuition is on overdrive, mulling over where he could be.

"It doesn't look like anyone's home. Would you like to stack the books on the wicker chair over there?" Alec is about to set the coloring paraphernalia on the chair cushion.

"And have a gust of wind blow it into the dirt? Too risky." I knock, expecting no one to answer.

A few moments later, the cook Bill and I met, wearing her blue pinafore apron, opens the squeaky door. She peeks through the gap with a pair of wary eyes.

"Yes. May I help you?" The woman's knit brows show the same agitation as before.

"We're sorry to intrude. Is Mrs. Hyde in?" I ask.

"The family has appointments in town today. Were they expecting you?"

Touché. That's what I get for rushing over here unannounced. How could a working sheep station be deserted? The police must have something to do with these appointments.

"We took a chance. Is it possible to leave gifts for Sutton? She's not expecting these, but I wanted her to have them before we went home. Can I drop them off?" I ask.

"Set them on the couch. There."

While I stand by the door, she directs Alec to one end of the sofa.

"I'll make sure she gets them," the cook says.

"Thank you. Please let the family know we stopped by."

Alec no sooner gets across the threshold and onto the porch when she shuts the door behind him, cutting us both off from the house.

"Friendly sort," Alec says with a smirk. "My money's on her for the tainted tea bags."

"Alec." I swat him on the arm. "She won't win the Miss Congeniality award, but I hardly think that curt and cold are enough to zoom her to the top of the suspect list as chief poisoner."

"It doesn't help. C'mon, I'm ready to scout out prettier scenery." He takes my hand and entwines his fingers with mine.

"Wait. I want you to see Dax the ram at least before we go. Ask Bill to come with us."

Alec stops at the driver's side to retrieve Bill from behind the wheel.

"The family would've moved him to get into the pen where Cooper died, but if you think he's still there… Okay then." Bill locks the doors and joins us.

"It's not far. I'd like to take a second look at that paddock anyway. Maybe it'll jog a memory about whether Cooper closed the gate behind him," I say.

When we approach the fence we stood by a couple of days ago, Bill's correct in his assumption. The ram is gone, and yellow crime tape streamers bar us from entrance.

"Be careful and don't touch the fencing," I remind him. "There's still fingerprint powder on the gate. I can see it from here."

"Anna, I don't think this is a good idea, skulking around a crime scene," Alec warns.

"We aren't skulking. If the station is closed to visitors, they would've set up a barrier at the entrance like they did at Walker Farm." My mind is still a blank about Cooper's actions when he showed us the ram. "I thought I might recall new information, but it's no use. I wasn't paying close attention to what he was doing before haltering the buck."

"Who's that?" Bill points to the car passing through the station entrance.

"This is a good time to go." Alec looks toward the car.

The three of us begin our walk to our SUV rental as the sedan slows in the drive. It's not the police, unless it's a plainclothes detective.

"Recognize it?" Bill asks me.

"No," I say, walking faster to our Toyota.

The tan vehicle's window rolls down, and some-one waves at us then pulls up alongside our group.

"Annalisse. I didn't know what day you were stop-ping by," Ellen says with a gleaming smile. "Allow me to park in the garage. Don't leave yet."

"Hi, Annalisse." Sutton's small hand waves crazily at me.

"So much for our quick getaway," Alec whispers to me.

I lower myself to see the girl in the front seat. "We brought something for you, Sutton. It's in the house."

She claps. "What is it?"

"We'll see in a minute," Ellen says to her daughter. "Meet us at the house, Annalisse, and bring your friends." She drives past us to the back of the home.

"We'll do this quickly." I'm assuring Alec, but his expression isn't buying it.

By the time we reach the bluebird wreath on the door, it swings open, and Sutton is squealing in delight.

"Books. Mum, look. Did you bring things for Livia too?"

"Just you." The girl's happiness is infectious and so is her grin.

"Would the gentlemen like anything to drink?" Ellen asks.

The question drops like a wet towel hitting the floor.

"Nothing for—" Bill's interrupted by Alec declining the offer at the same moment.

"Still full from breakfast, but thank you anyway," I add.

"Come sit next to me, Annalisse." Sutton scoots over on the couch and lays one of her new coloring books on the coffee table. "You take one page and I'll color in the other."

I glance up at Alec and find him smiling. He does have a soft spot for all children, not just little boys.

"For a few minutes; do you mind?" I ask him.

"Do you have time for a nickel tour around the barns, Mrs. Hyde?" Alec asks.

"Of course. Sutton, don't be too bossy to Annalisse, and don't hoard the pretty colors in the crayon box." Ellen smiles my way. "Thank you for thinking of her."

They pile out the kitchen door and leave me alone with Sutton.

"Here, you can use these red and blue colors for the birds, and I'll take brown and green for the tree." Sutton nods, quite pleased with her instructions.

"Sure. My colors match your shirt. A good choice."

I haven't had crayons in my hands for years. The action of coloring inside the lines brings back fond memories of my sister, Ariel, and me using colored pencils and crayons at the kitchen table in our Kensington home. Ariel was so gifted and had so much potential. Leaving us at the age of ten seemed unfair then, and more so now that I'm thirty and miss her friendship terribly. I hope Olivia doesn't squander away her time with Sutton and regret it later. In a blink, the world changes, and loved ones can be taken away.

Sutton's busy shading in the bark on her tree, and I'm painting the cardinal's wings in scarlet red when I spot a seed-starting kit with tubes on the table that wasn't there when Bill and I were here.

"Who's growing these plants? Olivia?" I study a see-through plexiglass unit with five tube chambers. All have different shades of soil and what appears to be a large bean seed.

"Not Livia. That's my experiment. I read how things grow. We study veggies in school; you know, botany? The dirt in each tube is soil I found in different places on the farm. The dark one is dirt from underneath Da's tractor. It had a lot of oil in it. That one there"—Sutton points to a tube filled with pebbles—"is from the stream bank. The light dirt came from two different hayfields."

"What about this one?" I point to flaky particles in the last tube.

"That's from Olivia's sheep barn. It's all manure."

"What's the purpose of your experiment?" I lay down the red crayon and wait for her explanation.

"That's easy. To see which dirt grows the biggest bean tree."

"Bean plant. They're big beans. What kind are they?"

She shrugs. "Whatever Mum gave me."

"I guess you'll know what kind they are when the plants grow their pods." I'm laughing at her creative mind. "Did you come up with this experiment yourself, or did someone help you?"

Sutton flat-hands her chest twice. "I do all kinds of tests and experiments. It's fun to watch veggies change from a seed into a plant. Then the plants get big, and we dig holes for them outside. I grow things in water too. It's called hydra… hydro-something."

"Hydroponics. That means growing plants in water and nutrients without soil." I pause, then go down a different path with her. "Sutton, I was wondering, did you and your mother go shopping today?"

Sutton stops coloring and her lips sour. "Not shopping. Policemen wanted to talk to Mum. They were nice to me, though. A lady in a uniform gave me candy and a donut with sprinkles. Then Mum stopped talking and she was crying. I hate it when people cry."

I slide my good arm around her shoulder. "I don't like that either."

"I want everyone to be happy."

"Wouldn't that be wonderful?" I ask. "Did you hear any of the questions they asked your mum?"

"Why do you want to know?" Sutton tilts her head, curious.

"I'm a history buff and love figuring out mysteries. It's kind of like being a detective." It was the first thing that came to mind without having the girl get suspicious of an interrogation and run to tell her mother. "I work in an art gallery with lots of antiques from other countries."

"Do you like secrets?" Sutton asks.

"Very much. But secrets only stay a secret if you don't tell anyone. Do you know a secret?" *Like who spiked the tea bags?*

I hope that Sutton can't hear my heart palpitations.

The screen door hinges squeal, and Alec's voice is above the rest.

"Thanks so much for showing us around, Ellen. Let's see how the girls are doing with their pictures."

My question to Sutton will have to remain our secret for now.

"In here, Alec. Tour over already?" I grasp the end of the table. "I need a break from my knees; they're numb." Holding the ledge, I push on the table with one hand.

Alec runs over to assist.

"We got sidetracked with Sutton's growing experiment. She's amazing at coming up with the idea on her own. I hope she'll write to me and let me know which plant grew the best and what kind of bean they are. My purse is in the car, so I'll write my home address here for her. She can send letters to me anytime, Ellen. I'd love to hear from her."

"Sutton likes email, too," Ellen says.

Bill walks over to the coffee table, studying the growing tubes.

"Ellen would like us to have dinner with them," Alec says. "And I accepted for us."

"You mean here? We don't want to put Ellen out." I must be frowning from Bill's wild look, so I jump into a smile to cover my thoughts.

"We'd like you to meet us at a restaurant, Annalisse," Ellen clarifies.

"She's figured that you and Bill have already eaten at every greasy spoon on the main drag, and she'd like to show us one of her husband's favorite restaurants. Known for their green-lipped mussels and seafood pasta." Alec's brow bump follows because mussels are my weakness, and he knows it.

A restaurant is safe enough, and I'll be in the company of the guys.

"An awesome idea. Thanks, Ellen. Seafood pasta is one of my all-time favorite dishes. Steamed mussels in a garlic sauce are a close second."

"Then you're going to love the Wharf Hideaway. Their local white wines are quite nice too," Ellen says. "Would you like to meet there, say seven thirtyish? It's movie and popcorn night for the kids. A night out with adults is a luxury I don't get often."

How sad for her. Her husband's position brings a lot of nights alone.

"We'll be there. Thanks again for the hospitality." Alec herds us out of the house and down the path to our vehicle, opening my door for me. "Why don't you give your arm a break from the sling? Are you game for some freedom?"

"You have no idea." I slide my arm out of its covering. Rotating my shoulder, he clicks the lap belt closed. "Circulation in my elbow again feels good."

He parts the hair from my forehead. "That lump on your head is almost gone. Barely a bruise."

"I forgot that I hit the counter tile first." I stretch to see myself in the rearview mirror; the spot is smaller and has yellowed.

In a matter of seconds, we're bouncing through potholes on the road toward town.

"That was a quick getaway. You'll have to tell me all about your grand tour from the lady of the station." I smile. "Sutton was quite forthcoming, and I've learned that she has a calculating way about her. She's miles ahead of me when I was her age."

"That's intriguing," Bill says. "What did she say?"

"I'll tell you all about it after lunch. Is anybody else hungry?"

"What do you feel like?" Alec and Bill are laughing at me.

"Hey, I have a few days' worth of missed meals to catch up on. A milkshake or one of those Hokey Pokey ice creams will do if no one else wants anything."

The guys are roaring in laughter.

I'm missing their joke.

CHAPTER TWENTY-ONE
Motivation and Cover

The Wharf Hideaway near the coast has dim lighting and an atmosphere of wooden magnificence. Muttering guests in dressy attire huddle over their individual rock waterscapes and candles placed at the center of each table. Shellfish aromas from the kitchen and diners' dishes waft throughout the eatery, enough to make anyone hungry. Each table is made from native lumber glistening from a coat of clear resin. Large sections have been joined together with no visible seams that I can see. Our table has five place settings, even though Ellen told us the kids were staying home tonight, and she's late.

"Any guesses who the extra diner is?" I ask a table of shrugging men.

Bill's perusing the restaurant's perimeter in sheer wonderment. "Did you notice how many tiki carvings there are? I've counted over fifty, and that's just along the walls."

"Reminds me a little of the Hawaii coffee table books I've seen. Lush plants and wood carvings," I add.

"Tahiti is similar. I should take you there, Anna. You'd enjoy the huts over the water. Very romantic." Alec speaks from experience, but I doubt that he went solo.

"Tahiti is one of my bucket list places to visit. I'd like that. Hawaii is on that list, too." Taking his hand in mine under the table, he acknowledges with a squeeze.

A female server in a midriff blouse and flowing long skirt arrives, directing her introduction to Alec. "I'll be your server tonight. Can I start you off with a specialty drink from the bar?" She tilts her head. "Do I know you? You're so familiar." She asks the same question I've heard many times in so many countries. "I know. You're that Zavos... Alex guy from Greece." She sways in her long flowery skirt, just enough to show a little more leg through the dress slit.

The curly blonde with sharp cheekbones doesn't have a Kiwi drawl. An out-of-towner probably working here in the off-season.

"We're waiting on a friend for dinner. Would you like a drink, babe?"

"Anything but champagne. I've had enough headaches and spinning since I fell." My comment brings his smile. "I'd like to try a glass of local wine."

"Our guest." Bill's head tips toward the auburn-haired woman in a square-neck red sleeveless dress and black stiletto heels. "Cleans up well."

The room erupts into applause, and some diners rise to stand beside their chairs in awe of Mrs. Hyde.

Hair stands on my arms from the spectacle. This room doesn't seem to care about the Bluebasin controversy. Maybe the picture that Alastair painted is an exaggeration from his point of view. Ellen's celebrity status equals genuine royalty, and it's on display tonight. The applause confirms the influence she and her husband have in Temuka. According to Kate, politics does have its perks, if feeding the ego and acquiring wealth is the goal.

We join in on the clapping to be cordial but stay in our seats.

Has the copper tea poisoner come into our midst, or is my imagination on overdrive? I stifle a shiver from between my shoulder blades. This evening has a surprise element to it. A simple evening with Ellen alone is too much to ask of a politician's wife. We're visitors on full display for the townspeople in a popular establishment.

Ellen waves to the crowd and bows with palms together in a thankful moment, then notices us at the table in back of the establishment.

Someone calls her name, and she's off to greet one of her husband's constituents.

A somewhat handsome man in an impeccable gray suit, his brown hair flawlessly coiffed, enters the restaurant behind Ellen, and again the place goes wild in applause. The show is wearing on me to the point that my wrist pounds from the cheers sparking around us.

As the well-dressed man makes his way around the room, he shakes hands with all who'll clasp his.

I recognize his face from online photos and family pictures at the Hyde homestead. Finn Hyde accompanies his wife to dinner when he told Ethan he wouldn't come home to help shear sheep, and it's only the middle of the week. He's the fifth dinner place setting and a drastic twist from what Ethan said yesterday.

The police interviews might have something to do with Finn coming home to put out the dumpster fire ablaze at Woolcombe Station.

While driving, Alastair made a comment about the House of Representatives being in session in the north. Not for everyone, it seems.

Alec stretches and whispers, "The man himself."

"This ought to be interesting," I say to Alec and watch Bill trying to read our lips.

"I predict a long evening ahead," Bill utters. "But it's shaping up to be one amazing reveal." He lowers his voice and leans closer to us adding, "Stay alert and take note of anything that smells of a cover-up."

I shift and whisper to Alec, "Do we know how Ellen's first husband died? I'm going to find out."

"Don't ask her," Alec says.

Bill looks at us with a blank expression. "Guys, she's headed this way."

Alec and Bill rise from their seats in old-fashioned politeness when Ellen glides next to her chair.

"Oh please." She motions for them to sit. "I'm so sorry we're late. Sutton had one of her tantrums, and Finn had a business call that couldn't wait. He wants to meet you."

Is his business political, personal, or dragging brush with the Temuka Police Department? I'm dying to know which.

"An unexpected pleasure. We're looking forward to it," Alec says. "He has a lot of admirers in this room; you both do."

Ellen glances at the empty place setting at the end of the table then her eyes scan the restaurant, more on edge than she was at the station. "You must be starved. Finn won't be long."

Our meals are amazing fare, as promised. The conversation is light banter about current events outside the sheep station. Occasionally, Finn answers a few of the guys' questions regarding New Zealand politics. Finn's wearing his politician's hat and has his practiced mannerisms down, perfectly. He knows when to pivot from an uncomfortable query and when to answer a question with another question. I've never seen a smile erupt as fast as Finn can conjure his.

Strangers who smile too much run headlong into my intuition as being suspicious. He has clear blue eyes that can look right through a person, and Finn's charismatic to the umpteenth power with his native accent. A gracious host and hostess who are skillful in table etiquette and politeness, but what is the real Finn like when not in a public setting?

Alec's notoriety has taken a front seat with Finn, and I gather that soon Alec will be hit up for a donation to one of the many causes this politician champions. Alec knows the drill, so he'll handle any situation like that with class. So far, no one has brought up the two incidents of foul play or next week's protest at Bluebasin Lake.

"Alec and Annalisse, how did you meet? I'd love to hear you add your side to the story?" Ellen asks.

"Getting to know Anna that night at Mom's gallery opening was the most momentous evening of my life." Alec squeezes my hand and his eyes twinkle. "Although, she might have a different account."

I can't help but chuckle at Alec's self-assured grin. I had so many emotions during the party, it's a wonder how I made a good impression when the celebration ended on such a terrible note. We haven't spoken about my old boss since.

"Annalisse?" Ellen inquires. "Tell us your thoughts."

"Alec took my breath from me most of the night."

Laughter spills from around the table.

Heat rises to my cheeks when I realize what I said has two meanings. Alec learned I'm notorious for double entendres during our first intimate liaison on Crete.

"I can't add anything to that, Miss Drury." Finn laughs again and turns to Bill. "We're so happy you were able to rearrange your schedule to see our humble station. It's an honor to have Americans stay at the station cottage." The politician's gaze lands on me. "I hope you haven't been too bored with the place," Finn's Kiwi drawl is heavier, or it's the wine talking.

Bored at which place? The cottage or sheep station? With murder investigations popping up everywhere, who could be bored? I'm afraid to look at Bill or Alec in fear of giving away my thoughts. Finn must be short of words to make a cold statement like that.

Ellen's questions during dinner feel so put on and awkward, as if she's staging theatrics like a blocker on the football field does for a teammate, keeping her husband running downfield. Since Finn has come on the scene, Ellen's more mundane and reserved about the sheep station. Police interviews can do that to a person.

We order coffee but pass on the dessert tray, and Ellen continues to check her watch.

"Is everything fine?" Finn asks Ellen from across the table. "Livia can handle Sutton."

"I'm sure you're right." Ellen straightens in her chair as if she's been struck by an arrow and it's resting near a vital organ.

"Representative Hyde, what can you tell us about a lake we passed on the way from Christchurch? I think it's called... Blue Canyon or something like that. A bluish mountain range sits beside it. Do you know the one?" I direct my question to Finn alone, not making eye contact with Alec or Bill, but I can feel their eyes urging me to stay clear of land mines. "I might have said the name wrong. It's right off Highway 1, about twenty minutes before Temuka."

"You're speaking of Bluebasin Lake," Finn says.

I lift my index finger. "That's it. The area is one of the most beautiful we've seen in your country."

"As it is, the lake draws fishermen and hikers. In the future, we might preserve its magnificence while adding more activities and another income source to our small community." Finn wipes his lips with a napkin and places it beside his plate.

Before I can ask more involved questions, he all but blocks that avenue off. "It's in the planning stages, so I can't go into details. Our first agenda is for the environment. We must do this without disturbing the natural habitat."

The rehearsed political answer to cover all bases.

"We're very sorry to hear about the loss of your sheep manager," Alec says in his own style of digging. "What a shock. Do you plan to keep your ram under the circumstances?"

Ouch. That's a place I didn't see Alec going.

"Annalisse and I were introduced to Dax when we got here. I don't know anything about sheep, but he's a magnificent creature." Bill adjusts Alec's directness to a much safer discussion.

"Yes, he is," Ellen says. "Olivia's pride and joy. Dax was protecting his domain."

In one phrase, Ellen disregards Dax's action. The family doesn't believe the ram did anything wrong. From their side, what happened to Cooper was purely a ram protecting his turf.

"How's Sutton coming with her coloring books? She's such an intelligent girl. I found it easy to forget she's still a child and not an adult," I add.

Ellen nods. "I couldn't have said it better. Our children's personalities differ greatly." She gropes through the black clutch in her lap with an unsteady hand and pulls out a small rectangular piece of paper from beneath the dining table.

I notice it's folded as she passes it to me where no one can view the exchange.

"For your trouble," she whispers, looking at my cast.

At first blush, it appears to be a check. Unfolding it underneath the table, I see my name on a bank check, then note the amount. It's a breathtaking sum. Does she expect us to open a New Zealand account and transfer funds to the US? My mind is swirling—with payoff as her motive.

Ellen smiles and pats my hand, like I'm supposed to know what the money's for.

247

My first inclination is to give the payment back to Ellen, but something stops me. This insulting bribe is as if a bucket of cold water splashes my face for Ellen's enjoyment. A freezing cold sheet of ice flows down to my chest like a monster glacier. Concealing the action, I reopen the check and concentrate on the amount because I must've misread it.

While I think about what's happening, Finn is telling Alec and Bill what it's like to be a representative in Parliament. I'm glad for the diversion so I can sort out what Ellen is doing.

Finn's wife glances toward her empty plate and joins the guys' discussion without missing a beat. Did her husband tell her to make my fall and broken wrist disappear with the offer of money?

I fold the check and drop it into my tote's side pocket, but inside I'm seething. Wiping my hands along my slacks, I jump into the table discussion by adding a few remarks about our country's politics, but my seafood pasta and white wine are gurgling in the depths of my gut.

"Here's a brilliant idea. Would you like a private tour of the lake?" Finn looks straight at me.

Tours aren't working well for us this week, and I have plenty of photos of the area from when Alastair drove us there. I hear his invitation, but I'm too distracted by Ellen's generous *gift*. I don't trust Finn Hyde or Ellen, for that matter. A private tour of any kind from this controversial Parliament rep creeps me out.

"Thanks, but we can't take your precious time away from family," Alec answers for us when I don't reply right away.

I smile at Alec because that's all I can think to do. My mouth hurts from pleasantries, while my head is spinning with ideas of espionage and politics coming at me from high levels of corruption. The best option is to play it cool and finish this curious outing with the Hydes.

Leaning back, I spend less effort engaging and more time listening to absorb Finn's and Ellen's words for alternative meanings and clues. If I allow myself to show how I genuinely feel, I will blow it. It's the check I can't get off my mind.

"How's your wrist, Miss Annalisse? It must be painful and awkward with the cast." Finn breaks my reverie by bringing attention to my wrist for the first time this evening. "Ethan said something about feeling crook just before your fall. I trust your stay in hospital was good?"

"I'm fine, thanks for asking."

A bizarre thing to say. *No stay in the hospital is good.*

Ethan might not be aware of the spiked tea and never mentioned it to the family. It depends upon how much Bill told Ethan at the emergency room. The Hyde clan might not know I drank the coppery tea, but I find that hard to believe due to Ellen's police interview. Another question for Bill later.

I stare at my watch for a long while, hoping that Alec notices. I need to tell Alec and Bill about the bank check while I can still keep my eyes open.

Alec tosses his napkin beside the silverware in a grand gesture. "Thank you, Ellen and Finn, for a gracious evening, but Anna's exhausted, and we should get back to the cottage."

Finn and Ellen bid us goodbye and wander the tables, working the room full of constituents again like good politicians. What a display they're putting on for us and everyone else.

I slide past the guys and into the night air, taking a gulp of salty sea breeze, allowing the stale air to leave my lungs.

"Is your wrist bothering you?" Alec's hand flies through his hair.

"No. I could hardly contain myself in there. You're not going to believe what Ellen did."

"Tell me." Alec searches my eyes for clues.

I lay my head on his shoulder. The fresh air is brisk and cools my skin. "I'll give you a hint; they're as corrupt as those we left in Italy."

Bill strolls out of the restaurant and acknowledges us in the parking lot.

"Once Ellen fumbled with her purse, we lost you in there." Bill expects me to dish, and when I don't, he ambles to the car.

"I hope it wasn't that obvious." The cast feels too heavy on my arm for a stroll in the parking lot. "I need exercise, but not here."

CHAPTER TWENTY-TWO
The Ripple Effect of a Tidal Wave

"Bill, would you park behind the cottage?" I ask, as he takes the turn onto the dirt road toward the house.

Alec looks over his shoulder at me from the front seat. "What's worrying you, Anna? Why don't you want the Toyota seen?"

"I don't know if there's a spot to park in back, but I'll make one," Bill says.

Throughout the drive from the restaurant, I keep what passed between Ellen and me on a verbal hold. The guys don't inquire further, as if they understand when to allow me to stew for a time. Alec knows this about me, and Bill is learning all my quirks and mannerisms on this trip.

My first instinct is to approach the police with this new development, but the discussion belongs in a roundtable with the guys. It's touchy bringing a bribery accusation to authorities when people in high places are concerned. Finn didn't get to his position in Parliament without a willingness to fight his election opponents. He and his wife will battle to keep their status untarnished in the community and retaliate if threatened, so we have to be extra cautious.

Whatever Alec and Bill recommend is what I'll do.

We have a full moon tonight, not unlike the huge supermoon we experienced in Crete over the Adriatic Sea. Bad things happen during full moons, which isn't much comfort in my current dilemma.

Bill stops the SUV in a secluded corner behind the cottage and beneath the tree's hanging foliage. During the day, it looks like a typical shade tree for the area. In the moonlight, the massive Rimu shrouds us in its shaggy beard like a pensive old man with lustrous long hair, watching and listening to us. We are hidden and veiled from the entrance road, which makes me feel better.

"This should work for seclusion." Bill unbuckles his seat belt.

"What happened with Ellen?" Alec clutches the upholstery, waiting for me to explain myself.

"Not here; outside is better." Strange looks fly between the guys. They think I've gone insane, I'm sure. I raise a finger to my lips. "Shh." I unsnap my belt as well, bring out the bank check, and slide to the right so that I can climb out without help.

"I'll give you two some privacy. I'm going inside and catch up on email. Good night." Bill's wish to leave us is less than convincing, but he waves and vanishes.

We'll have to discuss the matter and get Bill's thoughts later.

Alec and I traverse the pond in silence for one entire revolution, then he follows me to the tree where the Toyota sits.

"They are playing us," I announce, leaning against the ridges of the tree trunk. "Ellen offered me a bribe."

Alec nods. "It looked like you were passing notes back and forth."

"You could say that. Here." I hand the bank check to Alec and watch his reaction.

Alec holds it up in the moonlight for a good long while, twitching his mouth now and again as his mind works through it all.

"Is she afraid I'll sue her for my fall in their home, or is it something else? During Ellen's interview, Karena might have told her that I got sick from the copper tea. Sutton explained that she and her mother were talking to the police today, so Ellen must've been told. Tonight at dinner, they were closemouthed about both deaths and made not a mention of the tea. I find that unbelievable when you offered your condolences for Cooper, and they barely acknowledged you. Plain weird, not to mention cold."

"If Ellen's the one behind the tainted tea, the bribe's large enough to cover your silence and to forget about the victims in the morgue—all in one drop," Alec says.

"Finn is here because Ellen wants him home, the police requested his presence, or Finn himself had to cover tracks leading back to him." I lean against the tree's rough bark and look up at the stars. "His family is involved in something ugly, and Finn has to make it all go away fast before it ruins his career."

"Is Finn your reason for not discussing this in their cottage?" Alec pauses to reflect. "I was right to have Bill check for spying devices."

"Before you got here, our rental car was all over town, parked for short and long durations. It's as easy as they make it in crime shows to place a GPS or listening device within seconds. In this small town, our rental Toyota stands out among the local vehicles. For all we know, they've wired the cottage and are recording us. It was built for a station manager to live in or entertain guests from Parliament away from the homestead. I won't take the chance."

"A powerful family in town will do anything to keep their reputation clean. If Ellen orchestrated hit jobs, Finn will fix it if he can. The bribe money is a good start to keep nosy visitors from asking questions," Alec says. "A quarter of a million dollars would stop most people." He hums, scratching his head. "What are you going to do with a check drawn on a New Zealand bank? An amount of that size can't be cashed and is impossible to deposit without an account in this country."

"I'm not accepting the money, but Temuka police should know about it. The Hydes don't hand out that kind of dough for nothing, and I can't think of any good reason to pay me off other than to keep me quiet. Even corrupt law enforcement can understand that. If I tell the police what happened and show Karena the check, they might look more seriously into two out-and-out murders, not accidents of happenstance."

"If you tear up the check and don't go to Karena with it, it's as if we're condoning their possible involvement in at least one murder. Cooper's." Alec kicks at a weed. "But show it to Karena as evidence of a bribe, and if he's a dirty cop, he could inadvertently paint a target on you if he runs to Finn. The commissioner is in charge of investigations, so we have to expect Finn will be informed about the check."

"The commissioner has been clear about my meddling into Alastair's affairs. He wants us to leave soon. I don't know how deeply Finn and Karena are tied together, but we have to take that chance and offer the evidence after I make a copy of the check."

"The police will want the original or at least a copy to pursue a crime. We'll know a lot by how they handle the evidence." Alec passes the check over to me.

"Sutton mentioned her mother crying at the police station. Ellen had to be spooked by what the police were implying during her questioning. Ellen, Olivia, Finn, or Ethan—one of them could be diabolical enough to take people out of the picture. I expect Karena pushed Ellen hard for answers." I groan. "Poor Sutton. That little girl shows signs of mental abuse. She wants everyone to be happy. It breaks my heart." I lay a hand over the weight pressing on my chest. "What will it do to her if someone in her family is behind what happened to Cooper or Alastair?"

"I like Sutton too, babe, but it's not our job to protect her no matter how innocent children are. We could be dealing with a group effort and not just one person."

"Alec, I think the commissioner knows more about the medical examiner's report than he's telling us. I don't buy that their findings were *inconclusive*. I have no proof of the fact, just a strong feeling the ME absolutely knows Cooper's actual cause of death. They're trained to know." I bump my cast against the trunk and suck air through my teeth as pain zings through my wrist. I take a slow breath and continue. "If these two men were sickened on purpose or meant to die from a slow death, by finding the tea box, my fall accidentally shed light on how the copper was used in the tea poisonings. Would the medical examiner have noticed it in the corpses without knowledge of the bluestone powder?"

"They should in Cooper's case, but not if the ME was instructed to keep all findings of wrongdoing off his record. That's a big *if*. I'd like to think this department isn't involved in a major coverup."

"Bill found one in the forensics group very helpful. That same man might be approachable again for the real medical findings. I'd like to talk to Bill about it and hear what he recommends," I say.

Alec's phone vibrates in his pocket and he seems to recognize the caller's ID.

He wraps one arm around my waist and says, "Garrett, thanks for returning my call. I know it's late." Alec's head bobs in the affirmative. "Time to take the lid off and get the paternity results to me as soon as possible." He turns away a little. "I know. Yeah, I've changed my mind. Looking forward to what you find. Thanks, Garrett." Alec stows his phone and engulfs me with his overwhelming presence in the darkness.

I'm trembling in a cool wind that flutters my blouse over sticky skin. This is the first time Alec's been awake and this close to me since he got here, with a bonus—Bill's unable to hear us.

"It's crystal clear what I have to do," Alec says. "Virena is either factual or an opportunist."

Gen isn't mentioned in his decision. Alec's putting himself above her innermost wishes by allowing fate to close the issue. Whatever happens is the truth.

Garrett has to be the man running the paternity test on Noah. I don't press Alec further on his change of heart, but inside I'm dancing in relief—we'll soon know if Noah belongs to Alec.

He twists, resting on the bark, his forearms on either side of me. Alec's body heat spreads over the area between our hearts, the beats thudding in my ears. The very air around us is electrifying and sensual at the same time. In two short weeks, I've forgotten how his magnetism affects me head to toe.

His gaze rakes my throat and he inhales the cologne he gave me last Christmas. Inches from my lips, his penetrating silver eyes meet mine, alight with desire.

This intense Alec Zavos has transformed since our first weeks together. He's always attentive, but something's missing in his cheerful heart. When Pearce Zavos died, I'm more than certain that some of Alec died with him on that yacht. It explains Alec's hesitancy with matters of the soul, and adds to my uncertainty about us as well.

Alec places his palms on the tree and pushes away; the moment breaks bitter memories.

"To be continued later," Alec says in a sultry tone. "We can't stay out here all night, although that supermoon over us is tempting me." He chuckles, running his thumb over my cheek. "I forget myself when I'm with you under the stars."

"You can forget where you are with me anytime, Alec."

He backs away, readjusting the shirttail slipping from his belt.

"Do I have your blessing to make an appointment to talk to the police? It's as if Ellen tried to hand me a suitcase filled with cash without the container to hold it."

"We get a copy made first and then make the appointment. I'm in." Alec snugs me against him by the waist. "You're shivering. Let's go inside and see if Bill's still awake."

Rolling my shoulders, I stifle a yawn.

"I hope I didn't hurt you against the tree. Turn around."

"How could you hurt me when you never touched me?"

Recalling his unforgettable touch sends me reeling where I stand, but my mind is working overtime on the personal check.

He grins. "Get ready, Anna, that's all about to change." Alec rubs my shoulders and the base of my neck, relaxing the tight knots put there at the restaurant.

"I'd like Bill next to me when I go to the police. Karena won't appreciate charging the wife of a Parliamentarian with bribery. I may need Bill's tactfulness if things get hot in there."

He nods. "Fine by me. Tomorrow ought to be an interesting day."

Misty clouds blanket the moon as I huddle against Alec. I search my mind to remember the last time we were *completely* alone outdoors under the stars. That night in Greece happened two years ago. Has it been that long? Having Helga on the second floor above

Alec's bedroom suite is always in my thoughts when I stay over. In such a huge estate house, it's a conundrum I don't understand. Helga's bedroom should be upstairs at the other end of the hallway. Perhaps the addition of a housekeeper came after he built the Tudor-style home. We'll have to adjust that when we get back to New York, but I'm not sure how.

Bill's thoughtful and kind to leave the night to the three of us—Alec, me, and my fiberglass cast.

CHAPTER TWENTY-THREE
Sleight of Hand Times Two

The smothering gray interrogation room walls of the Temuka Police Department are without windows or a mirror, and I'm regretting my decision to come here. The last time Bill and I came to the department to give our statements, I was in control of the narrative when irrefutable facts were on our side. This time the strange set of circumstances surrounding the deaths of Alastair and Cooper include us being the last people to see either man alive. I expect authorities will be defensive when they hear my accusation. Police are protective of their citizens, especially when it's leveled at one of the town's respected families. I'm here of my own accord, and Bill agrees it's our duty to mention Ellen's large check, no matter how uncomfortable the meeting may get.

I'm certain nothing gets past an observer watching the camera feed on monitors in another part of the building. With the door being shut in a small room for the past twenty minutes, it's stifling hot in here. No fan. No air movement. I hope the commissioner won't keep Bill and me waiting in this cubby for too long. The skin beneath my cast is sweating and itchy, and I'm sticking to my plastic chair.

Alec stayed behind at the cottage, using my laptop to catch up on email and tie up loose ends that he left behind at Brookehaven. In his quick exit from New York, the only device he brought along was his smartphone. I've yet to find out what Alec's plans are for the vet clinic or how the work from Garrett is going. It's too soon to have results, but we're in a solid position now that the paternity process has begun.

We can't go forward until we work out the unknowns about Noah.

Alec understands that now more than ever.

Last night, my long-awaited and overdue romantic evening with Alec was more than enough to fuel the energy I need to get through the meeting with the commissioner. The wait for Alec was worth it. Sensual, sexy Alec is back. It feels as if our relationship took a giant step toward a rebirth of sorts. No matter what Garrett finds, Alec and I can work through it because here and beyond, his needs come first as this thing with Virena breaks one way or the other.

Without fanfare, Commissioner Karena steps into the room with his two notebooks and shuts the door. "Hello, Mr. Drake, Miss Drury. What do you have for us?"

I can't get over Karena's stiffer-than-usual manner, and his false smile is anything but warm. Have the Hydes been in contact with him since our dinner at the restaurant, or is he just getting tired of seeing us?

My skin crawls with an eerie sense of uncertainty.

Bill glances at me with the same trepidation that I'm feeling.

"We won't take up a lot of your time, Commissioner," Bill begins. "Something has happened that must be brought to your attention. The sooner, the better."

Karena leans back and folds his arms. "Continue. You can say anything in this room. Nothing leaves here without my consent, should you worry about that."

I want to laugh. When he learns that we're here to point fingers at the Hydes, all bets on the rumor-mill explosion at the police station flush down the toilet.

"Annalisse." Bill cues me to tell the story.

I give Karena a little background into the restaurant outing and what happened while waiting for Ellen Hyde, meeting Finn, and fast-forwarding to the hand-off of the check.

"I didn't know what Ellen was giving me at first because she handed me folded paper. I was blown away by the check amount." Reaching into my tote, I place the folded check in front of me.

"Mrs. Hyde gave you money for what purpose?" Karena asks.

"That's a very good question. I fell in her home, as you know. But she gave no explanation for the check. There was no discussion, and I wasn't about to question it as dinnertime small talk. I was stunned to the point of silence about it. That's when I thought you should see it and give me your recommendations. We aren't talking about a few hundred dollars. She made the check out to me for two hundred fifty-six thousand six hundred sixty-six dollars."

The commissioner's brows rise on the figure, but he reserves reaction other than that.

"Does the amount mean something to you, Commissioner?" Bill asks. "Annalisse can't figure it out."

"A strange number, I agree."

"The only thing I could come up with is the satanic sixes, the mark of the Beast."

"Are you sure Mrs. Hyde didn't tell you what the money was for, and maybe you forgot?" Karena's either expecting to hear a different answer or wants me to hypothesize.

"I'd remember that number, Mr. Karena, but I have to assume it was a bribe so I wouldn't sue her. Do the Hydes know I drank copper-laced tea from their cupboard and that I fell as a result of it? Neither she nor her husband mentioned the tea last night. Do they know why I fell?" I shift a glance sideways at Bill, wondering how Karena would respond.

"I can't discuss an ongoing investigation," he barks.

And just like that, I have my answer.

"Commissioner, you have strong circumstantial evidence implicating someone in the Hyde home in at least one death because *I brought it to you*. We presume that Mrs. Hyde was made aware of Annalisse falling, either by someone in your office or her son, Ethan, who accompanied us to the emergency room. The family has been interviewed; her youngest daughter said as much to Annalisse." Bill's shaking mad and slides his hands into his lap to cover the agitation.

"We expect your department will be factual with us since I was personally injured in this matter," I say, coming to Bill's aid.

"Here's what I *can* tell you. You'll be relieved to hear that the Alastair McGregor incident is a closed matter. We have proof that his death was an accident due to being hit by a driver only once. That should give you some solace that he wasn't run over with malice."

I glance at Bill, who has steam rolling out of his ears. That's not what eyewitnesses told him. Karena's department is doing its best to make a possible murder, or murders, go away.

"Once was enough to kill him." The temple throbs I'm experiencing tell me my blood pressure is high. "Aren't you going after the driver? How can the case be closed when someone drove that vehicle over another human being? This doesn't feel like justice to me."

Karena rests his arms on the table and entwines his hands one finger at a time. His irritation at my hammering him on how to do his job is as strong as Bill's anger.

"I understand your frustration, Miss Drury."

The commissioner is talking to me like a child.

"Getting back to Ellen's check," Bill says, "it's my belief that the Hyde family is trying to make several regretful things disappear such as Annalisse's injuries and the stay in the hospital after ingesting the poisoned tea taken from the Hyde cupboard. A syringe found in the box carries traces of copper sulfate. The same substance tested and found in the unused tea bags I produced for Temuka forensics. The very same diluted bluestone consumed by Annalisse from her used tea bag—and found in the bodies of Cooper Dunn and Alastair by the examiner. Would you rather we call a press conference with the media and tell them the facts as we know them?"

"Rubbish. Watch your tone in this meeting, Mr. Drake." Karena slams hard against his chair back. "I cannot go into any details involving an open investigation. You're a detective. Surely you understand this."

"Ordinarily, that's true, but we're part of that investigation. Look, it doesn't matter if Ellen knows about the copper or not; she's trying to pay Annalisse off so that she won't make waves for the family dynasty. Her husband's career and their livelihood are at stake," Bill says.

"An interesting theory," Karena says. "It's a sizable sum we shouldn't ignore."

"We came here because offering a quarter million dollars to a virtual stranger from another country set off major alarm bells for us. If it doesn't for you, I'm confused by that," Bill says.

"May I see the check? Is that it?" Karena eyes the folded note.

"By all means." I slide it across the table, grateful that Alec made a copy.

Karena studies the front and back and sours his lips. "I'll personally call Representative Hyde and find out his wife's intentions behind the check." Karena's nervous mouth tic shows cracks in his calm facade and a betrayal. I suspect that Finn hasn't brought him into the plan to bribe me. Even the best police training melts away when a powerful man like Finn acts behind his back. Ellen would never offer this much money to me without Finn's blessing.

"I plan to call Ellen privately. Last night at dinner wasn't the time to discuss it," I say. "We came here to show you the check and report the strange behavior. May I have it back, please?"

"We can't do anything about this without proof." The commissioner places one hand protectively over the check.

If he secures the original in police custody, it's possible no one will ever see it again, including me. It's appropriate to tell him we're one step ahead.

"Should you decide to act on the bribe in the future, we'll gladly share the photocopy we made of the check," I say while looking at Bill. "But I prefer to keep the original check in my possession. It's my property, after all." I hold my hand out.

Karena hesitates, then slides it across the table. "Miss Drury, we don't know that she intended to bribe you. That's merely a supposition on your part. May I make a copy for our files before you go? Until I make inquires—"

Interrupting him with a smile, I say, "You have my number."

"The commissioner's time is valuable, and we'll leave him to it." Bill solidifies our exit.

I'm careful as I zip the check into an internal purse pocket, then push myself up with my tote in hand. "Should anything else come up, we'll be sure to alert you."

"One more thing before we go." Bill sits back down. "How did you arrive at the case conclusion on

Mr. McGregor if witnesses said the vehicle hit him twice before fleeing the scene? That is intentional manslaughter, not an accident."

"The driver gave us his statement. Witnesses aren't always reliable and can be confused by what they observe when watching a horrific tragedy play out. Their eyes deceive them. Upon reflection, these witnesses agreed that Alastair McGregor was struck only once by the young man who confessed to the incident."

"You got a confession? Why did he drive off?" I think another payoff might have taken place with the witnesses or driver.

"Because he took to the streets without permission. The car isn't registered for the highway. Offroad use only with a very old license plate. That's why we couldn't find it in the registry. When the boy hit McGregor, he was shaken up and drove away in a panic. His conscience brought him and his parents into the office. There's not much we can do to a fifteen-year-old without a driving license, other than fine the parents and put him in juvenile detention for a stint."

"It's still hit-and-run." Bill shrugs off the comment. "How did the copper get into Alastair's blood and, I assume, his organs?"

"We don't have all the answers, Mr. Drake, but the examiner has determined the cause of Alastair's death is a result of his head injuries. End of case."

I want to start up the conversation again about Cooper's injuries, but I don't dare. The commissioner is in no mood for niceties once I went rogue about keeping the actual check. Information regarding Cooper's investigation is off-limits to us, and whatever is taking place between the Hyde family and the police is being held on a need-to-know basis.

"Thank you for taking our meeting," Bill says, pulling out my chair.

"Cheers. Have a pleasant flight back."

On that finale, Bill and I exit police headquarters and enter the rental car in silence, each of us mulling over the interview and if presenting the check to authorities was wise. Karena wants us out of the country in the worst way.

"Did you happen to notice a drugstore or office supply in town?" Bill asks. "I want to make some notes retracing our steps in case this blows up into a major scandal."

"We're irritating Karena. You had him squirming when you threatened to go to the media. I sensed from the commissioner that Finn Hyde has spoken to police or a go-between recently. If he's a good politician, he'd get ahead of any brewing scandal. Ugh." I scrunch my nose. "The bad tea pun wasn't intended."

"If Finn's wife or children are involved in anything as nefarious as poisoning people, he'll do whatever it takes to protect them, as anyone would." Bill starts the car and backs out of the lot. "Karena has a lot to lose if the town finds out their police department is covering up Alastair's murder, if it leaks to the media. Two murders in a small town like this is big news. I'll check inside the drugstore for a newspaper."

"His backside is exposed. We know there's a poisoner in his community, which is a problem for Karena if he's involved in a cover-up," I say. "Turn down the street to the right." I point to a shopping area. "Try over there; a *chemist*, as they call it, should have note-books and writing materials. I'll wait for you in the car. Maybe when you return, we can find a bank and exchange a few US dollars for the local currency."

"Almost everyone takes credit cards, Annalisse, but if you feel better using the local currency, sure, we can exchange some for you. It won't hurt to have a little for small purchases."

Bill steps out of the car and enters through the glass doors.

Watching shoppers cross in front of the car on the sidewalk, I notice a couple reading newspapers as they walk. Whatever they're reading seems fascinating to them.

I unbuckle, and open the car door. "Excuse me. Can you tell me if the drugstore sells newspapers?"

"We have two. Here ya go, miss." The man in an ivy cap folds his paper into thirds and hands it to me.

"May I pay you for it?" I'm hoping he won't ask for money that I don't have in his currency.

He shakes his head. "No worries. Cheers." The couple continues their walk as I slip back inside the Toyota.

"Let's see what the local media knows about this week's events." I unfold the paper and gawk at the headline. Reading it over again, I allow the bold words in all caps to sink in. "Rugby Stadium Donated on Behalf of Fallen Officers." I don't have to dig too deeply to find out who the benefactor is. "My, you do work fast, Mr. Hyde."

Rugby is New Zealand's number one pastime sport, and anyone associated with the All Blacks rugby teams is royalty in New Zealand. Home decor, road-way billboards, and advertisements hail rugby players as men to adore and aspire to. I liken the phenomena to a cult in popularity, much like our sports figures in the States but at a higher level.

Bill opens the driver's side door and drops a paper bag on the console.

"No dice on the newspaper. Where'd you get that?" he asks, peering over at the paper on my lap. "Leave you for one minute and you manage to get what we need." His smile turns sober. "Is there anything earthshattering?"

I turn the headline toward him and watch his reaction.

Bill exhales in disgust and leans his head against the headrest, closing his eyes. "It's as bad as we thought. Sad thing is, I don't know if there's anything we can do to change it."

I shake my head. "Our day just got more challenging. When Alec gets his hands on the paper, he's going to jerk all of us out of this country on the next flight home, and I'm not sure he wouldn't be right."

"Then we'll have to decide whether we leave the media a little gift before we go."

"Sourced anonymously," I add.

"Is there any other kind?" he says with a chuckle.

CHAPTER TWENTY-FOUR
Discovery

I concentrate on the SUV's engine purr and the air conditioner's cool air to distract me from the dread I feel about going inside the cottage where Alec is. Bill is deep within his thoughts as well. Having Finn donate a rugby field to a community of this size is huge news. By now, it's all over town.

"Which of us breaks the news to Alec about the stadium?" When I don't answer, he continues. "I think we should start by telling Alec how the meeting with Karena went, *then* show him the newspaper, not the other way around. If he's looking at the local news online or watching it on TV, he already knows about Hyde's stadium donation, and he'll bring it up."

"If Alec suggests we go home, I'm ready to talk about it," I say in defeat because I know it's the best thing to do, all things considered. I was right to come to New Zealand but wrong to do it before talking with Ethan—and having that long discussion with Alec. I laugh when one of Kate's sayings comes to mind. "We all jumped the gun." A great escape without a solid plan—and rotten timing.

"He'll honor your wishes, whatever they are. He's not going to push you into going against your will. He's not made like that." Bill's phone rings. "Bill Drake." He has a question on his face. "Yes, I remember. How are you, Tane? I'm putting you on speakerphone."

I have no idea if Tane is a man or a woman and wait to determine which it is.

"I'm decent, Bill. Do you have time to meet up today?" the male voice asks.

"Sure. We're at the Hyde Station cottage. I can introduce you to Annalisse and her friend Alec."

"I'd like to meet somewhere else. Do you know where the Pleasant Point Reserve is? Park benches and picnic tables and we won't be disturbed."

"Annalisse and I drove into Pleasant Point the first day we looked around. We'll find it. What time?"

Tane doesn't speak at first, then says, "I can be there in an hour."

"An hour it is. See you then." Bill ends the call. "That was Tane Otene. He's part of the forensics team I met with while you were in the hospital."

"Why haven't we met him until now?"

"I tried to bring him into your hospital room, but he declined because he didn't want the department to know he was feeding me information about your case. Sorry, I should've insisted."

"Who could blame Tane for staying out of sight in order to keep his job? A higher source than the Temuka Police Department might've told them to shut up about these investigations. They're rare, so it wouldn't surprise me. How much does Tane know about us?" I ask.

"Nothing more than the tea evidence I gave him. He's been most helpful, and I think he knows about more mischief within the department. It's just a feeling I get. Forensics has been instructed to stay away from me from what Tane said."

"It smells like a cover-up, doesn't it?" The redundant question doesn't bring a reply. Bill feels like I do. "Tane must want to share investigation information or warn us about something. What other reason can he have for a secret meeting? I'd like the three of us to go, okay?"

"Absolutely." Bill checks the clock in the dashboard. "It takes about fifteen minutes to get to Pleasant Point, add a few more to find the park. Let's bring Alec in on what we know."

Our earlier assumptions are correct.

Alec has already heard the news about the stadium donation, and couple that with how our consult went at police headquarters, he's in agreement the police are making deals with Finn Hyde.

"I know you want to leave New Zealand, Alec, but why don't we hear what Tane has to say before we look for return flight reservations?"

He seems to be in a receptive mood this afternoon and scoots his chair under the table and closes my laptop with a click. "Your trip, your timeline. I don't have any set schedule anymore, remember?" Alec smiles at me in earnest. "I have so many new proposals to toss at you that I'm about to burst."

One of them left dangling is his marriage proposal from December. I wonder if he's lumping that in with other ideas.

Bill looks at his watch. "Hold off on the bursting, bro. If we don't leave soon, we aren't going to make it."

I didn't expect to find Alec in such a peaceful mood as dual murder investigations swirl around us. Did he have a heart-to-heart with himself while we were away?

An even more exciting consideration zooms into my head.

Did Alec get results back on the paternity test?

The picnic area is almost deserted, save a couple of kids on the swing set. We're sitting at the table in the most remote place, beneath a tall, native Totara tree, it's needlelike clusters throwing shadows on the ground to shade us in the soft breeze. It's a comfort to do nothing but think about being in nature, watching gray squirrels chatter with each other and birds chirp in the tippy-top branches of the park's overgrown woods.

Alec's hands are fidgety and his sighs are more frequent. I can't blame his irritation. Tane asked for the meeting, and he's keeping us waiting.

"Something happened," I say to Bill. "He's twenty minutes late to his own meetup. Do you think the team overheard him talking to you and stopped him from meeting us?"

"Things come up. We'll wait a little longer before we take off. He might have been sent out on another call. He'll be here." Bill's more positive than I am.

My spirits lift when a blue compact parks next to our Toyota in the designated grassy area. One person gets out in summertime clothing, wearing beige shorts, sandals, and a black T-shirt.

"Darn. I thought that was him, but it can't be." I expect an officer in uniform.

The guy surveys the picnic area and heads in our direction. He has a steady gait and a Māori tattoo that covers the front of his right leg below the knee.

"That's Tane," Bill says, sitting more upright.

Alec perks up as well.

"We about gave up on you," Bill says to Tane.

"Couldn't be helped. I thought I was being followed. Had to ditch into town for a bit to be sure. Popped into the chemist for a fizzy while I was there." Tane's close-set eyes fall on my cast. "You must be Anna. Tough thing, that. Sorry you were hurt." He checks out Alec, who's already on his feet.

Bill waves his hand toward us and makes the introductions.

Alec shakes Tane's hand and then sits on the bench again. "This vacation for my girlfriend has been not only eventful but deadly. It's not the trip I wanted for her. I hope you'll explain why the Temuka police seem uncooperative and secretive when Annalisse is a damaged party in the matter of Cooper Dunn. If Bill hadn't been quick to take her to the hospital, we could've lost her. I might've... lost her." Alec's voice breaks.

My heart swells from Alec's caring words. He seldom rants at a complete stranger on my behalf. I've known him to be private and not confrontational with personal matters, keeping his opinions guarded, except when matters involve his mother. I'm more family to him than I realize...

Tane rubs his blocky jaw. "Mr. Zavos, you're no longer in the United States. On the South Island, we work cases in our own way at our own speed. I did some research on you and your lady friend. Movie-star-type Americans snap their fingers and get results. I understand how crime scene investigations may frustrate you. Forensics is a science that takes time and logic to look at all possibilities. I can tell you that we are certain what happened in both cases you're referring to," Tane says to Alec. "I'm on your side. Believe me, I am. There are powerful people who drive a heavy mallet in our department. No one can find out that I'm here with you. What is said today is strictly on the hush."

Tane's cop ego and attitude won't get him far with Alec. I hope Bill jumps in soon before we're asked to leave without any new information.

"What do you have for us?" Bill asks.

Tane huddles closer to the center of the table, bowing his head of short, cropped, dark hair, clasping his hands. "You've heard about the donation made in the name of fallen officers?"

We all answer in the affirmative.

"Miss Annalisse, you were at the sheep station when Cooper Dunn was injured, yeah?" Tane doesn't wait for me and continues, "As Bill probably told you, we spent the better part of a day taking prints at the scene. After the warrant to search was obtained, a team went inside the homestead and recovered more evidence. Evidence we aren't allowed to mention."

"If you're going to repeat the same spiel as the commissioner did with us, we're wasting our time here," Bill says.

"The evidence, ah, leads straight to... Mrs. Finn Hyde," Tane says.

"We figured that part out ourselves," I add to Tane's obvious statement. "Did Ellen administer the copper in the tea and make people drink it? We saw Olivia, the oldest daughter, bring out a mug of something to Cooper the day he died. She had the hots for him, so I find it hard to believe that she would want to hurt him."

"Someone in the family did it, but no one will admit to it except Mrs. Hyde," Tane says.

"Wait a minute. I'm confused," Bill says. "Didn't you say the evidence leads to Ellen Hyde?"

"That's who's confessing to it, but I don't believe her. Neither does our team." Tane plumps his tanned cheeks in a nervous squint. "We can't find the box of tea bags Annalisse used. No other tea bags were located in the dwelling. We found the loose tea in a tea canister on the counter where you said it would be, Bill. We tested it all. It's clean. Tea leaves and no copper."

"Ellen's jumped in and confessed already? Don't you find that suspicious? Did you test Cooper's beverage from the scene?" I ask.

Tane nods. "We found tea spiked with copper sulfate similar to your tea bag in Copper's insulated container. A jar of bluestone was underneath the kitchen sink. Easily accessible. Not many uses for it in a kitchen." He smirks, wrinkling his offset nose. At some point in Tane's past, he broke it. I'm thinking while playing rugby since everyone seems to enjoy the sport.

"It's the source for the copper. It has to be," Bill declares.

"Fingerprints from every family member were found all over the bluestone jar, including the help. We think it was moved around to get to other items under the sink. The outside of the container was stained blue and dusty, like it wasn't from the house."

"Did you check the fireplace or any burn receptacles?" Alec asks.

"We frown on burning outdoors during a dry season like the one we're in now. The fireplace was recently cleared of ashes. Spotless. If anyone burned paper, it is long gone," Tane says, then turns toward Bill. "If you hadn't picked up the syringe when you did—"

"A lot of good it did. The prints are washed off," Bill says.

"Here's what's interesting," Tane says. "We obtained a partial, but the part we have doesn't match anyone from the family. We printed members when they came in for interviews. Finn Hyde is already in the database because he's a public official."

"So you're back where you started. What makes you believe that Ellen Hyde isn't your poisoner when she's confessed to it?" I ask.

"During her interview, an officer quizzed her hard about what copper sulfate is and asked how she administered it to her victims." Tane laughs. "She doesn't know how a sheep foot rot remedy wound up in the kitchen. We waited for her to mention the tea bags. It never came up. If Mrs. Hyde used the substance, she doesn't know how she did it."

Ellen has lived on a sheep station for years; she's trained in foot-bathing sheep, copper sulfate's uses, and how ingesting copper is poisonous to sheep and humans. She's lying by omission to the police as cover for another family member. It's the only thing that makes sense. Ellen's familiar with what's beneath her kitchen sink and would know a sheep treatment didn't belong there.

"Ellen confessed; therefore, she has a good idea who tainted the tea and is covering for that person," Alec says.

"Do you believe Cooper Dunn's death was an accident?" I ask Tane, who's taken aback by my directness. He delays his answer as if he's afraid to give an honest opinion.

"No accident. The trauma caused by the ram didn't help him, but his heart gave out due to myocarditis. His entire body, especially his liver, was fouled with copper. The ramming caused his death a few days sooner. The medical examiner said as much."

"Bill, Commissioner Karena—"

"He told you that Dunn's death was an accident, didn't he?" Tane asks me. "Accident is the *official* cause of death going forward. We were given the word yesterday."

"The commissioner wouldn't speculate on ongoing cases," Bill says. "We had dinner with Representative Hyde and his wife last night and found it odd that he'd be in town when Parliament is still in session."

"I didn't know he was home," Tane says.

"Were you also involved in Alastair McGregor's case?" I ask Tane.

"We're a small outfit. Yeah, McGregor had plenty of copper in his system too. We're unsure how he was dosed, but there's a connection to the Hydes. The eldest daughter works at the sweet shop that McGregor owned. I hear there's already a bid for that business since the man's passing."

"Ellen Hyde told me *they* wanted the business for their daughter, but Alastair wouldn't sell," I say. "Makes me wonder if your boss isn't lying even more. I don't believe anything the commissioner said today."

"McGregor died of his wounds. He sustained irreparable damage," Tane says.

"Too coincidental. The Hydes wanted his store, and someone conveniently confesses to running the man down—a boy too young to go to prison for the crime," I say. "If Finn Hyde can make a sizable donation on behalf of law enforcement, he won't flinch about paying a family to take the fall for running over poor Alastair, or putting the kid up to the task."

"I'd like to offer sound advice." Tane is speaking to all of us but looking at me. "Don't get involved in Temuka town politics. Do your sightseeing and then go home. Forget about Dunn and McGregor. They're gone, and you can't bring them back." Tane looks at his wristwatch, almost a duplicate of Ethan's, and frowns. "Shift starts in an hour. Do not pass along the information I've shared with you. I could lose my job."

"Why do you trust us with the truth?" Bill asks.

Tane pauses for what feels like an eternity. "The department I work for is corrupt from the top down. I plan to take my family out of this town and away from the politics, but for now, I need this job. Miss Drury, you sustained an injury due to this copper business. I wanted you to know what we've uncovered in the cases."

"We understand," Alec says. "Thank you."

Tane nods to Bill, ignores me, then ambles to his car.

"I have to digest this." Bill walks in the opposite direction as the officer.

Alec slides closer to me and strokes my hand, staring through me as if he was trying to read my thoughts.

He's waiting for me to figure out where we're going next. Do we stay a while longer or leave the country? I'm swaying toward the go-back-to-New-York camp, but the same thing Bill's struggling with is getting me down too. This police department is under orders to break any fingers pointing at the Hyde family for crimes that would land any other citizen in jail for murder, and that's only the first charge.

"This Hyde *business* has got Bill messed up," Alec says. "I don't think I've seen him so at odds with himself. His compass direction is all over the place."

"He wants to tell the media about the corruption and knows he can't," I say. "He's such an honest and good guy. You should've heard him talk about the little girl in his arms, lost to the fire. Losing that child and her mother tore him up."

"He mentioned that?" Alec widens his eyes. "Bill's tight-lipped about the fire and doesn't bring it up unless he trusts that person. You're a good listener, so I get it."

"I have ways of poking about without sounding like I'm meddling." I lean into his shoulder, lifting my brows.

Alec plants a kiss on my temple. "Bill gives me space when I need it, and we should do the same for him. It's a great friendship that I don't want to lose because of stepping over boundaries. He'll open up more about his past when he's ready." Alec glances away. "We can talk more in private."

Bill approaches the hardwood table and plops onto the bench, making it creak. "I needed some alone time. We've been lied to by everyone, including Tane. He knows who the real poisoner is."

"Bill, he can't divulge everything, and he told us why," Alec says.

"I'd like to research the death of Ethan's father, the first husband in the picture with Ellen. He owned the sheep station originally. I don't trust Ellen." I swivel and scramble over my bench. "Ethan said it's been in the Fawdray family since the 1800s, starting with his great-grandparents. Records should say how Mr. Fawdray actually met his demise. Ethan was a small boy when he died, so Fawdray probably didn't live into old age unless he was decades her senior."

"The police aren't going to tell us any more, Anna," Alec says.

"I see where she's going with this. If Fawdray died of poison or accident, we'll have more to go on," Bill says. "Check it out."

"You guys are scaring me; you're starting to sound alike." Alec hikes over his bench.

I take Alec's hand and say, "This is something I have to do."

"Do your research, I understand."

CHAPTER TWENTY-FIVE
Declaration without Fanfare

I'm reliving the research we did on Gen's family ties while we were in Italy, searching through the obituaries for the men of the Fawdray line.

As I recall from a conversation last year with Ethan, his father's name is Robert Fawdray. Fawdray is a popular name from the several Robert Fawdrays in the South Island archives. Considering Ethan's age, I look through the past two and a half decades. Olivia was born a few years after Ethan, which places Ellen's introduction to her second husband shortly after Robert Fawdray's death, or she might have known Finn from before. If Finn Hyde had his eye on Ellen while she was a married woman with a child, it's possible they could've conspired together to get rid of Robert Fawdray. That would make Ellen a schemer and evil.

I hope that isn't the case and she had nothing to do with her first husband's death. It seems noteworthy that a young woman would lose a husband at their age unless he lost his life from an accident or a sudden heart attack or maybe cancer. That's possible too.

"I'm turning into a conspiracy theorist of the worst kind," I say under my breath. "This is all conjecture, but it fits if she had a financial motive to move on to another man."

"Are you talking to yourself?" Alec wears a silly grin as he pulls out a chair at the table. "You may not know this, but I can always tell when you're researching a subject. You mumble and think out loud."

"It's a bad habit." Nodding, I say, "It must be one of my tells. Bill noticed how I run a sweaty hand down my leg when I'm unsure or afraid."

Alec sits in silence as if he's contemplating what I've said.

"My hand, not his. I have two *tells*, it seems."

"We all have them."

"Your biggest one is the hand-through-the-hair thing you do. It allows me a window into your mind. I know exactly how you're feeling at the time."

"We're acting like an old married couple." He laughs.

"In the two years we've been together, you and I have experienced more than some married couples do in their lifetimes. I don't know if that's a good thing, but I can honestly say that we've seen each other at our worst and best. That's a plus." I pat his hand in a motherly way.

"Can I help?" Alec asks.

"I'm overwhelmed by how many Robert Fawdrays there are. I've searched by narrowing down how old he could've been at the time of his death. If I stay within a parameter of Temuka, I should be able to pinpoint the right one because the sheep station has been in the same family for over a century. Cause of death is primarily what I'm after."

Alec twists his mouth enough to dimple his cheek. "Okay. I could get in the way. You have a system."

Leaning back in the chair, I come up with another option for him. "You *can* do something for me. Would you check on return flights?"

"Seriously?"

"Yeah. My mother is gone, and Ethan is too preoccupied for any tour of the sheep at the station. We've seen enough of Temuka for a lifetime, frankly. There's nothing more for us to do in this town."

Alec's already scrolling through the internet on his phone. He's not making eye contact, but I can see the twitch of a happy grin.

"The station began in 1884 with Ethan's great-greats. I'm going to work it backward to the present and see how much I can learn about the people in the Fawdray family. Where's Bill?"

"On a Saturday sabbatical walk. He's steamed about how law enforcement works around here. He's not used to getting his hand slapped when all he wants are the facts."

We leave each other to our devices, literally, and I continue my records search of the Woolcombe Station founders. There are a few articles from the early 1920s, birth and marriage announcements, death notifications—mostly from natural causes at young ages by the standards we live under today. The harder the life, the shorter their lives. In its heyday, Woolcombe Station held fifty to sixty thousand head of Merino-Corriedale crosses. An article written in the 1930s, after the US stock and economy crash explains the hardships that occurred on this island continent.

"I found a couple of options," Alec says. "We can fly out of Auckland in four days or Christchurch in three. If we book soon, these flights have openings where all of us can go on the same aircraft for all connections."

"Auckland is on the North Island," I say. "We'll be adding another leg to the flight if we have to fly to the north."

"Yes, but you'll love this." He drops his phone in front of me. "How many times have you watched the Hobbit movies and read the series? Would you like to take a tour of the Shire? It's not that far from Auckland." Alec's eyes light up. "So the trip won't be a total waste; we should try to see it."

"See where they filmed the Lord of the Rings Trilogy? Are you serious? Do we have time to plane hop and make a scheduled tour? I'm sure we have to make reservations ahead." My spirits lift for the first time in days. "Talk to Bill before we get too excited. He has a business on hold for me and paying clients waiting at home. You can discuss and report back. It would be the upside for an unpleasant trip."

His kiss grazes my lips, and he scratches my chin with the beard I love so much.

I'm alive with anticipation of something to look forward to finally.

Watching Alec leave through the sliders, I scan article after article from the 1980s that brings me closer to Ellen's part in Temuka.

"Woolcombe Station breaks the South Island record for a high-selling Corriedale hogget," I mutter. "That's a cool record to hold." I search for the price paid and can't find it listed. That's when I come across the seller's name, Robert Fawdray, Esquire. "I'm in the right decade." Scanning more articles in print five years later, I find the marriage announcement for Robert Fawdray, Jr. and Ellen Taylor of the US. "Yay, it fits." My heart rate picks up. "Ellen Taylor is the sister to Thomas Taylor." My father, *supposed father*.

I reread the marriage announcement for confirmation. "It's them."

Fast-forwarding through Temuka news following the marriage, I find a small article four years after they're married. It mentions a farming accident at Woolcombe Station. No name is given in the paragraph, just that a tractor accident left one person injured in the hospital. People drive tractors.

"Who was—"

"Hi, Annalisse!" Sutton Hyde explodes into the room with an armful of books. "Whatcha doing?" She runs into the kitchen and dumps her armload on the table. "Are you surprised? Ethan said we could come over."

"Whoa, girl." I close my laptop, taking in her smile stained with a cherry essence. "Have you been eating candy?"

She bumps her head up and down. "Ethan gave me a big, all-day lolly, but I left it in the truck. Wanna see?" She grabs me with her sticky hand.

"After we wash your hands."

We undertake a thorough battle with soapsuds at the sink and dry off with a towel. The candy forgotten, Sutton's sitting next to me with her coloring book and papers in front of her.

"Where's your brother?"

"Outside with that nice man who thinks I'm pretty." Sutton's grin is full of pink-stained teeth.

Ethan's with Alec. Alone. I shudder to think about that conversation.

"Did you bring the book we colored in together?"

"Yeah. I finished the whole book. Look." She flips through the pages, pausing at a few here and there, offering her accounts of each colored rendering. "See, that's the cardinal you started. I finished it for you." She flips into a family of squirrels having a picnic on a tablecloth. Sutton adds another character to that page with her crayon.

"Why did you draw another squirrel by himself?"

"He's on a timeout. He did a bad thing."

"May I look?"

She offers the book to me. It's not long before I see a pattern. On every page where there are two or more animals, Sutton has drawn an extra one alone, cast out in the background. Turtles, horses, starfish, you name it, she's making her own story as she colors.

"Sutton, this turtle has his arms folded like he's mad. What happened to him?"

"He was arguing, and they didn't like it." She folds her arms to match the turtle's.

"Who didn't like it?"

"His mum made him clean his room." She pouts over the turtle's made-up situation.

Ellen asked Sutton to clean her room the first day I met the family. Closing the booklet, I gaze at the other things she brought with her.

"Great job on your coloring book. Tell me about the rest."

Sutton slides the coloring book to me. "I want you to have it. Do you have any biscuits?" Her eyes dart to the kitchen counter.

"No, sorry. We didn't buy any cookies. What's in the binder?" I point to the thin, open ring-binder filled with printed pages. "Are you writing a story?"

Sutton shakes her head. "I made you a copy of my experiments. I like doing experiments with plants and growing stuff. I told you that." She releases the end of the binder and rearranges the pages on the rings then folds her hands in her lap and sighs. "I thought you liked me."

"Show me your experiments. I like you a lot, Sutton. I think you're a smart girl with a great imagination. My sister, Ariel, was like that. You remind me of her."

"Crikey. Really? Okay, these are the first experiments I tried. They didn't turn out so good, but they got better. See?"

Sutton hands me her binder, and I read off the list: from growing experiments to testing bugs swimming in flavored water to learning how to make the perfect cuppa.

Tea? She's experimenting with bugs in tea. That's creepy, but the idea of tea mixed with other matter strikes a chord with me.

I read further, and she continues to test how bugs and animals respond to loud noises, especially when she yells at them. Sutton has a fixation with angry words and arguments. The list in front of me shows how she experiments with sound on plants also, but it's the tea experimentation that I want to know more about.

"Hon, did someone want you to learn how to make the perfect cup of tea, or did you want to do this yourself?" I ask with cotton in my mouth.

"Livia runs around all the time, asking me to make tea for her work." Sutton huffs, crossing her arms like the turtle in her coloring book. "When I don't want to, she gets mad."

There's that word again. Mad.

"When people argue, how does it make you feel?"

Sutton wrinkles her nose. "I hate it."

"Does it make you walk away or try experiments?"

Please say you walk away.

I hold my breath when she doesn't answer, and an iciness passes over my skin, lifting bumps on both arms. Sutton's calculating something in her head like she's gauging what I'll do if she tells the truth. It might be my suspicious mind, but there's a devious side to this little girl.

My phone buzzes from a random email, and I slide it into my lap, swipe the screen, and tap the Record symbol. An internal pang nudges me to save evidence from the rest of our talk.

"Can you keep a secret?" Sutton asks, sliding the binder across the table. "I'll only say it if you promise not to tell."

I nod, glancing into my lap. It's better to be non-verbal about a promise I can't keep.

"Mum and Livia argue all the time. It hurts my ears. Mum says the bad man Livia works for won't sell the candy store to us. Livia wants to run it, but the man makes her do what he says. Every day they yell about it." She licks her lips of leftover sugar. "Make him sick and Livia gets to run the shop."

I'm trying hard not to freak and flip my straight hair over one shoulder as cool as I can be.

The bizarre tea puzzle pieces are fitting together from a direction none of us dared to consider. Did Sutton taint the tea so her sister could run the shop without Alastair getting in her way? Cooper was given the copper tea, which doesn't quite fit. As unemotional as possible, I sit waiting for the rest of the girl's story.

"Livia likes boys, even the dodgy ones." Sutton makes a face. "Mum wants her to go to college, and she wants to play with the boys. Livia wants a boyfriend because they do stuff." She puckers her lips like a fish, making kissing noises. "Mum hates that Livia liked the mob boss, and they argued so much my head hurt." Then Sutton says the next words with a weird gleam in her eyes. "Make him sick and it stops."

Sliding both hands down my jeans, I'm unsure if I should interrupt or let her talk. I have to hear from her own mouth how she made it all stop.

A part of me doesn't want her to tell me the details.

"I know what you mean, Sutton. I don't like arguments either. I never know how to help make people happy again."

"You know what I do?" Sutton asks but doesn't wait for a response.

My heart is chugging in my chest, but I have to hear her out.

"I put medicine in their tea."

"Really? What kind of medicine? Like honey or lemon?" My hand under the table clutches my thigh. I sense what's coming.

"No. Not that. Feet medicine for sheep."

My breakfast is lurking at the base of my tongue. Did the police fingerprint the youngest daughter or dismiss her because she's a child? Tane said the partial print on the syringe didn't match anyone in the family.

She might've told her story to Ellen or the police, thinking that it's okay to make someone sick if there's a good reason for it. No way would Finn Hyde allow what his daughter did to reach the media. Sutton describes a premeditated attack, worthy of a mother's confession to protect her. From Finn's point of view, better for Ellen to take the fall than him.

I back my chair from the table, adding distance between the girl and me.

"Does your arm hurt?" Sutton knits her brows together as she looks at the cast.

"I don't know that sheep medicine. What's it called?" I lie to her, hoping she doesn't see through me. I'm such a bad liar, and she's eerily shrewd for an eight-year-old.

"Bluestone."

"Do the sheep drink it?" I want to see how much she knows about copper sulfate.

"Bluestone kills the rot." Sutton laughs. "Miss Annalisse, sheep don't drink it; we wash their feet with it. It's quite brilliant."

I'm shaking from her admissions, and it's getting harder to cover.

"Who are you giving the bluestone to? I thought you were making tea." Trying my best to sound like a city girl who doesn't know sheep, I have to be careful not to lead Sutton. She must explain her actions in her own words, no matter how difficult they are to hear.

The temperature inside the house has dropped since Sutton arrived, and I'm so close to a case of the teeth-chatters.

Shaking her head, she says, "Don't be *sook*. I put the bluestone *in* the tea. You know, with a tea bag? It makes people sick, and they turn into a *wally*. They get the trots too. It's funny to watch them."

"Hon, you have to stop doing that. People are being hurt. Please don't use this tea on another person. Let me put it another way; if someone gave you the bluestone tea and made you sick, would you like them after that?"

"I don't like getting sick."

"Bugs and living things don't like being sick either. Make people and animals smile instead. If you want people to get along, showing them love is the better way." I'm watching her soak up my words and hope they take effect.

Sutton shuffles the binder aside and draws out a book hidden at her waistband beneath her blouse. "I have something else for you from a long time ago when Mum and Da went to his work. She thinks she lost it.

I can't put it back, or she'll know I took it. Take it to New York." Sutton holds up a small diary that's lockable, but the lock is missing. "It doesn't lock anymore. I've already read it ten times. I don't need to look at it again. Put it in your purse, or I can. Where is it?"

Setting the phone carefully in my chair, I stand. "That's a personal diary, and I suggest you return it where you found it."

She gets red in the face and slams it on the table. "I can't."

"Then hide it somewhere, but I can't accept the diary, Sutton. I'm sorry."

Ethan and Alec enter the cottage in discussion, and Sutton spooks, running beside the arm of the couch. The natural reaction of someone who's hiding bad deeds and about to get caught in the act.

There are personal and private writings in Ellen's diary; whatever happened to Ellen's first husband might be chronicled in that book, but no one wants their secret musings read by anyone but themselves. I won't delve into a diary to find out what happened to Robert Fawdray. That's stepping over the line even for me. Ellen didn't lose her diary; Sutton took it, and by now, she's aware it was taken.

"Anna, I hope you don't mind Sutton visiting. She was brassed off when I told her we shouldn't bother you. Threw a hissy fit until we came." Ethan has a dirty face, and he's in a pair of dusty overalls as if he's been on a tractor all day.

"She showed me the coloring books. I loved seeing them." In a huge effort, I manage a weak smile for the mini serial killer in training.

Sutton notices and smiles at her brother. "I showed her the stuff," she says, then asks me, "Are you leaving soon?" She frowns, wearing the heart of a little girl on her sleeve but thinking nothing of getting her way by any vile means.

I've read about murderers who begin their careers by torturing bugs and animals before they graduate to taking down humanity. This child needs help, and I hope she gets it before her fiendish deeds escalate into those of an adult psychopath.

Sutton is nothing like we thought.

"We don't know when we're leaving; don't worry," I say to make her questions end. Giving her possibilities won't upset her as much. She's a smart kid who travels her own little world while there's negativity along the way. "If we have time, we'll say goodbye before we leave."

Sutton tilts her head for a moment. She's working on my answer in her mind. "You're my favorite friend." She hugs me around the hips and waves as the Royals do. "Ta-ta." She leaves my side and takes her brother's hand, who turns to me and shrugs. Ethan has his work cut out for managing the station and babysitting in his off-hours.

"Cheers, Anna," Ethan says over his shoulder.

Sutton leaves her pages on the table.

"Wait. Don't forget Sutton's books and papers over there." I point to the kitchen.

"I have copies," she sings. "You keep 'em."

"I meant to show you more of the station," Ethan says with a crooked smile.

"Some other time," Alec responds for me.

"Leave the key in the pot near the steps." Ethan's in anguish and doesn't smile this time.

Brother and sister depart, and I plop onto the sofa cushion to relax every muscle clenching in my body. Nothing feels normal, and I'm having trouble getting enough air while I process my conversation with the little Hyde darling. Her warped ideas and careless attitude about sickening others are too gross to be joyful about.

Alec is gawking at me in horror as Bill steps through the glass doors.

"Babe, you're as white as that lap robe over the couch, and you're sweating. What happened with her?" Alec asks.

"Pick up my phone on the kitchen chair. It's still recording." I cross my legs and arms in unison. "There's so much; you have to hear it for yourself."

"What's up?" Bill asks, closing the slider doors.

"I could use a drink. Something harder than soda," I reply.

Never in my life have I experienced a foretelling from someone this young. Sutton carries the dark aura of pure malevolence at work within her. I saw her eyes turn for that split second when she spoke of making Cooper sick.

I can't stay in a state of fear, but Sutton Hyde scares me to the marrow of my bones.

CHAPTER TWENTY-SIX
The Verdict

Some vacation I'm having.

The guys listen to the recording of little Sutton with barely a raised eyebrow, which unnerves me, unless she was always on their list of suspects, and they kept it to themselves. It's a warm day for sitting outdoors, so I suggest we hit an air-conditioned bar to discuss, regroup, and consider our options.

Instead of pulling up a barstool, Alec and Bill head for a booth at the back of the establishment in the darkest crevice with the dimmest light source. It's easy for anyone to find out about private scandals with a single inquiry at the local pub. Bartenders overhear, and those I've met blab. At least there's no fear of listening devices in a public place like the neighborhood pub. At three in the afternoon, we're the only patrons in the building.

After finishing his beer, Bill breaks the uncomfortable silence around the booth. "Sutton was on my radar at first, but as time went on, the adults in the family had the most to gain from the poisonings."

"How did you arrive at a sweet girl like Sutton?" His comment dumbfounds me. "She had me completely fooled."

"When the fingerprints didn't match the obvious suspects. Like you said a few days ago, accusing a little girl was far-fetched, so I discounted the idea," Bill says. "Here's what I think: Finn and Ellen Hyde know what their youngest daughter did. The scandal is so huge they concoct a narrative for Ellen to use the copper tea to sicken Alastair and Cooper. Just enough to make them ill so they'd leave the sweet shop for Olivia to run and send Cooper packing because he was too interested in Olivia. They tell police Ellen believed the tea was a harmless game and had no intention of killing them."

Alec sets his martini down. "What if Finn is behind Cooper's tea, using his young daughter as a scapegoat? For the same reasons you mentioned. A family member could've noticed Sutton working with the tea bags in one of her experiments, asked her to explain, and used her for cover."

I wipe my chilled fingertips on the drink napkin. The crazy woman in me wants to laugh at the bizarreness of it all, but I can't. There's nothing funny about a vindictive girl so neglected she plots against those she wants to hurt.

If Sutton did this on her own.

"This child has no patience. I think Alastair took too long to get sick, or die, so he was picked off at the side of the road by other means," I say. "The Hyde clan had reasons for both men to fade into the sunset as nothing more than a memory."

"I'm sorry you had to endure that with Sutton," Alec says. "Why didn't you call one of us in?"

"I couldn't. Sutton trusts me enough to tell me things she wouldn't say to you. If we were interrupted, she would've clammed up. I had to know what really happened since the police are sworn to secrecy."

"You have the girl on record making tea for both men should the authorities ask for it," Bill says. "Because Sutton's a minor or didn't consent to the recording, it might not be admissible in court anyway. The Temuka Police Department appear to be corrupt, and we'll know for sure if both cases are addressed to the public as accidental deaths. Finn pledges the stadium donation, and police flip the incidents into the solved-case files. Karena's already done this for Alastair McGregor. What's one more?" Bill grazes the bottom of the beer bottle on his napkin.

"We might never know who was truly behind the poisoning," I add.

"Did Sutton say she won't use the tea again?" Bill asks.

"No. She's proud of herself because the discord went away." I shiver. "It's like a horror show for a child to do such a lethal thing. Each time she makes the copper tea, she rids her world of the source of anger. In her mind, she isn't doing any harm with the tea. She's happy to make them sick enough to go away, and the good life returns to Woolcombe Station once more." Lifting both shoulders, I clench my teeth.

"Does she know the difference between sickness and murder?" Alec asks me.

I shrug again. "Maybe. I saw with my own eyes how calculating and calm she is about her tests on living things. Trying not to spook her from the truth, I decided not to mention that two men had died, although she might know about Cooper because of the police activity on their station. That's her parents' job to tell her about his death. You both heard the recording. Sutton may not know Cooper and Alastair died. She didn't imply that she wanted them dead. Sick, yes, but killing them, I didn't feel it was the goal."

Bill and Alec nod in agreement.

"If it goes deeper than Sutton and the Hydes encouraging their daughter to make the tea, they're the villains," Alec says.

"She'll make a heck of a politician one day. The little flake off the Parliamentarian's block." Bill sighs. "What a crime to cover up no matter who hatched the plan. I can't believe Finn and Ellen aren't wise to Sutton running amok, poisoning the township. They must know what she's capable of. Before you started recording, did she say how long she's been making the copper tea? There may be more who've died."

"When Sutton mentioned secrets, I didn't want her to get off track for a minute, so I didn't go there." A yawn sneaks up on me and I stretch. "The drink is zapping my energy. Sorry. She tried to give me one of Ellen's private diaries, but I didn't want a part in it."

"Sutton wants desperately to share her secrets. That's why she left you a copy of her list of experiments and confessed to the tea," Bill says. "You won't tell because you're her special friend from another country. She's emboldened and feels untouchable when bringing you into it. While you're far away in the US, her secrets are safe."

"I'd rather be an imaginary friend, thank you very much."

"Anna was searching for information on the death of Ellen's first husband this morning. Do you think the answers are in the diary?" Alec asks me.

"If they are, that's where they're staying. Robert Fawdray's obituary is almost a blank page. His death might not be nefarious, but I'm the suspicious type."

Bill hums. "Sutton's shrewd for a girl her age."

"Yes, probably because she's around adults most of the time. She can come across as an immature innocent, but Sutton schemes to the end like an adult."

"Changing the subject, I checked on the Shire tour. Reservations are closed until next month," Alec says.

"Like every other tour in this country. It was a nice thought," I say with regret.

"Not to worry," Alec says. "Auckland and the surrounding areas are teeming with activities and sights to see. They have a zoo and aquarium, peninsula tour, safari, and an awesome Rotorua geothermal area. That's off the top of my head. There's even more to do if we stay longer than a day or two. It's up to you, Anna."

The napkins I've been shredding look like a mountaintop piling with snow. Do I even want to stay longer?

"I'm on the fence. It's more up to Bill." I defer to his opinion. "He's here because you asked him to come. I don't know what you guys talked about before he showed up for my flight, but Bill should be the decider. If he has anything pressing at home, we'll check out Auckland another time."

"I blanked out my schedule for two full weeks. Whatever you want to do, Annalisse, I have time," Bill says.

"Let's do food. Is anybody else ready for dinner?" I ask. "I'm starving."

Alec utters a hearty, baritone laugh. "Pretty lady, you wouldn't be *you* otherwise. What do you feel like? Fish, pizza, Italian?"

"This might be our last night at the cottage. Someplace with seafood." I grin at both men. "Hard to break old habits. I'd like to go back to the place we had dinner with Ellen, as soon as I can change out of these scrubby jeans. Sound reasonable?"

"More than fair for me," Bill says.

"I'll put possible itineraries together," Alec says, "and we can discuss them at dinner. If you're up for the stopover in Auckland, we should have no trouble getting out of Christchurch tomorrow. Think about what you'd like to see and how much we can fit in. I can book the trip home from Auckland when you're ready." He rubs his forehead. "Your wrist. I'm not thinking. Do you even want a stopover? We don't have to. It's just an idea I had to put a happy face on an otherwise rotten few days. Nothing is holding us back from hauling out of New Zealand altogether. There might be a way to do it with a short layover in Auckland."

"We'll talk about it. My head is swimming with all that's happened today. I'll leave the details to you since you're the international-travel-reservations man. I think better on a full stomach."

My purse is ringing.

I turn the phone around to show Alec the caller's name. "Do I answer or let it go to voice mail?"

"Up to you."

"Hello? Hi, Ellen." Speaking to her is unsettling, but I listen, curious about how much she's willing to divulge since she believes I've accepted her check.

I don't like what she has to say and make a sour face at Alec.

"Sutton wants to come by tomorrow? She was just here... I don't know—I'll have to run it past the guys. We have activities planned all day."

Scribbling on Alec's napkin, I tell him my thoughts.

"It'll have to be late morning, say eleven thirty?" I ask Ellen and stare at Alec. "Fine. See you tomorrow." I throw the phone inside my tote, wiping that hand on my leg.

"I saw that," Bill says. "Ellen's a smooth operator. By now, she's learned how to be a corrupt politician's wife."

"Ellen says it's because Sutton wanted a chance to say goodbye. I already told her that we'd do it if we had time. What is Ellen up to?"

Alec levels his gaze at me. "You think there's more to it, don't you?"

"Yep. Sutton might've mentioned what we talked about. If that's true, Ellen will have to "drag brush" as Kate says, to cover what Sutton told me. Assuring us it's her daughter's wild imagination, a child telling stories, things like that." I mound up the torn napkins to a higher peak. "We can't be at the cottage when they get there."

"Where do we go?" Alec asks.

"We have a nice dinner tonight, get a good night's sleep, and pack our things. I'd like to be on the road early even if we have to wait in the terminal for a flight."

"As far away from Woolcombe Station as we can get." Bill finishes my thought.

Far away from Finn Hyde and his band of morally corrupt kinfolk that I *allegedly* happen to belong to.

The seafood at the Wharf Hideaway is as spectacular as the pasta from the other night. My plate of abandoned mussel shells has a festive look, with their green edges lining the dish one at a time. I give each empty mussel a shove to the side, making a circle, as I consume garlic chunks and eat my way through too many of the delicacies steamed in white wine. Alec won't be able to stand me. Guaranteed. Boy, it's easy to overeat when shellfish tastes this fresh and buttery. A savory, rich treat from New Zealand's sea to last in my memory until the next time Alec and I make the trip on our own. The right way.

Other than Alec showing up, the flight over with Bill was the high point of my stay. If I knew that then, we could've saved ourselves the expense, turned right around, and flown back to New York. Remembering the shock and good vibes when I saw Bill on the plane brings a hint of a smile. If he wasn't along, I don't know what I would've done.

Everything has detonated around us, lighting small bonfires each day since landing in Christchurch. If it's possible to be mentally exhausted to a greater degree than our Italy trip, that's where I am. My body is totally void of energy, partly from the wine, but mostly because we're about to leave this continent on such a low note. I came a long way to live the life of a New Zealander for a short time, only to find another crime family operating here.

"I've never seen you polish off a kettle of mussels that quickly," Alec says, beaming at my pile of black shells. "And I've seen you eat a lot of shellfish."

He's having such a good time tonight, smiling and laughing at my bad jokes as well as Bill's wisecracks.

I can get used to this Alec, who goes with the sexy beard.

I dab the corner of my mouth with a napkin, having finished the last sea creature on the dish. I'm so full there's zero room for dessert. Alec's right; I've broken a record after eating this vast kettle of shellfish in one sitting.

"It's true what they say about great food tasting better when it's local. I've lost count of how many green-lipped mussels shipped from New Zealand I've downed in New York's best restaurants. None of them tasted like these, not even in Italy. Little pink delights in a shell. I'll never forget this dinner with my two favorite men on the planet." I hold up my glass of Sauvignon Blanc. "Thank you, Alec and Bill. This is a crazy adventure for the books. I hope we never repeat it, but I'll never forget it."

"Neither will we." Alec and Bill recite the words, lifting their glasses.

Alec touches his glass to mine. "We'll do it better next time." He stares at my cast and the fingers on my left hand—that should hold his ring. "I promise you won't break any bones on the next trip."

"Will you ever go back to Woolcombe Station?" Bill asks me with a straight face.

"Are you seriously asking me that? It's a rule of mine to run the other way from the demonic realm."

"Ouch, that's harsh," Alec says.

"You weren't in the room with Sutton and her pile of books and papers. She's gravely messed up and in need of a shrink. I doubt anyone in that self-absorbed family cares about her mental psychosis. She's been left alone to create a perfect world for herself, distorted in make-believe that she engineers through experiments." I thumb off some condensation from my glass.

"Taking down anyone who gets in her way," Bill says what I'm thinking, again.

He has an uncanny habit of doing that. Maybe Bill's more quiet tonight because of the alcohol, or he's soaking up our conversation in small bites.

Alec flags down the server, who is wearing a customary long skinny skirt and tied bandanna for a top. He asks for the bottle of the French champagne I can't pronounce, which sends her scurrying off to another table.

"Alec, I can't do champagne tonight on top of all the wine and what I ate. I'll watch you enjoy it if that's all right."

"I think you'll want just one glass." A sly smile crosses Alec's face.

No romance ahead, just Headache City for me tonight. I'm glad I keep plenty of ibuprofen on the nightstand for my wrist.

"I spoke to Mom while you guys were at the police station."

Oh no. What's he doing?

"Is there something wrong at the gallery?" I'm hit by the guilt complex again. "When I called Chase from the cottage about how Boris is doing, he didn't mention the shop. I hope they aren't out of their minds in client appraisal requests with me out of the country."

Alec shakes his head. "It's all fine. Mom's good with the time to yourself. We all need mental health breaks, like the one you gave to me."

"Is that what I did?" I'm curious about where he's going with this.

"At the time, I didn't like it, but while you were away the first couple of days, I saw beyond my own feelings and more of the big picture you were painting for us—by leaving me behind in New York. Funny thing about wanting it all and the realization I'm working against us. I woke up. Outside of you… without you, the rest is meaningless."

His words cover my heart in a toasty blanket of pleasure.

We were separated less than two weeks, and although I took off like a brat, the time apart has enriched us.

I take Alec's hand, filled with bliss, too swept away by his love to utter a reply immediately.

"You've been so sweet, Alec, considering how I left you. I shouldn't have blown up. Look where it's gotten me." I spread my arms wide. "I'm in New Zealand; I've reached my basic goal, but what a shamble I'm leaving. I bolt down here and still miss seeing Kate. Who knows where she is now?" Closing my eyes, I feel Alec's hot breath as his lips graze my left cheek.

"Others let you down too. I'm gonna work on not doing that again. I love you, Anna." Alec leans close to me and whispers in my ear. "Don't worry about Kate. That meeting will happen when it's supposed to."

The bottle of champagne arrives in an ice bucket, and the server sets it at the edge of the table next to Alec. She extracts three champagne flutes, places one in front of each of us, and carefully pops the cork, securing the bottle in a cloth.

After pouring our flutes half-full of the bubbly wine, the server says, "Let me know if you need anything else, Mr. Zavos." She smiles at Alec and speeds away.

As always, his celebrity status follows him to the restaurant. Our last server might have put the word out to the rest of the staff.

I push myself farther into my seat cushion, fondling Kate's golden locket.

"Alec, I have no room."

I'm getting more uncomfortable by the minute. The wine and mussels have swollen to the size of a small melon deep inside my belly.

"We're celebrating," Alec announces. "Take your glasses."

Bill and I grudgingly raise ours and look at each other in our misery.

He's overindulged in food and drink as I have.

"What are we celebrating?" Bill asks. "To a safe trip home."

"Yes, a safe trip home," Alec says.

We sip from our glasses, and I'm about to put mine down when Alec continues toasting.

Ugh. The next sip will be with a closed mouth. I can fake it.

"To Virena and Noah—wanderers, who will remain that way."

I spill some of the wine as I set the glass near my plate of shells. "What?"

"I'm not his father." Alec looks over his glass, smiles at me, and takes a gulp of champagne. "Garrett sent me a text a little while ago."

The massive, invisible barbell pressing down on my chest since that December afternoon in the new sheep barn lifts. It rolls up and off my shoulders as if a miracle has blessed us while in this eatery. The colors throughout the restaurant are more vivid, and the other diners seem happier than when the server showed us our seats.

My intuition came through for me once again. Keeping good thoughts and barring the negative ones *will* manifest the chosen outcomes. Bad things still happen, but in the end, we get what we want and deserve.

From deep within, tears spring to my eyes in a steady flow, streaming down my cheeks. There's so much relief pouring out of me I can't speak, but Bill says it in his own way for both of us.

"Alec, congrats…ssulations." Bill slurs while sipping his drink, holding me in a one-eyed wink longer than needed. Bill is hammered, or darn near close to it. "Great news. Chapter's at an end, and we close that mystery for good."

Finding a tiny space for more champagne, I say, "Alec, we're wasting our time down here, and my heart can't take another minute of the Hyde clan when we should be at Brookehaven with Helga and the horses. We'll have several days together before I have to get back to the gallery. I miss Harriet and her foal so much. And I miss Boris." It's a little tricky but I manage to hug Alec around the neck, telling him, "Thank you for showing me the way home. I want to be with you most of all." Resting my forehead against his, I remember that we're in a public place and draw back.

"We might not find a flight with connections for all of us on the same plane. We're at the mercy of airlines on such short notice," Alec reminds us. "But I'll get to work on it. We might get lucky since we're having a good night."

"I don't mind a s… sseparate flight. I can leave before or after you." Bill's knuckle hits the table. "It's settled." He holds up his glass to me and toasts the air. "Anyway, I have the Thomas book to read." He grins at me sideways.

"What did you talk to Gen about while we were with the police?" I ask.

"Mom has decided to help out Noah and his mother. She wants to ensure that he has a good education fund once he's ready to go to college."

I hear Kate in my mind saying, *Cheaters never prosper.* In the short term, Virena has won a battle with her ruse to toss her son at Alec as a legitimate heir to the Zavos fortune. But for all that she gains from Gen's generosity, Virena will be miserable once she no longer has money.

"Does Generosa know Noah isn't yours?" Bill asks.

Alec pours himself another glass. "I haven't told her yet. Mom has the freedom to give her money to whomever she chooses. I'm not surprised that she wants to help Noah, but when Mom finds out he's not mine, she might reconsider, but I doubt it. She's gotten attached to him."

I nod. "Alec, I think I'm going to need a wheelchair to roll myself out of the restaurant. Did you see one for emergencies near the coat check room?" I'm giddy with laughter, and my lips are numb. Too much wine has left my brain floating above my body.

Alec's eyes close, and he slowly opens them. "If Bill will kindly take on his chauffeur duties and bring the car around, I'll carry you to the car myself, Anna." He observes his friend swaying in place and adds, "I feel like getting some air, on second thought. Bill, stay here with Anna, and I'll bring the car around. I have chauffeur duty tonight." He grins at Bill and slides out of the booth.

"Don't worry; we've gotcha." Bill tosses his napkin aside and rests his head on the back cushion.

We need two wheelchairs waiting because Alec can't carry Bill's dead weight.

CHAPTER TWENTY-SEVEN
Four Weeks to Serenity and Justice

There's a great sense of serenity and clarity to gain from the top of a horse. No matter how overwhelming the day is, riding in the cold morning mist makes everything come into sharp focus. When my world is aligned, and I'm on horseback, I'm propelled into a state of extreme happiness, same as when I visit Harriet in her stall—pure, unadulterated, blissful peace. My thighs are sore from the long ride, but I don't care. Owning Harriet and caring for her are some of Alec's special gifts to me.

I shift the reins into my right hand and wriggle my brace high in the air, relishing the freedom of movement. My arm feels so good to part with the fiberglass monstrosity. I'll never know how I kept myself from ripping it off during the past four weeks.

"Be careful," Alec warns, sitting high on Kristol Magic, the stable's premier stallion. "The doc said to limit the movement or you'll end up in another cast."

"Two more weeks with a flexible brace, I can handle. You have no idea how liberated I feel. Oh, I almost forgot about your ankle. You understand that feeling well." I reach down and pat Harriet's withers, taking in her pungent aroma of horse sweat. "What did you decide to name Harriet's filly?"

"That's your job." Alec unzips his jacket.

"During the flight I thought of a few ideas." I slow our canter to a walk.

"Oh boy. Let's hear it."

"We don't have to use it if you'd like to tweak it more."

"Anna, the filly belongs to you. Tell me."

"When Harriet's foal runs in the sunlight, her hair coat reminds me of a shiny piece of copper. I can't get over how much she looks like Kris when he's galloping freely in the pasture. Your daughter's quite magnificent, isn't she, Harriet?" I scratch behind my horse's ear, then gaze over at Alec, staring at me.

"She's a beauty, but we might be a little prejudiced." Alec laughs.

He's happier these days.

I like the change in him since Italy. He's no longer the corporate guy with deadlines and company decisions to make since selling his dad's car company. Alec has become a free spirit with no firm plans to go anywhere or finish anything that he doesn't want to. The Zavos Gallery is his new hangout when I'm in Soho, where we can go to lunch or take the afternoon off and shop or walk Central Park.

"On the flight over, my first inclination was to combine Kris's name with copper, but it's not right anymore since the word *copper* conjures sickening memories. I'm working a new angle for her name."

Horse's hooves pound the hard portions of our route through the field as dragonflies dart in front of us. The air smells of wet rye grass sprouting in the pasture.

"We should nail her name down soon for the Jockey Club because they'll need to check it against the current names in their registry. If you want, I can bring Hank in and see what he comes up with for marketing. His instincts are better than mine."

Alec tugs on the reins and slows Kris's pace.

"Whoa." I stop Harriet on the path. "You'll ask Hank to help us? Would he do that?"

"He's actually quite clever with names. He would consider the task an honor. Work on more ideas, and if we can't find the right one, Hank's our man."

"I love that idea. It takes the heat off me."

"Good," Alec says. "Race ya back to the stables. Are you up for it?"

I whip Harriet around and gallop against the wind in a head start, even if it's only a temporary lead. Kristol Magic is much larger and faster than Harriet once he gets his powerful legs under him. In a matter of seconds, my barn coat is covered in Kris's mud as he passes us and pulls away. The wind whistles in my ears, and Harriet's gait smooths as if I'm sitting on a comfy cloud. She's an amazing mare.

The race ends when they beat us to the breezeway by an easy two lengths. Harriet makes a much better showing than the last time Kris met Harriet in a race, not too long after Alec weaned her from the foal.

"Not bad, Harriet. You've picked up some energy." Alec dismounts on the concrete in front of the stallion's stall. He has the prime location and a fancy brass nameplate over his stall door.

I'm huffing in giant gulps and laughing, out of breath. "Give me a minute to—" I puff some more, coughing the dryness from my throat while hanging on to Harriet by the neck.

"You're supposed to close your mouth so you won't…" Alec's laughing so hard he has to grab Kris's bridle.

"I don't know what's wrong with me. Harriet did all the work. I'm out of practice."

"That's my fault. Stay there while I tie Kris in his stall. I'll come back to help you down. Don't try to get off on your own. Your wrist isn't strong enough."

I walk Harriet to the end of the breezeway near the indoor arena while Alec takes his stallion through the stall opening.

Instead of tying him, Alec removes the saddle, exposing the wet area on the horse's back, and carries the rest of his gear out, hanging it all over the tie-out post.

"Your turn." Alec beckons me with his index finger and a mischievous grin.

"Hey, be nice now. I haven't done this in a while and never one-handed," I say, smiling.

Harriet's ears perk when vehicle tires roll onto the brick driveway at the stable entrance. The car has paper plates and is not a vehicle that I recognize.

"Do you know anyone in a gray Lincoln?" I ask.

Alec ties Harriet to the long post next to Kris's saddle and blanket.

"Not sure. Whoever it is isn't getting out." Alec reaches for me to slide off the saddle.

"My thigh muscles aren't functioning. Give me a second."

I twist in the smooth leather saddle, and Alec helps my outer leg over Harriet's back, sliding me from the mare the rest of the way. Operating with one good arm is a pain. I'll be glad when I'm fully functional again.

Bowlegged and unable to put my knees together, I try to force them to no avail.

Alec wraps an arm around my waist to steady me. "How do you feel?"

"Like I've been on a horse too long and need a giant clothespin for my legs." Glancing down, I look ridiculous.

"Walk it out; you'll be fine. Harriet almost caught us this time," Alec says, strolling us out to the end of the concrete and into the sun.

The driver's side door opens, and Bill Drake steps out, sporting a black leather jacket and a shorter haircut.

"Huh, he's in town. Did you know?" I ask Alec.

"I haven't spoken to him since he landed."

Bill retrieves a gift-wrapped package and a book from the car.

"He's bearing gifts." I wonder if we've forgotten a birthday.

"Drake." Alec waves at him. "Meet us in the office."

Stopping between the car and the barn, Bill's frozen where he stands.

"Alec, he's petrified of horses. You'd better put Harriet away first. I'll take him into the office and wait for you there."

"Hi, Bill." I step off the concrete and brick and meet him halfway. "You're out of your turf." I give him a hug. "And you smell good." The woodsy cologne is a new one for him.

"Thanks. I came to give you this." He hands me the big book I recognize as the Thomas Taylor hardcover.

"Did you enjoy it on the plane?" I ask.

"The photos are amazing, and I've learned a lot about Egypt's and Turkey's history. He's actually quite humorous throughout the book. Maybe one day you'll get a chance to meet him." Bill thuds the dust jacket with a single knuckle. "With your love of history, I think you'll find a lot in common with him."

"I hope I get that chance."

He lays the other package in champagne-colored paper on top of the book. "A mutual friend sent the contents to me."

I motion for Bill to follow me to Alec's office in the barn and set the hardcover and box on the corner of the desk. My mind is whirling through the possibilities of who our *friend* might be and what is so important to warrant Bill's surprise visit.

"That's a long drive for a delivery. Have a seat." I drag a chair forward from against the wall. "I'm dying to know what that is, but we'll wait for Alec. He shouldn't be long."

Bill has a golden-brown tan and seems rested, as if he's been hiding out on a warm island beach in the Gulf for the past few weeks. The leather jacket is a new accessory for him, but it's still cold out, and I'm used to seeing him during warm summer months. The jacket might be his usual gear.

"Did you find out any more about the investigations in New Zealand?" I ask him. "I'm dying to hear about it."

Bill twists his mouth in an odd smirk, but he doesn't answer.

He knows something.

"What brings you out this far?" Alec shakes Bill's hand as he gets to his feet.

"That." Bill points to the wrapped package, then shoots me one of his looks. The kind he uses when we're thinking along the same lines. "We left New Zealand with *some* things untidy and lots of loose ends. New developments since we left." Bill takes the box. "Who'd like to do the honors?"

Alec accepts the box from Bill and hands it to me.

Sitting on the desk corner, I slide my fingernails through clear tape on the wrapper and lift the lid on a carton the size of a ream of paper. Inside are various periodicals from New Zealand, folded neatly.

"*New Zealand Bugle, the Christchurch Starlight, Wellington Newsline.* Even the Temuka local paper is in here." I look toward Bill with glee. "Someone or something has made their national media."

Bill chuckles and sits back down. "You could say that."

I set the box in my lap. "Who is the mutual friend who sent these to you, Bill?"

"Tane Otero from Temuka forensics." He clears his throat and adds, "*Formerly* of Temuka forensics. He's taken a new position with the Timaru Police Department. The flames got too hot in Temuka when the story broke." Bill nods toward the box. "On a side note, Commissioner Karena suddenly found the need to retire after we left." Bill's signature smile is wide, and he's enjoying himself.

Alec is awestruck as he mutters, "Karena went down."

I scan the headlines from the front pages and read the first few lines of each article.

My heart is heavy for what this news means to Ethan.

"Oh. My. Gosh. There's so much Finn has been charged with." I draw a long breath. "Bribery—payment and receipt of bribes, theft, conspiracy, insider dealings and taxation offenses, but I notice they haven't charged him with murder." Laying the newspapers in the box, I set them aside and look at Alec. "Finn Hyde is in jail, awaiting trials for multiple crimes by a Parliamentarian." I'm blown away by the depth of his corruption. He is abusing his office in Parliament to the max and is about to meet his fate. Oh, how karma can bite.

Bill passes me a sticky note. "This came with the papers."

I read the printed words more than once. "Sutton acted on her own. That's why they couldn't pin the murders on Finn." A cold shudder overtakes me. "I hope they get that girl some help. Did Tane say what happened to her?"

"No mention. Once *Da* was charged, the adults must've fessed up. Finn is in enough trouble without adding murder charges to the list," Bill says.

Alec gazes at his friend. "Did you have anything to do with—"

"Absolutely not." Bill shakes his head. "Not in my purview. When we met with Tane in the park, I could tell he was contemplating something big. He moved his family and researched the best police organizations that were on the up and up. That's life-changing. If you ask me, I believe Tane is the anonymous source as Hyde's whistleblower, but I don't know that as fact. There might've been many who came forward."

"The only good news I can see is what Alastair was trying to stop," I say. "Bluebasin Lake is safe from development if Finn was the hinge pin. Developers who might've paid Finn off won't want that stain on them while the man is being prosecuted. How are Finn's crimes going to affect Woolcombe Station? Is Ellen implicated in any of this?"

"They aren't mentioning her yet. I hope she's not directly or indirectly involved. The station became hers when Fawdray died, and Ethan is Robert's descendant. Let's hope that Ethan can hold it for his family," Bill says. "Tane will keep us in the loop on future news."

"We have our answer on the copper poisoning. That talk I had with Sutton… She had the opportunity to tell me her father coerced her into making the tea, and when she didn't, it all made sense. Whatever it's worth, I'm convinced Sutton didn't know bluestone could kill. Her child mentality is to make people sick to get her way. Did Tane say?" I ask Bill.

"Not in so many words. The girl is a minor—a devious one at that. Your recording of Sutton says she made the tea and had her own reasons for doing it. Blaming a child might be more than authorities want to do in a small place like Temuka. The international media would go wild over that one. Ellen has a confession on record, whether she actually had anything to do with it. Police have the accident theme for Cooper's and Alastair's deaths without mentioning the tea to the media. They won't or can't prosecute a minor for murder even if they can prove it circumstantially."

"There's an open question about Dax the ram that no one is talking about. Was he let in to the pen with Cooper, and if so, by whom?" I purse my lips. "We'll never know the answer to that. Dax's role in the death could be as simple as an unlatched gate. Cooper had enough bluestone in his system to kill him, or perhaps it was the blow by Dax that ended his life. Only the medical examiner knows for sure. I don't trust Karena's version of the incident."

"Sutton as a sociopathic twenty-year-old is a scary thought." Alec shakes his head. "By then, or before, she's going to have problems in society unless she works with a therapist. I'm glad you didn't accept the diary from Sutton, babe. Cutting ties from her is best."

"Let's hope she doesn't show up on the estate doorstep. Having to look over our shoulders is a scary thought." Both hands ride down my thighs from the sudden case of the sweats. "I left her books and papers on the kitchen table at the cottage. Ellen must have been shocked that we left without a word when she planned to stop by. It had to be this way."

"She and her husband are neck deep in scandal. Ellen knew why you left the country fast, trust me," Bill adds. "What have you decided to do with the pay-off check, if you don't mind my asking?"

"Anna's going to frame it as a memento," Alec says.

"And hang it in Alec's office." I laugh. "It might be an interesting relic for someone in the future. Centuries down the road."

"One other thing. I took the liberty of taking a photo of the Māori statue that Charlie Sinclair gave you when we were in Massachusetts, and texted it to Ethan. He'll research it and let us know what he finds. Sinclair having this statue must've originated from Ted Walker in the short term. A relic that belonged to Kate, now that we know about her New Zealand connection."

"The knowledge that Thomas Taylor is an explorer of sorts could link the carving to him since it came to me via a man who hated Kate's lover. I feel a connection there. We know the origin is Māori, and who better than Ethan to look into it? I'd like to know what it has to do with me and why Ted Walker sent Charlie to deliver it. Thanks, Bill. Who knows? The Thomas Taylor book could give us clues."

When we found Kate last year, I asked Bill to keep the statue for me. We believe the carving is considered a death mask, and holding it might bring in bad luck or bad karma. Alec and I don't need more of that. The mask is safer in Bill's hands while Ethan checks it out.

I close the lid over the box, pushing the wrapping into the trash can beside Alec's desk. It's hard to know how to feel now that justice is working its way as it should.

"Anna, are you all right? You seem disappointed." Alec leans against the desk next to me. "I thought you'd be relieved about Finn."

"Ellen's husband is a rat; no getting around it. The warning signs were flashing at us while we were down there. It's Ethan I'm worried about. What a shame if he loses the sheep station that's been in the Fawdray family forever. I know you aren't fond of Ethan, but he'll have no means of support if someone else takes over the station after they're finished with Finn. Ethan doesn't deserve that." I rest a hand on Alec's thigh and give it a squeeze.

"It hasn't happened yet. We'll monitor things, and should the worst happen, I'll make it my business to see that he has other options down there or in the States. Let's hope the station is safe for his sake." Alec covers my hand with his. "That's a promise."

"What's the latest on the vet clinic, Alec?" Bill asks. "You never explained why you sent all the furnishings back. I see the building hasn't progressed since January. What's up with that?"

"The spot for the clinic has been repurposed for our stable manager, Hank. He and the workout jockeys need a larger space for their Brookehaven Stables bull room. They've outgrown the jockey quarters and Hank's tiny office where the foals are. I'm waiting for his ideas before we renovate the interior walls," Alec says.

Bill glances at me, and all I can do is smile.

"Months ago, Anna and I talked about building Hank a new office and quarters. While you guys were away, I reconsidered my clinic project for another purpose. Hank and the workout jockeys won the day. Anna actually came up with the idea first, and it's a good one."

Bill widens his eyes. "No foolin'?"

"Alec's solidly back into horseracing once again," I say. "I have no idea what the racing business is about, but I'm going to find out and can't wait. Alec put his veterinary dream on a temporary hold so that he can get more involved in the day-to-day of running his stable. Hank has great managerial skills to take Brookehaven Stables to the next level." Raising my fist in the air, I add, "And I'm going to bet on my first horse, sired by Kristol Magic. How cool is that?"

"It'll be a blast for both of us," Alec says with a grin. "Thanks for hand-delivering the newspapers, Bill. We wondered how that investigation turned out. It's a relief to hear that justice is making it through their channels."

"Your cast is off. How does the wrist feel?" Bill asks.

"A little feeble from the inactivity, but it's healing and getting stronger. I'm sure glad you were there when I fell. If I haven't said it enough, thanks for taking such good care of me. And thanks to this handsome guy." I wrap my bad wrist carefully around Alec. "He had the good sense to send you with me." The rest of what I want to say clogs my throat, so I leave it at that.

"How long can you stay?" Alec asks Bill. "Helga would love nothing more than to make you one of her authentic German dinners."

"Pork sausage and potatoes with strudel for dessert?" Bill slaps his belly. "Man, that sounds great. I didn't bring enough antacids with me though."

Alec and I laugh, and Bill joins us. Bill loves Helga's meals but she cooks with full-fat and lots of it. He has a touchy stomach, and his indigestion soars when Helga dishes extra helpings for him. The food is so good, Bill overeats to the point of waddling from the table—miserable from the meat sweats.

"Don't worry about the antacids; we have that covered. Alec keeps them in every room of the estate." I stand, taking Alec's hand and holding the other toward Bill. "I hope you brought an overnight bag. Alec's gonna get you on a horse yet."

"Well…" Bill begins a protest.

"We'll talk about it later. Are you guys ready to go to the house? I was warm when I got here, but now, not so much. As I recall, there's a fire blazing in the drawing room. We have so much to tell you, Bill."

An odd thought strikes me as we're walking. I flew thousands of miles to see actual sheep stations in operation with their huge flocks of sheep. Trouble was, I got close to only one sheep: a beautiful Corriedale ram named Dax, and that introduction went from exhilarating to deadly. I'm better off at Brookehaven, content with my own mixed flock of thirty sheep.

As for Alec and me, we have more work ahead to mend a few hiccups in our relationship. Jumping headlong into horseracing together is a fantastic start. We'll do that in earnest—*better together than apart*. Boy, is that ever true.

Alec mentioned at breakfast today that he's heard from Kate again, and she wants to see us. Together.

THE END

Ewephoric Publishing

Dear Reader,

   If you've enjoyed *Copper Waters* and other Annalisse series installments, please consider leaving an honest review on your favorite book site. Every review means the world to this author!

   Be sure to sign up for free books, giveaways, and news on future releases in the Annalisse Series as well as other books by Marlene M. Bell. Visit Marlene's website at: https://www.marlenembell.com

SOCIAL MEDIA LINKS
Facebook Author Page: fb.me/marlenembell
(Personal Page) https://www.facebook.com/marlene.bell.3194
Twitter: https://www.twitter.com/ewephoric @ewephoric
Bookbub: https://www.bookbub.com/profile/marlene-m-bell
Goodreads: https://www.goodreads.com/author/show/17642396.Marlene_M_Bell
Instagram: https://www.instagram.com/marlenemysteries/

ACKNOWLEDGMENTS

Elizabeth Kracht of Kimberley Cameron and Associates is the only editor to read my first drafts. She's a gifted developmental editor and soon-to-be screenwriter! I'm so thankful to have Liz's Big Picture recommendations for every novel in the Annalisse series.

Thanks to my huge team of editors and proofreaders who went over the updated version of *Copper Waters* with keen scrutiny to point out areas needing an adjustment in the ARC (advance reader copy) published in late 2022. I'm grateful for your comments.

Kristine Hall of Hallways Bookworks, LLC has the final manuscript critique before a finished installment becomes a book. Her editing unit, bloggers, and book reviewers are simply the best of Texas, and the Lone Star Literary Life book tours are awesome!

A big thank you to *Celine Sicard* for your sheep character name suggestion. The ram in this book is DAX, thanks to Celine's unique take on naming sheep. There's something about a *Dax* in *Copper Waters* that feels right for a four-legged bloke from New Zealand.

To my readers ~ Thank you for your continued support for my writing in this series and my children's books. I sincerely appreciate every book review and always appreciate your feedback for future installments. Readers are the lifeblood of authors, and mine are the best!

Any and all mistakes are my own.

BOOKS BY
MARLENE M. BELL

Stolen Obsession ~ Annalisse Series Book One
Spent Identity ~ Annalisse Series Book Two
Scattered Legacy ~ Annalisse Series Book Three
Copper Waters ~ Annalisse Series Book Four

Trading Paint ~ a short story,
Volume 5 Texas Authors

Mia and Nattie: One Great Team!
A Children's Picture Book

ABOUT THE AUTHOR

Marlene M. Bell is an eclectic mystery writer, artist, photographer, and she raises sheep on a ranch in wooded East Texas with her husband, Gregg.

Marlene's Annalisse series boasts numerous honors including the Independent Press Award for Best Mystery (*Spent Identity,*) and FAPA— Florida Author's President's Gold Award for two other installments, (*Stolen Obsession* and *Scattered Legacy.*) Her mysteries with a touch of romantic suspense are found at her websites or at online retail outlets.

She also offers the first of her children's picture books, *Mia and Nattie: One Great Team*! Based on true events from the Bell's ranch. The simple text and illustrations are a touching tribute of compassion and love between a little girl and her lamb.

Made in United States
Orlando, FL
11 June 2023

34052879R00211